The Duty of Love

RONALD NEAL GREEN

Outskirts Press, Inc.
Denver, Colorado

This is a work of fiction. The events and characters described here are imaginary and are not intended to refer to specific places or living persons. The opinions expressed in this manuscript are solely the opinions of the author and do not represent the opinions or thoughts of the publisher.

The Duty of Love

V3.0

Outskirts Press, Inc.
http://www.outskirtspress.com

ISBN: 978-1-4327-1259-4

PRINTED IN THE UNITED STATES OF AMERICA

PROLOGUE

She felt small and afraid.

So much blood.

The mangled body frightened her. She'd seen it before but she hadn't understood it at all. She stared, horrified, at the blood that dripped down the body, at the open wounds, the lacerations and the cruel punctures.

How many times had she seen the body and the blood that flowed so freely from it? But this time was different. She was seeing it truly for the first time. She could have seen it before, but she hadn't. Why not?

The blood.

It beckoned her and demanded her acknowledgment. It was more than she could bear.

Please, she thought. No, I can't. I won't.

She closed her eyes and turned her head away.

"Go away," she whispered.

Even with her eyes shut she could still see the blood. She clenched her teeth and shook her head back and forth.

No, she thought. I won't. You're not real. You're just somebody's nightmare, a bad dream, a fairy tale.

You're just a fairy tale.

Just a fairy tale.

Chapter I

A Strange New Creature

"You see, it was the slither hither and thithers that nipped the little prince in the magic forest."

Charles wrinkled his brow in puzzlement. "What's a slither?"

Father was quite prepared for the question. "It's like a snake does when it's crawling along on the ground. On its belly like this."

Father illustrated his point by making a waving, forward motion with his two hands to imitate the crawling of a snake.

"Oh," said Charles, thinking he understood. "They were snakes then?"

"Well, not really. Slithering can just be moving real close to the ground. Like this."

Father got down on all fours and moved about on his knees and hands with his stomach only about an inch from the floor. Charles did not laugh. He was a very serious boy, which was, perhaps, why his schoolmates thought him odd, and wanted to come to grips with this strange new creature.

"What's a hither?" he asked.

"A hither is going this way—to something," Father said as he hithered over the floor to Charles, "and a thither is this way—from something," he further explained, as he turned about and thithered away from Charles.

"Oh," said Charles, tucking his knees up under his chin as he pondered this new knowledge.

Father arose, brushed off his clothes and plopped into the red leather easy chair he kept at the foot of Charles's bed. Crossing his left knee over his right he picked up his red cherry pipe.

"What do they look like?"

Father struck a match and puffed away at his pipe, trying to get it lit, as he answered. "Well, let's see. They have small heads, with four eyes, two little ones and two big ones."

"Why do they have four eyes?"

"Well the two little eyes are real tiny, and those are for watching themselves, and the really big eyes are for watching their neighbors."

"That makes sense," said Charles.

"Indeed, it does." Father took the pipe out of his mouth and blew a big cloud of blue, sweet smelling smoke at the ceiling, and put his free hand behind his head. "Let's see. Oh, yes, they have six legs--four real legs and two tiny legs up front, not for walking, but for grabbing things."

"Like Prince Cha Cha?"

"Just like Prince Cha Cha."

"How big are they?"

"Oh, well I'm not exactly sure. Big enough to eat the

Prince anyway."

"Did they eat the Prince?"

"I was just getting to that…"

"Is there a beautiful Princess, daddy?"

Charles groaned. It was his sister, here to spoil the fun like always. He turned to see her standing in the doorway to his bedroom, dressed in her night robe and pajamas.

"Why aren't you in bed?" he growled at her.

"Why aren't you?" she answered him.

"Because Dad's telling me a story."

She ignored him.

"Daddy, I couldn't sleep. Is there a Princess in the story?"

"Of course there is, sweetheart. Come sit on Daddy's lap."

She padded solemnly in her slippers over to Father, who put out his pipe and lifted her up onto his lap. He pulled her bathrobe tight about her chest, then felt her forehead with the back of his hand. Then he kissed her on the forehead and said "I guess it'll be alright for you to listen to a story tonight."

Charles looked resentfully at his sister. Why does she always have to wreck everything, he thought.

"What was the Princess's name, Daddy?"

"It's about a Prince!" Just like always. She was taking over. She always did, Charles fumed.

"There's a Princess in the story too. Daddy said so."

"Not until you came in."

"No, no, son," Father said in a soothing voice. "There was always a Princess in the story. She just doesn't show up yet."

"When, Daddy?"

"In due time, sweetheart. You see, children, it all happened like this..."

"Once upon a time, in a land ever so far away there was an evil wizard. He had a long, red beard and long, red hair that hung down over his shoulders, and an evil rat lived in his hair and ran around in it. He, the wizard, not the rat, wore a bright red robe that was so bright it hurt people's eyes to look at it. And on his feet he wore huge red shoes with points that curled up way over his toes."

"Were they the same red as the robe, daddy?"

Charles struck his forehead with the palm of his hand. Why did she always ask such dopey questions?

"No, sweetheart. Even though they were red they were a wrong shade. They didn't match at all."

"That's sad."

"Yes, it is. And to make it even worse, they were hard to walk in. He was always tripping over them. That made people laugh, of course. But he'd hear them, and he'd clench his fists and glare at them, and they'd stop right away."

"Were they afraid of him, Daddy?"

"Oh, he'd think very horrible thoughts about them."

"I bet he thought about turning them into frogs," Charles opined.

"Not just frogs, Charles. Much, much worse--pigs and goats and mosquitoes and squirrels."

"I think being a squirrel would be fun," Charles said.

"That's because you already are a squirrel," his sister taunted from the security of her father's lap.

"Shut up, Tanya!"

"Don't fight, children. That's just what got Cha Cha and Ta Ta into so much trouble."

"Is Ta Ta the Princess?"

"Yes, sweetheart."

"Does she come into the story now?"

"I'm getting to that. Listen carefully."

"Now the evil wizard was very lonely. To tell the truth, he was very tired of having a rat running around in his hair. But it was his trademark. When he was a young wizard, he wanted to be different. He wanted to stand out from all the other wizards, so he got the rat for his hair and named it Typhus. At first, he dyed the rat red, but no one could see it very well in his red hair, so he dyed it black. Well, it was a sensation. Everybody in the court noticed it and were both disgusted and fascinated by it, and he got all manner of clients who wanted to be in the avant garde and au courant and that sort of thing. Naturally, the other wizards were both jealous and afraid of losing all their business to the evil wizard, Rigirus. So they too tried all manner of outlandish things—tattoos, crazy hairstyles, earrings all over the body. But no matter what they tried, none of them could come up with anything as grand as a rat in the hair. One wizard tried a parrot, but everyone just said he looked liked a pirate. Another wizard even tried putting a baby slither hither and thither in his hair, but he forgot to feed it one night before he went to bed, and, during the night, it ate him."

"Like they ate the princess," Charles said with a wicked smile.

"They didn't eat the princess! Daddy, make him behave."

"How do you know, smarty? You haven't heard the whole story."

"Did the slither hither and thithers eat the princess? Or the prince? You both have to be very quiet and I'll tell you the whole story."

***

So the wizard was very lonely, and he decided he

needed a mate. He looked all around the kingdom. It was a tiny kingdom, but he couldn't find anybody, for all the beautiful young maidens, even the unbeautiful young maidens, would hide from him. This made the evil wizard very angry, and even the rat would become afraid of him and hide deep, deep in the wizard's long red hair, not moving or making a sound.

This went on for some months and the evil wizard, his name was Rigirus, was on the point of giving up in defeat and resigning himself to a mateless existence when he came up with a strange idea--a brilliant idea, actually. He would send his rat out to spy for him. He'd been looking for an excuse to get the rat out of his hair anyway, and this would do quite nicely. As a spy, the rat could go all sorts of places he couldn't and find out just what the young ladies thought of him. Which ones liked him and why, and why they insisted upon hiding it from him. That sort of thing.

And, he rather suspected the rat in his hair wasn't helping him any with the damsels. This caused him no end of worry. Did he dare do without his trademark? Should he lose the rat altogether? Or would that reduce his visibility so that he was only a commonplace wizard? Why is life so complicated, he would whine to himself. If only he'd adopted another trademark. But then he'd think about it and realize he couldn't think of anything better. Oh, well, he thought, if I'm stuck with him I might as well put him to good use. Yes, a spy. Just the thing. Well once my mind is made up, it's made up, he told himself. Which actually wasn't true. He was a most indecisive wizard, in fact, and usually gave up on his projects much too early. But not this time. He really was very lonely.

So, he began looking through all his sorcery books,

hunting for a recipe to turn a rat into a human and change him back again. He rummaged through book after book and scroll after scroll but could find nothing really right. There were recipes for turning all manner of animals into humans and humans into animals and back again. For example, fish into humans, and vice versa, and also snakes and lizards, turtles, birds, wolves (there were many of these), newts, salamanders, frogs, toads, peacocks, oysters, camels, elephants, horses, pigs, flies, mosquitoes, dragonflies, gnats, cats, and even bats, but nothing, absolutely nothing, about rats.

RATS! screamed the evil wizard inside his own head. Nothing about rats? How could this be? He had the most complete sorcerer's library in the Seven Higher Kingdoms. He was absolutely sure of it. Except for the library of Sarnus, and there was no point in even thinking of that. It was totally inaccessible to him. So, in despair, he almost gave up. But he was lonely, and he did so want to get the black rat out of his red hair. Well then, he decided, I shall simply have to invent my own recipe. It can't be all that difficult. I'll just borrow a little from here and a little from there. A little of this recipe and a little of that. I'll come up with it, he reassured himself. After all, am I not the greatest wizard of all?

So, in the summer, the evil wizard began to experiment. As the days turned and the crops and fruits grew and ripened, and while others enjoyed summer sun in the clear mornings, and shaded themselves under broad leafed trees by the water's edge in the hot afternoon, he stayed in his tower all the day, shivering in the morning chill, and sweatily sweltering in the afternoon. Then the days shortened and cooled, the trees turned glorious yellow and red, and the air was crisp and delightful. But the evil wizard stuck his nose ever deeper in his musty books and scrolls, or held that very same nose over foul, smoking, steaming cauldrons and pots, full of boiling bits and pieces of plants and animal remains. As it turned to winter, and others sought the warmth of fireside, cheerful company at dinner and warm covers at night, the evil wizard stayed alone in his bitterly cold tower, the stone, untapastried walls covered with frost, his breath steaming as much as his cauldrons, except when his nose and face became red and unbearably hot from being thrust close to the simmering brews as he watched over them, while his back and red hair turned as white with frost as the walls.

And nothing worked right. He turned his rat into, to name just a few, a shrew, a cat, a gnat, a mouse, a louse, a dog, a hog, a goose and even a moose. At last, on the coldest night of the year, as the wind howled and the full moon was completely shielded by thick, icy, black, billowing clouds, and the snow came down almost sideways, and a thin layer of ice covered the inside walls of his tower, and the snow blew into his room and swirled around in eddies and currents, at last, he'd had enough. He broke down and buried his face in his soot-blackened hands and began to sob.

I'm such a failure, he thought to himself. Nothing I do ever works. I only became a wizard because I'm no good at anything else. Why does everybody else have it so easy? Why not me? Stupid rat in my hair. Hair! What happens when my red hair starts to turn gray? Do I dye it or what? Do I dye the rat again? Stupid rat. Stupid recipes. Stupid women. Who do they think they are? Who are they to judge me? What have they ever done? Do they have any idea, any idea at all, just how hard it is to be a wizard?

By now, the evil wizard was becoming quite worked up

and began to pound his hands on the table in front of him. Upon it stood many pots of potions and jars of spells, and as he pounded harder and harder, they began to jiggle and wiggle and bounce and jounce closer and closer to the edge of the table--and to the steaming cauldron that held his latest concoction.

In fact, the pounding became so loud it woke the evil black rat who'd been sleeping sound and snug in the evil wizard's hair. There, he'd been well protected by the wizard's thick red hair, from both the cold of the winter pouring through the open window and the hot blast of the fire by the table. Drowsily, he stirred and tried to reposition himself when the wizard, at last beside himself with rage, violently began tossing his head about. Suddenly, the rat found himself thrown down upon the table and into the path of the wizard's pounding fists. Terrified, while still half asleep, he scurried about with the huge fists hammering about him. He darted about the table in a frantic panic and then, horror of horrors, he bumped into a few pots and jars and knocked some of them into the cauldron.

Catastrophe!

A terrible silence. The rat looked up and saw the horrible red eyes, the fiendish scowl, the bared teeth, the death-wishing stare of his master whose fists were suspended in mid-air. The rat cringed, paralyzed with fear, breathless and trembling.

Then the evil wizard exploded.

"You stupid rat! You dumb rat. You ruined my recipe! I hate you. I hate you. You ingrate rat." And the wizard picked up the rat and flung him into the cauldron.

How many scientific discoveries and breakthroughs are the result of blind chance? Of happy fate? Of fortunate happenstance? The telephone, penicillin, the law of gravity. The evil wizard, of course, knew of none of these, but if he had, he would certainly have made the comparisons himself.

For there was a scream of fear and pain, and a full grown man leaped naked out of the cauldron and sprawled on the floor. Quickly, he came up on his hands and knees and scampered to a corner of the room. There he huddled on all fours trembling, but with a defiant snarl on his lips.

The wizard gasped. His jaw fell open as far as it could go. He collapsed back into his chair and stared. They stayed that way, the naked man snarling, and the wizard staring, for the longest time. Finally, the wizard noticed the wind and the snow had stopped, and the first rays of light were visible through the window.

Then he began to laugh--great big roaring gusts of laughter that shook his body. Tears rolled down his cheeks and made tracks through the soot that dusted his face. Then he got up and threw his hands up in the air and began to dance and prance and jig and skip about the room.

"I did it! I did it!" he half shouted, half sang. "Oh, I'm the best of the very best. I am the greatest wizard of them all. None greater than me. No, siree, none greater than me."

Then he froze.

"Wait. How did I do it?" he asked. "Which pots went into the cauldron?"

Quickly, he rushed to the cauldron. He noticed that the fire had gone out long ago. This was good for it meant that the potion would not be boiled off, and there was still some left in the bottom of the cauldron. Grabbing a pair of tongs he fished about and pulled out two little bottles and a jar. The jar was newt's tail powder he was sure. He looked at the pots still remaining on the table and surmised that the two bottles in the cauldron must have been dried bat blood and powdered black boar's heart. But which of the ingredients had done the trick and which made no difference? And in what quantities? These were crucial questions. Oh well, he had plenty. Just make sure to save it. He put a lid on the cauldron. It would take a lot of experimenting, but sooner or later he'd get the proportions right. Then, he heard a rustling noise behind him.

He whirled about and saw the man trying to crawl out the narrow window.

"Stop!" he roared.

The man stopped and turned to look at him. His eyes were pleading, tortured and confused.

The wizard noticed for the first time that the man's skin was turning blue and covered with goose bumps, and he was shivering. Quickly, the wizard became frightened. What if his creation froze to death? What if the formula wouldn't work on another rat? Quickly, he grabbed a blanket and threw it on the naked man. It hung on his shoulders for a moment, then fell to the floor. The man did not move but stared at the wizard, uncomprehending.

"Well, Typhus, why are you just standing there?' the wizard asked. "Pick up the blanket and put it on. Do you want to freeze to death?"

At the mention of his name something stirred in the creature's eyes. But he still didn't move. He stared for a bit more at the wizard, then dazed, looked down at the blanket.

"Pick it up," the wizard ordered. But then it struck him what the matter was. Of course! Typhus still thought he was a rat.

He stepped forward and grabbed Typhus's hands and held them up in front of his eyes.

"See, these are hands. Hands."

Typhus looked at his hands, and his eyes went wide in horror, and he shook his head back and forth as tears welled up in his eyes.

"No, no, Typhus, it's all right. You're human now. You're a man now. Like me. Pick up the blanket. Oh, here, let me show you."

The wizard bent down and picked up the blanket and put it over Typhus's shoulders and pulled it tight around him. Then he stuck the folds of the blanket into Typhus's hands, which instinctively clutched them. Then Typhus slowly sank to the floor with his back against the wall and began to sob.

The wizard shook his head.

"Typhus, Typhus, I know this is quite a shock to you, but you really mustn't carry on so. You're no good to me if you can't control yourself."

Typhus only sobbed harder.

"Typhus, you should show some gratitude. After all, last night you were a mere rat. Now, you are that most magnificent of creatures, a human being. Aren't you going to say something? Aren't you going to say anything at all?"

A horrible anxiety quickly filled the wizard's mind. What if Typhus was still a rat inside? What if he couldn't speak or, just as bad, would require years of training. Then all his effort was wasted. He screamed, "Speak up, Typhus! Speak!"

Typhus looked up from his crouch and his jaw began to move.

"Uh, uh, ah, ah."

"Speak. Speak."

"Ah, aah, I don't know how."

Immediately, Typhus let go of the blanket and clapped both hands over his mouth, his eyes wide in amazement.

"Aha," exulted the wizard. He bent forward in triumph and pointed his bony index finger at Typhus's mouth.

"See. You can talk. Am I not the greatest wizard of all? Say, thank you, Typhus."

Typhus did not say thank you. Instead he emitted a deep snarl. The wizard jumped back, startled. All the fear and confusion were gone from Typhus now. Full comprehension and human intelligence had replaced them, but in those eyes the wizard could see the ferocious soul of a rat.

"Who told you I wanted to be a human?"

The wizard was taken aback. The question was beyond his understanding. And his feelings were hurt.

"Why, you insolent wretch. Of course you want to be human. Who wouldn't? You little beast."

Typhus answered in an outraged growl.

"You arrogant goat. You're the wretch. Changing my state."

The wizard was amazed.

"You liked being a rat?"

Typhus fell completely silent, and the wizard knew he had him.

"Well, go ahead then. Tell me what was so wonderful about being a rat."

Typhus looked lost and his lower lip began to quiver.

"I can't remember," he said.

"What?"

"I mean, I don't know how to describe it. It's so different."

The wizard sensed that he'd better feign sympathy. Somehow, he felt something important was about to be revealed.

"Oh, my dear, Typhus, please forgive me for not understanding. You've been through a terrible ordeal. Of course, you don't understand. Who would? Here, sit on a chair like a proper human now," he added, as he slid a chair under Typhus.

"Would you like some hot broth?"

He began to bustle about and ladled up a small bowl of day old broth, which was only slightly warm, from a small cooking pot by the side of the fireplace. He did this quickly and shoved it into Typhus's hands. He continued to bustle about and suit his actions to his words.

"Now, let's get this blanket back on you. And I'll send for the tailor to make you a proper set of clothing. Now, what did you mean by different?"

Typhus now found himself warmer, strangely comfortable sitting in a chair, and the broth, while just barely warm, soothed his insides.

"Well, for starters, I can talk. I don't know how, but I can. All these sensations are crowding in on me."

He stopped and stared into space.

"Yes, yes. Do go on, Typhus."

"Suddenly, I know things. I make connections. I understand. All this is new to me. It's too much, too fast. Can I lay down and sleep, please?"

"But, of course, my dear, Typhus. But first, just a little bit please. What's it like being a rat?"

"It's so hard. You don't have a vocabulary. You just see an inch in front of your nose. You have a really tiny brain."

"Could you understand me when I talked to you?"

Typhus frowned as he tried to remember. He closed his eyes and tilted his head back.

"I see everything in a blur and a large shadow over me.

'Food, Typhus, my pet.' I remember those words."

He could also remember other words, bad words, but his innate rat instinct for survival kept him from mentioning those.

For his part, the wizard was very satisfied. Typhus could make out words as a rat and remember them. That, he was confident, could be improved upon over time and trained into perfection.

"Splendid, Typhus. Well, to bed with you now. You've had a long, tiring night."

Typhus moved as if to curl up on the floor, but the wizard made a grand show of putting Typhus in his own bed.

"No, Typhus, my lad. You are my honored guest now. You see how everything changes when you become human? You will sleep in my bed. No, no, don't object. Not another word. In my bed. I'll sleep in the attic. And here's another blanket for you. Don't worry about me," he said as he exited the room, "I'm not the least bit sleepy."

He closed the door with exaggerated softness as he left.

I'll bet you're not sleepy, you evil old goat, Typhus thought to himself. He shivered miserably, not against the cold, but against something he'd never felt before as a rat. He'd felt fear many times. It was part of being a rat. But this nameless dread, this trembling unease he'd felt ever since becoming human, he'd thought there was no word for it. But then the word for it had just popped right into his head.

Evil.

***

"Are you getting sleepy, sweetheart?"

"Uh, huh."

Charles noticed his sister's eyes had been getting heavy. Which was okay, because his own were starting to droop. He liked this story and was looking forward to hearing more. He didn't want to miss any by falling asleep.

"You didn't mention the Princess, Daddy."

"Soon, sweetheart, soon."

Charles watched as his father touched the back of his hand to Tanya's forehead again.

"Will I be able to listen tomorrow night, Daddy?"

"I think so. We'll see."

"I want to hear the whole story, Daddy."

"You will, sweetheart. Now, time for bed. Tuck yourself in, will you, Charles? Don't forget your prayers."

"Sure, Dad."

Father stood up with Tanya in his arms and quietly carried her out of the room, shutting the light off as he did so. Charles leaned partway out of his bed and gave the door a gentle shove to shut it. He lay upon his back and stared at the ceiling while his eyes adjusted to the light. As he did so he quickly hurried through his prayers.

He was troubled. For some reason, he felt guilty about his sister. She'd always irritated him. For one thing, she was a terrible snitch. Whenever you got into doing something really interesting she'd find out and either tell or threaten to tell. Charles could never get her to understand that just because you'd been told not to do something that didn't mean it was really wrong. It depended. Like if you were playing down by the lakeside; Mom and Dad didn't want you to do it when they weren't around because they wanted you to be safe. So, Charles reasoned to himself, if you were extra careful so you didn't get hurt, then it was okay. But Tanya couldn't see that. A rule was a rule no matter what. And when she said she'd tell Mom, she meant it. And, being a girl, Mom thought rules were rules too. And of course, Dad would take Mom's side, even though Charles was sure that Dad, deep inside, agreed with him.

So, why was he feeling so guilty now about being mad at his sister? And she didn't want to do anything anymore. Here it was, a beautiful September, and all she wanted to do was stay inside. When there was so much to be done outside. They had this huge backyard with a lake and woods on either side of the house. And another thing, school was going to start soon. How was she going to go to school if she stayed inside all the time? Everything about his sister made him mad. So why was it that when he looked at her sometimes now, he wanted to cry?

His eyes drooped shut and he dropped into a fitful sleep. He began to dream.

It was a beautiful summer day. He and Tanya were walking through a field of high, golden grass. It was silent. There was no sound of insects, nor birds, nor running streams. A high sun, directly overhead, gave off an intense light that reflected off the grass and made it hard to see. But the sun gave off no heat. Yet Charles didn't feel cold.

Tanya let go of his hand and began to run off through the grass. Quickly, because of the glare and the high grass, he lost sight of her.

"Tanya," he cried out. "Wait for me." He ran after her, running faster and faster, following the trail she made in the grass. He ran and ran breathing harder and harder, the sun now beating down upon him very hot, the sweat pouring down his face. Out of breath, he stopped.. The trail was gone.

And so was Tanya.

In her room, Tanya was not dreaming. Nor was she sleeping. She was sitting up in her bed, her knees drawn up next to her chest, her arms wrapped tightly around her knees. In her right hand she clutched a steak knife she'd taken from the kitchen. She fought sleep by poking the palm of her left hand with the knife point whenever she felt she was drifting off. Her eyes were staring at her closet. It was in there again. She could hear it rumbling around--growling, grumbling, poking about. One night it was going to come out after her, she was sure. And she wouldn't be awake. She wouldn't be able to drive it back. Sooner or later, her luck would run out, she'd fall asleep at the wrong time, and it would have her. Some night, maybe even…her eyes drooped shut and she fell asleep.

Tanya, too, began to dream.

"There was a fairy kingdom once," she heard a voice in her dream say.

And Tanya could see them. Moving softly, glowing like fireflies in the dusk, through a valley in the middle of a mountainous forest. At the end of the valley she could see a tall, blue castle, in front of a mountain, with huge turrets that rose high into the evening sky. And drawn to the castle in front of her were hundreds of fairies, glowing in the deepening darkness, flying gently down the valley between the forested mountainsides toward the castle.

Strangely, she realized she too now had wings, and her own body was glowing. She was flying gently towards the castle. It was so peaceful. She felt so light and so safe. Nothing could harm her now. Up ahead she could see the fairies in front of her moving faster and faster as they approached the castle, sweeping up and flying into the windows of the castle. She felt herself being pulled now, ever faster as her heart began to pound. Which window should she choose to enter? What was in the castle? She suddenly had the horrible feeling that she was not flying toward the castle but being drawn against her will, now much too fast. One window suddenly loomed up in front of her, and she realized that none of the fairies were flying into it. It had seemed so far away and small and now so incredibly large and black...

She awoke and looked down at her hand. She saw that she had pricked her palm with the tip of the steak knife. A thin trickle of blood ran out of her palm. It reminded her of something, but she couldn't remember what. Her whole body gave one wracking convulsive sob, and she rolled over, dead asleep.

Chapter 2

The Seventh Higher Kingdom

"How do you feel tonight, sweetheart?"

"Fine."

"Let me feel your forehead. Well, alright. We shall continue with our story. How about you, Charles? Are you ready?"

"Ready," said Charles hopping into his bed. Both children were in their pajamas again. Tanya's were white with pink teddy bears scattered about and Charles' were blue with red and yellow rocket ships. Father no longer smoked his pipe when Tanya was in the room, but it still gave off a faint, sweet smell of cherry from where it lay in an ashtray. Father sat, with Tanya in his lap, in the red, leather easy chair. The easy chair had sat at the foot of Charles's bed for as long as he could remember, and from it, Father had told him and Tanya stories for as long as he could remember. A table lamp at the side of the chair gave off a soft light from underneath its shade. Charles thought that there must be a new bulb in the light, because Tanya's skin looked extra shiny tonight. He paid it no more attention and waited for his father to begin.

Tanya snuggled in tighter into Father's arms.

"Did Typhus have a dream, Daddy?"

"Well, I don't know. Maybe."

"Did he dream about when he was a rat?" Charles asked. It would be so neat to know what a rat dreamed about.

Father looked thoughtfully up at the ceiling.

"Well, perhaps he did. Let's see now. Where did I leave off?"

"I know," Charles cried. "Typhus learned a new word—evil." Charles said the word with obvious relish. Tanya buried herself deeper in Father's arms.

"Well, I was going to tell you about Prince Cha Cha and Princess Ta Ta tonight."

Tanya brightened at the mention of the princess. But Father shook his head slowly and said, "But I think I'd better tell you about the dream first."

"But I want to hear about Princess Ta Ta , Daddy."

"And so you shall. But this is important. You really won't understand about Princess Ta Ta and Prince Cha Cha if you don't hear about the dream first. After all, you are the one that asked about the dream."

"Yes, I want to hear about the dream too, Daddy."

"Well, then it was like this."

"Typhus fell into a curious sort of half sleep. He wasn't really awake and he wasn't really asleep. He couldn't be sure if he was thinking or dreaming. And then, of course, his memories of being a rat would come flooding in, and he'd think being a human had just been a bad dream, a rat nightmare. But then, somehow, in his sleep he'd realize that didn't make sense. How could a rat dream about being a human? No, it must be the other way about. He was having a nightmare about once being a rat. That was it. But the memories, hazy memories, smells, sensations of dark caverns, and rubbing noses, and touching whiskers and eating cockroaches, and then being out in bright light once—he'd smelt food. It came to him very clearly, and he'd run to snatch the food, but once he had it and he turned to run away, something strange blocked his way. No matter which way he turned something blocked his way. And then some huge red shadow was over him, and these huge eyes were staring at him and then...Typhus felt suddenly very dull. His nose was assaulted by a riot of smells, and upon opening his eyes, everything in the room looked incredibly huge."

"Was he a rat again, Daddy?"

"Yes, he was. The formula wore off and he went straight back to being a rat. But now, I'm going to tell you about Prince Cha Cha and Princess Ta Ta."

Tanya squealed in delight and clapped her hands she was so pleased. Charles noted that this pleased Father so much he smiled bigger than Charles had seen him smile in a long time.

"Now, children, you must understand that Prince Cha Cha was a very handsome young prince, the handsomest in all the Seven Higher Kingdoms. He had soft, silky, blond hair that curled over his ears, a straight nose, a high forehead, a strong, but not pointed, chin with a little dimple in the middle and bright, clear, blue eyes. He also carried a short, jeweled sword that his mother let him carry."

"His mother!" Charles felt betrayed.

"Well, after all, he was still a young prince."

"How young?" Charles demanded.

"Oh, somewhere between seven and nine I suppose."

"Oh," said Charles. "That sounds interesting."

"How old was Princess Ta Ta, Daddy?"

"I'm getting to that, sweetheart. You see, children, it was like this."

***

Prince Cha Cha was very vain. He knew he was very handsome, and he knew that someday he was going to be king. And he felt that everyone should treat him like a king, even while he was still only a very young prince. This worried his mother and father, the Queen and King, very much.

"What kind of king will he be?" his father would moan and bury his head in his hands. "When he takes my crown, will he make his people happy or miserable?"

"I don't know what to do with him," his mother would sob. "If I punish him he just laughs and says, 'Someday I'll be the king and I'll do whatever I want.'"

"Maybe he needs more archery lessons," mused the King. "That way he'll learn how important it is to take careful aim to hit the mark. It's important for a king to think like that."

"Maybe more riding lessons," said the Queen. "Then he'll learn that ruling a country is like riding a spirited and dangerous horse."

"Chess lessons," cried the King. "He'll learn to always think ahead three moves."

"Dance lessons," offered the Queen. "He'll learn that to be King one must always take careful steps according to custom, and in tune with the same music as everyone else."

So, the King and Queen did all that and much more. They hired the finest masters in archery, horsemanship, chess and dancing; and also Latin, fencing, geography and all other things to teach him all that a prince could possibly need to know in order to become a good king. And Prince Cha Cha worked and studied very, very hard and was very, very good at all they gave him to do. But it all did no good. He just became more and more vain and more and more insufferable.

Now, up in the tower, watching all of this was Princess Ta Ta. She was the older sister of Prince Cha Cha, and she was as beautiful as he was handsome. In fact, except that her hair was longer and her chin daintier, they looked almost like twins. She would look down upon her brother from her tower window and sigh. It was all so very simple, she felt. Why couldn't father and mother see it? But she was only a year older than her brother, and she knew that no one would listen to her if she told them the answer. Even if she were older, the answer was so different and out of the ordinary it wasn't likely anyone would do it. Besides, while it was a simple idea, like many simple ideas it would be hard to actually do.

So, she would look down into the courtyard and watch her brother ordering people about left and right and sigh again. He was handsome, he was smart, he was brave, he was hard working--he was obnoxious. But for that last trait, he would not only make a good king, he would make a great king. And everyone in the palace knew it. Which, she supposed, was why they just didn't fling him into the moat. She was sure that everyone in the kingdom must have wanted to do it at least once. She wanted to do it at least once a day.

But she was only a little princess. And soon they

would send her to a neighboring kingdom to be a maid-in-waiting to a queen. There, she would learn everything she needed to know to be a duchess or a baroness or perhaps even a queen herself. But, she didn't want any of that. She loved their little kingdom. Her father was such a kind king, and it was well known that his peasants and subjects were the merriest, the most prosperous, and the best fed in all the Seven Higher Kingdoms. And she wanted that to go on, and she wanted her brother to become the great king she knew, that everyone knew, he could be. If only there were some way. And there was. That was the simple idea she had that she was sure no one would listen to.

There was a wizard, a very great wizard, someone had told her about. He was very wise, but no one had ever actually seen him. He lived over the mountain tops, past Sodarke Forest and Dark Wilde Forest, in the tiny little Kingdom of Fandon. Everyone knew he was the wisest and greatest wizard of all because his fireworks were the best in all the Seven Higher Kingdoms. Now the little Kingdom of Fandon stood close to the top of Mount Stalwart guarding the pass into the Land of the Mists where only, she was told, the Wizard of Fandon dared to enter. Surely, thought Princess Ta Ta, the wizard of Fandon, being so wise, would know what to do about Cha Cha. But, she knew that no one at the castle would take her suggestion seriously because she was just a little princess. So, she would have to go to him herself. But how? She was just a little princess and the Kingdom of Fandon was so impossibly far away. It was through Dark Wilde Forest, past the Kingdom of Ilwil and then over the Roaring River and then through Boulder Desert and up the steep, rugged trail of Mount Stalwart to Fandon Castle.

There was no one she could send in her stead. She was

only a little Princess, and no one would undertake such a mission for her, no matter how much they loved her, and everybody in the Kingdom did, except of course for Griselle, who was probably jealous of her beauty. And, even if she did tell them what she wanted them to do, she was sure they would only laugh at her suggestion. No. She must go herself. But again, she asked herself, how?

Her thoughts were interrupted by the sound of her brother screaming. She shuddered and going to her window, looked out, fearing the worst. Down far below, she saw her brother screaming at a serving man and brandishing his sword about his head. She could see that his face was red and contorted and the serving man was trembling. She could see a flask of spilled wine on the stone flagging of the courtyard and a red blotch on Cha Cha's bright white surcoat. She was glad she was so far above the courtyard that she couldn't understand what her brother was yelling.

Suddenly, she felt a cold clammy breath on the back of her neck.

"I think it was terribly careless of that serving oaf to spoil dear little Cha Cha's coat."

It was Griselle that spoke. Instinctively, Princess Ta Ta took a quick, deep breath and put on her biggest smile before turning to look up at Griselle.

"It's so nice of you to speak up for Cha Cha," Ta Ta said, "but you know how he rushes about headlong in the courtyard. He probably turned about and ran straight into the servant before the poor man had a chance to move out of his way."

"Tut, tut, my dear. It's the servant's job to anticipate our every action. It's what they're bred to do." Griselle leaned over Ta Ta's shoulder and looked down on the courtyard and shook her head in disapproval. "What's your brother waiting for? He should smack that wretch with his sword. He's the Prince and he has every right to do so."

A tight, thin smile appeared on Griselle's lips. "Look, he's going to strike him. Good."

Ta Ta whirled in alarm and leaned out the window. So upset was she that her hands clutched the window ledge like vises. Down below she saw that Prince Cha Cha had his sword all the way back over his head and was ready to strike the servant full force with the flat of his sword. It was a horrible moment. Even if the sword didn't hurt the servant, news of it would spread throughout the kingdom. In an instant, life would change forever in the kingdom, for all knew the Prince would be the next king, and everybody would live in fear of that day. She was watching a disaster unfold.

Suddenly, a figure in purple rushed in and swooped up Cha Cha and carried him off as he howled and screamed and flung his legs about in rage. It was mother, and not a moment too soon.

Before Ta Ta had time to breathe a sigh of relief she felt a sudden pressure from behind on her back. The only thing that kept her from tumbling out the window to the courtyard far below was the vise like grip her hands had already taken on the window ledge. Just as suddenly, the pressure on her back stopped. Griselle flung her arms about Ta Ta from behind and hugged her tight.

"Oh," Griselle crooned soothingly, "your mother has kept your darling brother from giving that oaf his just desserts. Well of course, she is the Queen, so she must know best."

All of Ta Ta's senses were taut and alert. Everything about Griselle had suddenly fallen into place. She now saw with complete clarity why she'd always been uneasy since

Griselle had arrived in the palace. That sudden, firm shove in the back told her everything. And inside, she was also beaming with happiness. For now she knew how she could get to go to the Wizard of Fandon.

But, just a little later, down in his bedroom, Prince Cha Cha was not beaming with happiness. Instead he was lying face down on his bed and sobbing in rage.

This was so humiliating. It was unbearable. It was insult. It was outrage. His jacket was ruined. His mother had taken away his sword! She had disrobed him like a little child and put on his nightclothes. In broad daylight! In front of the maids and servants! And when he warned her that he would be king one day and she'd better be careful, she lifted him up by one hand and struck him. On his backside! The insult! If she had struck him on the face, that would have been tolerable. But like a little child. And he had been nine years old for a month now. Then, the horrible word forced itself into his mind.

Spanked!

Like a little child. Like any child. Not like the future king. And the maids and servants had all smirked and nodded their heads to each other in satisfaction. They positively beamed at his mother in approval. And when he glared at them to make them stop, they just smirked all the more. This was wrong. This was intolerable. He would get even, and he wouldn't wait until he was king either. If only she were here, she could tell him what to do. She would help him.

Suddenly, he sat upright and stopped crying. An eager smile of anticipation settled upon his face. He could hear the stones slowly beginning to move. He was so glad he'd found that old, long forgotten, secret passageway that led throughout the castle. And he was so glad he'd only told one person about it. The stones stopped their rumbling and, from behind a tapestry of a wolf attacking a lamb, she appeared.

"Griselle," he cried happily.

"I don't like Prince Cha Cha , Daddy."

"But you do like the Princess don't you?"

"Yes, Daddy."

"Well, she loved the Prince very much."

"But, why?"

"Aw, shut up and let Dad tell the story."

"If you two start fighting, I'll never be able to remember how the story goes."

This was greeted by a frightened silence.

"That's better. What happened next? Oh, I remember."

"Griselle," Prince Cha Cha cried happily. He ran to her, and she knelt down to receive him. He threw himself in her arms and began to sob again.

"Look what they've done to me. They don't love me."

"Of course, not, dear," she crooned in a voice that was almost a singsong. "Haven't I always told you so?"

"Yes, you have." His lower lip trembled as he gave the next bit of horrible news.

"Mama took away my sword."

"From the future king? How dare she!"

"And, and…" Cha Cha looked away and down, uncertainly. It was too embarrassing. He needn't have worried for, as usual, Griselle had taken care to learn the whole story before she entered and, as usual, she took care not to let him know it.

"What?" Griselle's words dripped and clung to Ta Ta like honey. "What is it? What did she do to you?"

"She…she hit me."

"Where? Tell me where."

"On the face," he lied.

Griselle's face flickered only momentarily. She knew the truth, and she had plans to use his humiliation, but first, she had to stoke the fire to maximum heat. A lesser intriguer would have stumbled, but a lifetime at court, and a passion for deception saw her through.

"And you took it bravely, didn't you? I know you did."

"Yes."

"And she struck you hard?"

"Yes."

"Here, let me see your face."

She took his chin in her fingers and turned it side to side, pretending to study his face. A growing frown of displeasure appeared on her face.

"Cha Cha, are you lying to me?"

Cha Cha tried to turn away, tortured by guilt, but Griselle grabbed him by the shoulders and made him face her.

"Where did she strike you? Where? It's even worse than the face, isn't it?"

The prince sniffled, wiped his nose with his sleeve and looked down at the floor.

Griselle's voice rose to a fever pitch of pretended indignation.

"She didn't! She wouldn't dare. Not that! The outrage, the effrontery. Did she spank you?"

Crying and sniffling harder, Cha Cha nodded his head.

"Were others watching?"

"Y…y…yes," Cha Cha blubbered.

Griselle pulled the Prince tight to her bosom.

"Oh, my dear, sweet, Cha Cha. How do you ever bear it? You're so very brave. What a nightmare you must be living. No one but me loves you. No one but me knows what a great king you shall be. Poor humiliated Cha Cha. Spanked like a little baby in front of all your inferiors. How do they expect you to ever run a kingdom if no one respects you? Don't worry, Cha Cha. You're better than any of them. Be proud, Cha Cha, be proud. And don't worry. I'll help you to get your revenge."

As Cha Cha listened to the honeyed crooning of Griselle's voice, he found that, inexplicably, in the middle of the afternoon, he was falling fast asleep.

Now, a little later than this, in another part of the castle, after Cha Cha had fallen into a deep slumber, and Griselle had whispered soft, secret words into his ears before leaving him, later than that, Nana, the gray haired governess of Ta Ta and Cha Cha, was preparing Ta Ta for her afternoon nap. Unlike her brother, Ta Ta liked to take a nap in the heat of the afternoon, whereas he would never have slept at all if he could have avoided it. Griselle was there too. She insisted on spending time with the children. Without knowing why, that bothered Nana. She did not like the way Griselle always fussed about the children, especially Cha Cha. For a recent new comer to the court, she was much too familiar with the royal family, if you asked her. As Nana brushed Ta Ta's hair, and Griselle turned back the covers on the bed, the princess did something different. Something unexpected.

"Nana," she said, "bring me a cup of milk to go with my cake."

"But you never drink milk in the afternoon," Nana answered.

"Yes, but it is so warm. I think milk will help me to rest better."

"But I must prepare you for your nap."

"That's all right. Griselle can help me while you're

down to the kitchen getting the milk."

Griselle stifled a gasp, then crooned, "I'll be happy to do it."

Nana stood stiffly erect and stopped brushing. Her feelings were hurt.

"I can send a servant down for it," she said querulously.

"But, Nana," Ta Ta said, "you're the only one that knows how to mix it with peach and honey just the way I like it."

Nana chuckled softly, mollified.

"Yes, of course, dear. I'll go down and mix it up myself."

She gave Ta Ta's hair a last stroke with the brush and handed it to Griselle who put on her widest smile for Nana as she accepted the brush. Then Nana kissed Ta Ta gently on the top of her head and left, humming softly to herself.

Griselle tried to hum as she brushed, but it reminded Ta Ta more of the lazy buzzing of a wasp that has already eaten its fill, than of a tune that she could recognize. And Griselle bore down too much on her strokes so that it burned the skin. Ta Ta endured it patiently, though every nerve in her body was as taut as a sparrow being watched by a hawk. She bided her time, somehow knowing that Griselle would underestimate her and make the first move. She didn't have to wait long.

"It's so nice to be brushing your hair, Princess."

"Really? Why?"

"Oh, I don't know. It's a complement, I suppose, when a great princess lets you wait on her."

"Great? Do you think I'm great? I'm just a little princess, you know."

"Little princess! Come now, you must never think of yourself like that. You're already a great princess."

Ta Ta remembered a phrase her father liked to use about his conferences with some of the courtiers. "The butter was two fingers thick," he would say and then roar with laughter. Now, she knew what he meant. But she gave no indication of what she was thinking. She just smiled into the looking glass she held in her hands at Griselle who stood behind her.

"Nobody else feels that way about me."

"But they don't see you the way you really are, Princess. It's almost as if you should be Queen."

Then, Ta Ta almost gave herself away. Something startled her about what Griselle said about being Queen. But she didn't know what it was, and she had no time to think about it. She pretended to cough and then smiled into the mirror at Griselle again.

Griselle seemed to have a hint of suspicion in her eyes.

"Is something wrong, my dear?" she asked.

"I think you're brushing my hair too hard."

A look of fear flashed across Griselle's face, and she almost dropped the brush.

"Oh, dear. Why didn't…" she fumbled with her words, "…why didn't you say so?"

But she recovered quickly, her crooning voice resumed, and her brush strokes were much gentler.

"You know I'd never do anything in the world to hurt you. All I want is to help you."

Ta Ta was at the moment of decision. She hesitated. She realized how dangerous this woman was. She remembered Griselle's hands on her back that morning, and that firm, testing push. If her own hands hadn't been jammed into the window ledge…maybe she shouldn't do this.

"Why, Princess, what's wrong?"

Ta Ta came out of her thoughts and caught her own expression in the mirror. She realized that she'd let her smile slip away, and her expression was unguarded now. That decided for her. She knew now what she must do, and that there would be no turning back.

"Oh, Griselle," she wailed, and she turned about in her chair and buried herself in Griselle's arms. "I'm so miserable."

Griselle dropped the hairbrush in surprise and confusion and would have stepped back, but Ta Ta gripped her so tightly it was impossible.

"Why, child," Griselle croaked instead of crooned, "whatever is the matter?"

Ta Ta remembered the sharp edged brooch Griselle wore, and buried the top of her head in it as hard as she could until the pain brought tears into her eyes. While she did so she kept talking.

"Oh, Griselle, I'm so lonely. Nobody loves me. Nobody understands me. Nobody wants to be my friend. Nobody wants to help me."

Ta Ta could feel Griselle's fingers digging into her shoulders the way a hawk's talons dug into a sparrow when it carried it off. It hurt enough to bring even more tears to her eyes.

"But, dear, I want to help you."

Now that Ta Ta could feel the tears running down her face, she pulled away from Griselle and looked straight up into her eyes.

"Oh, Griselle, do you really mean that?"

"Oh, child, of course I do."

"Are you really my friend?"

"Yes, dear child."

Ta Ta buried her head in Griselle's bosom again and pressed the sore spot on her head against a metal button.

She sobbed loudly, and when her tears were increased still more, she pulled back and gazed again into Griselle's eyes. "Oh, Griselle, if only you meant it."

"But, dear, I do mean it. I am your friend."

Ta Ta abruptly pushed Griselle away from her and jumped out of the chair and stamped her foot.

"Everybody says that," she shouted, "but nobody means it!"

"I mean it, dear."

Ta Ta stamped her foot again. "You do not! You're just saying that. Just like everybody else."

"But no, dear, I do mean it."

Ta Ta looked at the floor as if doubtful. "Really?"

"Really, dear."

Ta Ta hurled herself forward into Griselle's arms again. "Oh, Griselle, you are wonderful. You'll help me won't you?"

"Of course I will."

"That's wonderful. We'll leave at midnight."

"Leave?"

"To go hunting."

"Hunting?"

"For unicorns."

"Unicorns!" Griselle quickly disentangled herself from Ta Ta and stepped back two paces in astonishment. "But, child, there are no unicorns."

"Are too!"

"No, child, no."

"You're just like all the rest. You lie!"

"Child…"

"Liar! Liar!" Ta Ta was screaming.

"But, dear…"

"Get out! Get out!" Ta Ta picked up the hairbrush and

hurled it at Griselle who just managed to duck out of the way. Then Ta Ta flung a pitcher of water at her. "Get out! You're banished from my presence forever."

Griselle's face was contorted with horror as she watched her golden opportunity slipping from her grasp. Now, a little voice inside Ta Ta's head screamed. Now! She hurled herself back into Griselle's arms.

"Oh, Griselle, please, please," she sobbed. "Please take me unicorn hunting."

Griselle tried to croon again but was too confused to do anything but speak in her natural voice, which was whiny and unpleasant.

"But, there are no unicorns."

"Up deep in Dark Wilde Forest, up towards the River Dangerous. Please, please. There are unicorns up there. I just know it."

Ta Ta felt the hawk's talons tightening into her shoulders again. She looked up at Griselle and saw a serene smile on her face, and when Griselle spoke again her croon was almost musical.

"But, of course, dear. I'll take you. How could I ever refuse you anything?"

And I, Ta Ta thought, will have two requests to make of the wizard of Fandon now.

***

"What was the second request for the wizard, Dad?"

"That, Charles, I shall tell you another night. Your sister's falling asleep. How about you? You ready to call it a day?"

But Charles was already fast asleep and couldn't answer.

The next morning, when Charles woke up, he came slowly to full wakefulness. From the total silence in the house, he knew his mother and sister had gone for the long drive into the city. He was, for some reason, not included in these trips, and he knew that he didn't want to be. He would spend the day by himself, but he wasn't really alone. He was careful to always have the cell phone clipped to his belt, and his mother would call at least once to check on him. Just as important to his mother, their house was in plain view of the Johnson's farm on top of the hill half a mile away. Charles knew, without being told, that Mrs. Johnson was functioning as a long distance baby sitter. He would see her sitting on the porch, peeling apples or whatnot. If he was in the mood, he would wave at her and she would wave back. Later, she might come over with some apple pie, and he was minded not to touch it until his mamma came home. He had no trouble complying with that request, for without his really being aware of it, he had lost his appetite over the last six months. Mrs. Johnson was aware however, and would run a disapproving glance over his scrawny frame whenever she came by.

Aside from Mrs. Johnson, he had no distractions. Along with food, he had lost his appetite for TV, games, companionship, hobbies and even the lake. So, he would wander around aimlessly, from the house to the porch, to the garage, to the woods, through the woods and back to the house again, lost in thoughts he couldn't recall five minutes later.

On this particular morning, he lay in his bed and stared at the ceiling until the heat of the day began to feel uncomfortable. Then he got up and dressed himself slowly and distractedly. He left his bedroom, went downstairs and passed through the kitchen, without thought of breakfast, and out the pantry. Once outside, he began a slow, meandering walk down the dusty trail to the little, weather-beaten dock and, beyond that, to the woods. He wandered with his head down and his hands jammed into his front pockets.

He thought briefly about his sister and pushed it out of his mind. He felt vaguely that he should be happy she wasn't around messing up his plans, but a deep sense of foreboding was welling up inside him, and already, he was dreading her coming home today. Other confusing thoughts were fighting for his attention. It seemed that something very unfair was gripping her and his family—something that none of them deserved—and yet it was happening anyway.

Suddenly, he looked up and realized that he was deep in the woods and it startled him to realize that he'd never come this far before. He looked behind him and realized he was off the trail. He felt quite lost.

At the same time, in the city, Tanya could hear her mother sobbing in the doctor's office. She felt a wave of relief, as if a terrible burden had been lifted off her. Not knowing, she realized, was the worst thing. Hope, she had come to believe, made you afraid. But when there was no hope, she thought, you became free. At any rate, she felt free. Whatever happened now would be bad. She could tell from her mother's crying. Was she going to die? Was she going to be an invalid? It didn't matter. Whatever, her life wasn't going to be normal. It would be bad. It would be painful. Perhaps short would be a blessing. It was odd. She instinctively knew her mother would gladly switch places with her, if it were possible. But she was glad it wasn't her mother. She felt watching her mother suffer would be the worst thing. Anyway, it was over now. In a moment, she would know everything, and her life's course would be settled.

The door to the doctor's office opened and the serious looking doctor beckoned to her.

"Tanya, come on in. Your mother and I have to talk to you."

Later in the same day, Charles had been walking about in the woods for he knew not how long. He wasn't worried. He knew the forest wasn't endless, and that, eventually, he'd come out somewhere into some farmer's field, and he'd find a landmark or a road to get his bearings. But he was tired, and mosquitoes were beginning to pester him. He was tired of being lost, and he couldn't understand why he was lost. He thought he knew the woods better than this.

Unexpectedly, he saw a strangely twisted tree he'd never seen before. It had a huge trunk, and at the base of the trunk was a large, rough opening shaped something like a triangle. A light seemed to be coming from within. Immediately, his curiosity overcame his fatigue, and he walked over to investigate. He stood by the trunk, leaned over and looked into the opening. The inside was hollow and appeared to be large, clean and dry. He took a stick and poked inside. Nothing growled or bit at the stick, so he decided it was safe to go in. Once inside, he found it was large enough for him to stand up and turn around in quite easily. But where was the light coming from? He scanned the interior and noticed another hole, higher up on the trunk, on the opposite side from the entrance. Standing on tiptoe, he put his face next to the hole and gazed out. Through an opening in the trees, he saw the lake below and, on the other side of the lake, his house.

"Neat," he whispered to himself.

He knew he was going to come back to this newfound treasure a lot. He just had to be careful to mark a good trail on the way out, so he could find it easily when he wanted to come back. Suddenly, he realized he was very hungry and wanted to go home.

Chapter 3
Out From the Castles

That evening, Father sat in the red, leather easy chair at the foot of Charles's bed and puffed on his pipe, filling the room with a sweet woody smell. Charles noticed that Father was very tired tonight. Charles bit at a hangnail on his thumb, and then pretended to study it, trying to hide his disappointment.

They weren't going to tell him, he realized. Something bad was happening, and everybody knew what it was but him. He swallowed something inside and forced himself to think about how he was going to decorate his newly discovered tree.

His thoughts were interrupted by the sound of Tanya running down the hall. She came giggling into the room and ran to Father and threw herself in his arms so abruptly that the pipe almost fell out of his mouth.

"Daddy, tell us the story."

Father looked confused for a moment, then relieved.

"All rightey, darling. The story you shall have. Are you ready too, Charles?"

Charles nodded his head, dumbfounded. Everything had been absolutely glum when Charles got home that afternoon. His sister had already been in her room resting, and his mother had a long, dreary expression and red eyes. When his father came home, his mother had a long, private conversation with him in the kitchen. When it was over, his father came out white-faced and went straight up to Tanya's room. Later, Tanya did not come down to dinner, and Charles and his mother ate a cold meal in silence. His father skipped supper and went down to the dock where he sat and smoked his pipe until sunset.

And now, here was Tanya, fresh scrubbed, bright eyed and looking happier than she'd ever looked. This didn't make sense, but before Charles could think anymore about it, Father had put out his pipe, cleared his throat and resumed his story.

***

After Griselle had left, Ta Ta was very busy the rest of the day. She took the cloak she was going to wear, and instead of taking her nap, she sewed some pockets on the inside where no one could see them. Then, she snuck down to the kitchen past Griselle and Nana. There, she got bread, apples, dried beef and roast goose from the cooks and wrapped them up very carefully in oil cloth. She brought them upstairs and hid them in the secret pockets she had sewn, where Griselle wouldn't see them. She also put in some flints, a candle and a hunting knife and scabbard she took from her father's collection. Then she lay down and took a quick nap before supper.

At supper, she noticed for the first time how Cha Cha and Griselle kept glancing at each other but never spoke to each other. She also noticed how Griselle would make a big show of helping the Queen, but was actually playing up to the King. Ta Ta wanted to scream. It was so obvious now. Why hadn't she ever noticed before? Why hadn't everyone? But she was only a little princess and could say nothing. No matter. She had a plan. She knew it was a good one. Indeed, it was the only one open to her. As soon as the meal was over she went back up to her room, double checked all her preparations and went to sleep. She knew Griselle would not fail to wake her.

And she was not wrong. No sooner, it seemed, had she fallen asleep than she felt the jerking of her arm and the sharp talon-like fingers digging into her flesh.

"Wake up, child. You'll find no unicorns in your room."

Instantly, Ta Ta was fully awake and all her senses alert.

"Oh, Griselle, I knew you'd come. Did you make everything ready?"

"Of course, child. I have horses waiting."

"And food?"

"Yes, of course. Plenty of food."

"No one must see us leave, Griselle. They'll tell mother and father."

Griselle's croon became a soft purr.

"Do not worry, child. They'll never know of our little adventure. Now hurry. Get up and dress."

Ta Ta flung back her covers and sprang up already dressed.

"No need to, Griselle."

"You think ahead, Princess."

"Quick, Griselle. Let's get to Dark Wilde Forest before dawn. I've heard the best time to catch a unicorn is at first light."

They slipped quietly down the hallway and down two flights of stairs, and abruptly, Griselle pulled back a tapestry. There, she slid back a panel in the wall to reveal a doorway that Ta Ta had never known existed. A hand reached out of the shadows and handed Griselle a candle which she lit. Ta Ta managed to smile up at her and giggle as if it was all a lark. Inside, she shuddered as she realized how much danger her father's kingdom was in. Griselle knew of secret passages in the castle and had already recruited at least one traitor. She had guessed that Griselle would be more than happy to get rid of her, but she had not guessed that her plans to take control of the kingdom were so far advanced. She now hoped that Griselle's plan was to take her to the woods and kill or lose her and not to bury her in some secret chamber. Her relief was great then, when after walking through many long, dark passages, they came out somewhere outside of the castle in a little stand of trees. A man stood there with two saddled horses. Yet another traitor.

"Oh, Griselle, do you think we'll get to Dark Wilde Forest by first light? I so want to ride a unicorn home tomorrow. Won't mother and father be surprised?"

"I can't wait to see the look on their faces, Princess. But we must ride, ride like the wind to do it. We won't be riding side saddle."

"Good. I hate riding side saddle."

The man hoisted Ta Ta onto her mount. Ta Ta noticed that Griselle had flung herself up on her mount without assistance. They whirled their horses about in the direction of the road, and Griselle put her horse into a bumpy trot.

When she saw that Ta Ta was a good rider and had no difficulty holding her seat in a trot, she sped up into a comfortable gallop. Ta Ta recognized both horses as being from her father's stable and knew they were bred for endurance. They could gallop at this pace all night. Griselle would have her deep, deep in Dark Wilde Forest before she disposed of her.

"Doesn't Prince Cha Cha ever do anything?"

"Indeed he does, Charles, but before we get to that we must go back to the wizard.

"The evil wizard, Daddy?"

"Yes, sweetheart, the evil wizard. He's been very busy. You remember it was in the last winter when he discovered how to turn his rat, Typhus, into a man."

"And then, Typhus turned back into a rat."

"Yes, Charles, you remember exactly right. And this presented the wizard with a very serious problem."

"He wasn't sure how to make the formula, Daddy."

"That's right. And, he wasn't sure how best to apply the formula and he also had to teach Typhus."

"What did he have to teach him, Dad?"

"Oh, many, many things. It was like this."

The wizard was very morose. Turning Typhus into a human had not brought him the happiness he sought. For one thing, Typhus would never admit to being grateful for being turned into a human, although the wizard suspected that such was the case. For another, getting the dosage right was proving to be a real problem. He had been appalled at how quickly Typhus turned back into a rat. It happened so frequently that he never bothered to devise a formula for it. One just waited until the original formula wore off. On the plus side, he was gradually getting Typhus to remember more and more details about his ventures back into the rat world. But how long would Typhus stay human? It was never predictable, no matter how accurately he controlled the dosage. And it was very disconcerting when Typhus changed back into a rat without any warning."

"Why, Dad?" Charles interjected. "He only needed to be human long enough to tell the wizard what he'd found out."

"That's a good point, but we are dealing with people and that is always more complicated than it looks at first. It was like this."

Typhus insisted that he had to spend more time as a human. He would say, "You don't understand. Everything looks so different as a rat. If I'm ever going to spy for you I have to know how everything looks from the human side. I have to go everywhere you go. Meet everyone you meet. Then I'll be able to place them when I'm a rat and tell you what you need to know."

Now the wizard rapidly agreed to do this, even if it was a bit risky, what with Typhus being prone to change back into a rat so unexpectedly. Why did he agree? Well, truth to tell, he was not really a very good wizard. His fireworks displays were meager and drab, his love potions weak and unpredictable, and he couldn't make anyone invisible, not even himself (if he had he wouldn't have needed to change Typhus into a human). As a wizard, he was a bust. In fact, turning Typhus into a human was quite the best thing he'd ever done. And naturally, he wanted to show Typhus off. But he couldn't, of course, if he was going to use him as a spy. However, he could settle for the secret pleasure of parading Typhus around, knowing something that no one else knew. For the time being, it would have to be enough.

So, as soon as he'd gotten Typhus decently trained in court etiquette and had him fitted out in the finest imported styles, he began taking him everywhere. He introduced him as his cousin from the Third Kingdom across the Fourth Mountain which was a strange, far away land with odd customs. That, of course, accounted for his social awkwardness and momentary lapses in etiquette, and for his slightly long and pointed nose.

In spite of his strangeness and awkwardness, or perhaps because of it, Typhus was a huge hit with the ladies. They would come over in twos and threes, or even fours and fives, and fawn over him and invite him to balls, teas, picnics and anything else they could devise. The wizard was never invited to any of these. All this irritated the wizard, of course. In any case, all the invitations were refused, by either him or Typhus. There was no way either of them wanted to risk the embarrassment of Typhus unexpectedly returning to his rat identity in public. Additionally, it would be very hard to invent a complete past for Typhus. There would have to be a whole family history and education filled in, and it was more than either wanted to attempt.

It might be thought that the wizard's resentment of Typhus's success with the ladies would prove his undoing. But, once his initial pique wore off, it did not. For his whole triumph became that it was his little secret. It made him feel superior that they were fawning over a rat. A rat that he, a great and powerful wizard, had turned into a man. How foolish these silly women were. How great, powerful and wise he was.

"Do men really think like that, Daddy?"

"Only in fairy tales, darling. But back to the story."

There were problems, however. The first was making more formula. The formula always had to be heated before using, which meant that a little bit evaporated off each time. This was in addition to normal evaporation and, although he had long since sealed the formula in small jars, it was disappearing at a fairly rapid rate. Faster than he would have believed possible. Naturally, he tried to make a new batch, but try as he might, he could not get it quite right.

Typhus was too valuable to risk testing the new formulas on, so the wizard would catch other rats with which to experiment. The results were terrible, grotesque creatures with too many eyes or noses, or missing arms, or legs, or twisted spines or other ghastly deformities. Even worse, when they changed back into rats they would keep the deformities, writhing in terror. Then, the wizard would chuck them out the tower window, and they would fall to their deaths on the rocks below. Typhus watched all these proceedings with great interest, even taking notes for the wizard's experiments. He was able to do this as he'd taught himself to read and write, a feat which both surprised and delighted the wizard.

Then came the second problem. Finally, Typhus asked the wizard, "When do you want me to start spying for you?"

The wizard was thunderstruck. His jaw dropped open, and he held up his hands at a loss for an answer. He finally mumbled, "Soon, Typhus, soon."

The wizard was horribly embarrassed. How could he possibly tell Typhus? That he had no luck with women. That he could not make a simple love potion for himself. That all this was about, was getting in good with the ladies. That he had gone through all this simply so he could have a girl friend. It was too humiliating. Especially since it was something that came so easily to Typhus. What was he going to tell Typhus?

Actually, Typhus had guessed the truth almost from the start. He noticed that the wizard was always eager to introduce him to the most beautiful, eligible women in the court.

He also noticed how they instinctively recoiled from the wizard's presence, how they pointedly and insultingly excluded the wizard from their invitations and how clumsily and ineptly the wizard behaved around the women. But, most of all, Typhus noticed how the wizard stupidly neglected to introduce him to the most powerful and influential personages in the court—the very people most worth spying upon.

So, Typhus had quickly decided the wizard was a liability to him. Long ago, he started stealing a little bit of the formula at a time and hiding it in little, glass vials of his own. Within weeks, he had worked out dosages to control the amount of time he spent as a human almost to the minute. He'd also found that the amount of the dosage determined his intelligence, and that the correct amount gave him an intellect superior to the wizard's, and indeed, superior to everyone else in the court. And, he felt he was very close to replicating the original, successful formula.

He told the wizard none of this. In fact, he'd always misled the wizard. Almost from the beginning, he retained his full human intelligence in his rat state. But, he made out it was a slow process, pretending to fumble for bits and pieces of information from his forays into the rat world, making the wizard coax one memory after another out of him. Even yet, he let on it was difficult, feigning to forget crucial pieces of information.

He did all this, because he didn't trust the wizard. He had no doubt the wizard would dispose of him whenever he had what he wanted, so there was no point in helping him anymore than he had to. Not until he was ready. Not until he had learned everything he could and could contrive to turn the situation completely to his own advantage. For Typhus, despite his human intelligence, still had the soul of a rat. And he too, had plans.

Meanwhile, the wizard was too preoccupied with his own problems to see anything more in Typhus than he wanted to see. And now, his biggest problem was to get Typhus to spy on the ladies without knowing that was what he was doing. He needed to think, and a day out of the castle and away from Typhus might help him do just that. So he said to Typhus, "I'm going out by myself tomorrow. On a walk. On a picnic. You stay here. You don't mind, I hope. Oh, well, I'm going to get some sleep. You do the same, Typhus."

The wizard went to bed, and Typhus pretended to do the same. As soon as the wizard was asleep, after he'd turned back into a rat, he scurried off into the nearest rat hole.

As he passed through the hidden recesses of the tower, Typhus marveled at how his human intelligence blended with his rat body and mind. He functioned as a rat and instinctively did all the things rats did, but he retained his human overview even while he interacted with the other rats. Intellectually, he was impossibly far above his fellow rats now. It was, he felt, like a man on a mountaintop looking down upon his fellow men. He could make out his fellow men, but how would he be able to feel anything for them? They were just tiny figures down below. Still, he was born a rat, and that natural affinity of all creatures for their own kind burned in his heart.

He didn't know what to do. He had no desire to return to being a rat, despite what he let the wizard think. But the feeling in his breast made him long for his own breed. For awhile, he'd entertained the mad idea of turning all the rats in the castle into humans and taking over. But, despite his mastery with his own personal formula, he was learning that duplicating it for others was no easy task. He'd had great success at changing it to make himself more intelligent and more stable, but it had to be modified to each individual rat. That had been amply proven by the horrors of the wizard's experiments, which he had witnessed.

He clambered across a wooden rafter, scampered through a hole, across a roof, down a drain pipe, turned and went through another hole and was in his old lair. The members of his clan eyed him nervously.

They know I'm different, he realized. Each time it's worse. Soon they'll turn on me. Within, he burned with pain. What could he do? He could never find acceptance among humans. He would always have a secret, unreliable identity. He needed someone like himself. He was afraid to try his formulas on his fellow rats. What if he produced a monster as Rigirus had done? Yet, he was sure his latest recipe would work if he introduced it in small dosages and adjusted it after each reaction. Only, what if he was wrong? If only he had more time. But the hostility in the eyes of the other rats told him he was running out of time.

He was in agony. He didn't want to die, but his life wasn't worth living. Then, another rat, younger than he, one he hadn't seen before, seemed to notice his distress. It crept cautiously over to him and nuzzled him to comfort him.

Now, this was the very same night that Griselle and Ta Ta left the castle to go to Dark Wilde Forest.

They rode away from the castle, across the meadows, past the fields of the peasants, and onto the main highway leading to the Third Kingdom. After a long ride, they turned off on a dusty fork to Dark Wilde Forest. They rode until they saw a dark, forbidding gloom that looked like a solid wall of trees. Ta Ta thought they would stop and look for a way in, but Griselle plunged straight ahead off the trail, and across the waist high grass of a broad field, to the forest. It loomed closer and closer and Ta Ta could see a wall of bramble and thicket, that showed no gap at all, which protected the forest. Still, Griselle plunged ahead and even sped up. Ta Ta put her heels into her mount and stayed close behind. Suddenly, Griselle veered her horse slightly to the right, into the thickest part of the brambles. Ta Ta gasped, thinking they would surely be impaled in the tangle of broken branches and sharp thorns. But suddenly, they were inside the forest, riding through a narrow opening between the trees at a full gallop. Ta Ta kept her steed close on the heels of Griselle's and realized with a chill that Griselle was no stranger to Dark Wilde Forest.

On and on they rode, turning this way and that. Now Ta Ta knew there was no way she could possibly find her way out. Originally, she had planned to run away from Griselle once they were in the forest. But now, she knew she must stay close to her until she could find some place where there was an opening in the trees where she could turn and make her escape. But so far, there was no room to flee, for the forest was very thick and the ground choked with impenetrable undergrowth.

Abruptly, Griselle halted and Ta Ta's horse almost crashed into Griselle's, stopping so fast that Ta Ta was thrown to the ground. She rolled over as she hit the ground, and her forehead struck a tree trunk. Dazed, she staggered to her feet. As if from a distance, she could hear Griselle gloating.

"So, you little wretch, you thought you could fool me with your pathetic, little story about a unicorn. I don't know what your real game is but it doesn't matter now. You're lost in Dark Wilde, and you'll be eaten by a monster before you ever find your way out."

Ta Ta tried to say something, but as she looked at Griselle everything began to whirl in front of her, and she swooned away with the sound of Griselle's laughter pounding at her ears.

When Ta Ta finally came to, she groaned. She didn't think about where she was. All she thought about was how much her head hurt. She opened her eyes and saw that she was in a small, gloomy, damp little space that wasn't much bigger than the space it took to hold two horses. She was thirsty and hungry. She felt into the secret pockets for the food she had brought. It was all gone. Obviously, Griselle had taken it. She wanted to cry and lie down and sob, but she said to herself, "No. You're a princess and your duty is to your kingdom and the King. You must keep your wits about you, and find a way out, and find the Wizard of Fandon and tell him everything about Griselle. That is what Mother would do. That is what you must do."

So she got up, stiff and sore, her head hurting. Then, she looked up to see where the sun was. The forest was so thick there was no shadow on the forest floor. So she tried to see the top of the trees. Just overhead she could barely see the top. It looked like the sun was just to her left. She didn't really care which direction she went just so long as it got her out of the forest away from Griselle and her henchmen. Then she would go find the wizard of Fandon, and he would help her get back to her kingdom and help her take care of Griselle.

So, after checking the position of the sun again as best she could in the thick forest, she began to walk, crying only a little as she did so.

Over in the Fourth Kingdom, Rigirus was setting off on his own ride. At first, he rode wildly, scarcely caring where he was going. Gradually, he let his horse slow to an amble, prodding it just enough to keep it from stopping to graze. His mind was a jumble of thoughts and emotions. But while his mind was full of thoughts, it wasn't really thinking. It was, rather, a kaleidoscope of images and impressions. Sometimes it would conjure up scenes of his childhood. At other moments, events of just the day before would flash past. Then just as suddenly, his attention would careen wildly into a future in which he was the king of the wizards and the secret power behind every throne in the Seven Higher Kingdoms. One moment, his imaginings would raise up some pleasant memory or image, and he would be filled with a sweetness so strong that his eyes would begin to moisten with the beginnings of tears. A moment later, he would be filled with a blind rage at the thought of some real or imagined insult or humiliation that had happened in the past or might happen in the future. At these moments, he would grind his teeth, growl, and shake his clenched fists in the air or pound them on the pommel of his saddle. None of this disturbed his horse in the slightest as it was quite used to this sort of odd behavior on the wizard's solitary rides.

At last, the wizard noticed that the day was becoming unbearably hot. Without realizing it, he had come to the edge of Dark Wilde Forest. Indeed, he had been totally unaware of his surroundings all day long. All he noticed was that he was dripping with sweat and the forest was shady. Absentmindedly, he tethered his horse and plunged into the forest looking for a good place to sit in the shade and cool off while he rested. But, no matter where he looked, the ground was too brambly, or too dusty, or too muddy. So, he plunged on, walking faster and faster, getting hotter and hotter, sweatier and sweatier and angrier and angrier with every step he took. Of course, he was hopelessly lost after a few minutes, but he did not know it. He just knew that he was hot and tired and sweaty, and that nothing ever worked out for him--not even something as simple as finding a stupid shady spot in the stupid middle of the stupid woods.

By the time the wizard got lost in the woods, some time had passed since Ta Ta had started walking, and she was finding it harder and harder not to cry. She'd been walking for ever it seemed and getting thirstier and thirstier and hungrier and hungrier. And the forest was so thick it was almost impossible to tell where the sun was. She was sure now that she was lost and that she was doomed. At last, she became too tired to walk anymore, and she sat down and gave in to her tears. And she cried not for herself but for her fallen kingdom. It was apparent now that Griselle was a cunning, vicious woman with her web of treason reaching everywhere, that there were evil depths to her no one suspected, and that she had designs on the throne. What would she do? Would she drive out or assassinate Ta Ta's mother, the Queen, and then sit by Ta Ta's father on the throne? Or would she eliminate both the King and Queen, and use her influence over Cha Cha to be his regent until he was old enough to assume the throne? And what sort of monster would she make of Cha Cha? With his intelligence and courage corrupted and at her service, he would be a menace to the entire world of the Seven Higher Kingdoms. What sort of burdens would she place on the people? They would groan, and all the happiness and laughter of the kingdom would be replaced by tears.

If only, Ta Ta thought to herself, she had been able to reach the Wizard of Fandon. If only she had been able to pour out her story to him, surely he would have been able to help her and set things to right. But now, everything was lost.

But wait!

What was that crashing in the woods?

What was that roaring?

What was that bellowing?

Was it a hungry bear? Was it a ferocious lion? Oh, no! What if it was that most horrible of creatures, a slither hither and thither? The crashing and bellowing came steadily closer. It must have her scent. If only she could have reached the Wizard of Fandon. But now, she was going to be devoured by a monster. Horrible, unkind fate! The tears flooded down her cheeks now. She could no longer be brave, no matter how hard she tried. Then, through the trees, she saw a flash of bright red.

Most strange.

What forest monster was bright red?

Wait! She was beginning to understand the bellows.

The monster could talk!

Immediately, her tears stopped, her cheeks turned bright red, and she promptly threw her hands over her ears.

Such language!

She waited for a while, then stood up, hands still over her ears. She caught a brief glimpse of red, and it seemed closer this time. Bad language or not, she reasoned to herself, he must know the way out of the woods, and she'd better get him to show her the way. She uncovered her ears and shouted.

"Hallo, hallo."

The roaring, bellowing and crashing continued unabated. She shouted again, as loud as she could.

"HALLO, HALLO."

More roaring, bellowing and crashing.

This time she screamed; the loudest, highest pitched, shrillest, most blood curdling scream she could muster.

Dead silence.

"Hallo, hallo," she shouted again.

An answer came back.

"I say, who are you?"

"I'm lost. Can you help me find my way?"

Some distance away, amidst the brambles and trees, she saw a face, underneath a tangled mat of red hair, appear.

"You're lost? What the devil is that to me?"

"Please, I'm a princess. I desperately need your help."

The eyes went wide underneath the tangled red hair.

"A princess! Oh, I mean, yes little girl. Of course, I'll help you. Stay there. Stay right there. I'm coming. I'm coming."

And come he did. Charging and lurching and stumbling, straight through the brambles and undergrowth, breaking branches with his body, mumbling and screaming when he pierced himself with thorns, stubbing his toes, barking his shins, and getting hit in the face by tree branches until, at last, he stumbled into the clearing, his bright red robe covered with dust, torn and ripped in a dozen places. His beard and hair were matted with sweat and dust, full of cockleburs and small twigs and leaves. He stood there for a moment gasping for breath. When he was somewhat recovered from his exertion, he started to take one last step forward, but got tripped up on the curled up toes of his shoes and fell flat on his face in front of Ta Ta.

She couldn't help herself. She laughed out loud.

"What!" the wizard shouted in rage. He started to raise himself up, tripped over his other curled up toe and collapsed on his face again. Ta Ta threw her hands up over her mouth but it was too late. She'd already laughed out loud again.

"That's it!" screamed the wizard. "I've had it. Do you know who I am?"

He started to raise himself up by grabbing a branch but missed it and grabbed a bramble instead, pricking his palm with a thorn.

"Ouch!" he yelled and sat down. "Why does everything happen to me?"

Ta Ta knelt down beside him.

"Here," she said. "Let me help."

She took his hand in hers, stroked his palm a couple of times, then pulled out the thorn with her fingers.

"There," she said. "It was just a tiny thorn. You'll be fine."

"Fine? That's easy for you to say. It didn't prick your hand. And it wasn't tiny either. It was huge. Look. I think I can still see a spot of blood. See?"

He tried to show her his hand, but Ta Ta was no longer interested. She'd already stood up and was brushing the dust off her knees.

The wizard looked around and sighed.

"At last, a place to rest in the shade."

"What?" said the princess.

"All day long I've been searching for a comfortable place to rest in the shade. I think I'll lie down here and take a nap."

"A nap? In Dark Wilde Forest?"

"Dark Wilde Forest? Oh, no, that's on the other side of the kingdom."

"No," Ta Ta said. "I'm pretty sure this is Dark Wilde Forest." She was speaking tactfully, for she knew good and well it was Dark Wilde Forest.

"It is?" The wizard jumped up and looked wildly around. "We could get lost out here."

"Well, I'm already lost. I was hoping you'd help me get out. It's really very important. I'm on a very urgent mission. If you help me, I promise my father will reward you handsomely."

At the mention of a reward the wizard's eyes went wide, but he shrugged his shoulders and shook his head and said, "Reward? That's not really necessary. But, of course, as a small token, or a large token if he wanted, of his esteem, that would be nice."

"That's wonderful," said Ta Ta. "You must help me find the Wizard of Fandon."

"The Wizard of Fandon!" shouted the wizard. "What on earth for?"

"Because he is the greatest of all wizards in the Seven Kingdoms."

"Is not! Why the Wizard of Fandon's a charlatan, a fake, an imposter."

Ta Ta chuckled softly as she answered.

"But everyone knows that his fireworks are the most brilliant and original of all, his love potions the strongest and most sure. Why, he can even make himself invisible."

The wizard stamped his feet upon the ground, and that made the pointed toes quiver so fast they became two red blurs. Ta Ta had to put her fist into her mouth to keep from laughing out loud again.

"Cheap tricks," the wizard snorted. "Totally unworthy of a true wizard."

"But I need a wizard to help me."

"Then look no further."

The wizard bowed grandly in front of her, almost touching his head to the ground.

"I beg your pardon," Ta Ta said.

The wizard straightened up, exasperated.

"I too am a wizard. In fact, I am the greatest of all the wizards in the Seven Kingdoms."

Ta Ta looked the wizard up and down, taking in the torn, tattered robe, the bedraggled, matted hair and beard, and the sweaty, battered face. She shook her head skeptically from side to side, held her chin with her hand and tapped the ground with her toe.

"I don't know," she muttered. "I just don't know."

The wizard gaped at her.

"Don't know? What do you mean, 'don't know?' What is there to know?"

"Do some magic."

"Do some magic?"

"Yes, do some magic, and I'll believe you're a wizard."

"You don't just do some magic," sputtered the wizard. "You need spells and incantations, and time of the moon, and tide charts, and seasons and proper ingredients."

"I bet you the Wizard of Fandon doesn't need those things."

The wizard's face became as red as his robe. "The Wizard of Fandon does too need those things. All wizards do."

Ta Ta eyed the wizard shrewdly.

"Do you make a good love potion?"

The wizard drew himself to his full height and spread his right hand over his heart.

"I make the very finest love potions in all the Seven Kingdoms."

"Do you ever use them for yourself?"

The wizard looked momentarily confused, then raised himself back up to his full height and entwined the fingers of both hands over his heart. Piously, he said, "An ethical wizard never uses his magic for selfish purposes."

Ta Ta folded her arms and tapped a foot impatiently on the ground.

"If you're a wizard how come you can't walk through objects as if they weren't even there?"

"Huh?" said the wizard, dumbfounded.

"Look at you. You're all cut and dirty, and your robe is all torn. Why can't you just walk straight through everything? As if it weren't there?"

It was too much for the wizard. He bent down until his face was only an inch from Ta Ta's face and roared at the top of his lungs, "Because we wizards walk like everyone else you stupid, ignorant twit!"

Naturally, little Ta Ta began to cry.

"You called me a stupid, ignorant twit. I'm just a little girl, and I'm lost and tired and hungry and thirsty, and you called me a stupid ignorant twit. I think I'm going to cry," she said between her tears. "I wish I'd left that thorn in your hand and let it kill you."

The wizard straightened back up, feeling confused and somehow hurt.

"It wouldn't have killed me. It was only a tiny thorn."

"It was a huge thorn. You would have bled to death."

"It hardly drew any blood at all."

"Go ahead. Leave me here to die. Let a monster eat me."

"Monster!"

"Dark Wilde Forest is full of monsters," she sobbed. "I'll just be a tasty little morsel. You'll be a real meal."

The wizard looked nervously about, as if seeing his surroundings for the first time.

"Then hadn't we better be leaving?" he said.

"You mean you'll take me with you?"

"Yes, yes, of course. Only just stop crying."

Ta Ta stopped crying and looked at the wizard expectantly. After a long pause she said, "Well?"

The wizard was looking nervously about. The truth of the matter dawned on Ta Ta.

"You mean you're lost too?" she wailed.

"It's not my fault," he whined. "You don't understand. All day I've been looking for a nice quiet spot in the shade to rest and now that I've found it we've got to go and it's not my fault if nothing ever goes right for me and I'm not as lucky as everyone else and and and…" The wizard would have gone on but he was starting to cry.

"There, there now," said Ta Ta and she took the wizard by the hand to calm him down. "Look," she said, pointing to the way he'd come. "You broke a good trail crashing through there. And look way back there. I think I see a little piece of your robe hanging from a brush. Let's see if we can follow the way you came in back out."

And so, going by the broken branches, brambles and bushes, and bits of red cloth and strands of red hair and beard, just before evening, with Ta Ta leading the wizard by the hand, they stumbled out of Dark Wilde Forest right next to where the wizard's horse was waiting.

"Are you tired now, sweetheart? Do you want to go to bed?"

"Not just yet, Daddy. Tell us some more."

"Yeah, Dad. When does Prince Cha Cha do something?"

"Funny you should mention that, son. I was just coming to that. Let's go back to the castle of Prince Cha Cha and Princess Ta Ta."

Back at the castle everything was in an uproar. When Nana woke up that morning, she couldn't find Princess Ta

Ta. She had looked everywhere; in the garden, by the pond, in the kitchen, in the pantry, in the stable, in the attics(and there were many of them), in the lofts, in the blacksmith's shops, in the drawing rooms, in the ballrooms and in the dining rooms until, at last, she could think of nowhere else to look. So, she told the King and Queen, and they had the whole castle searched again. And still, there was no sign of Princess Ta Ta.

"Quick," said the King and Queen to the knights. "Ride out through all our lands, and check in every hut and cottage, and find our little Princess Ta Ta." And out rode all the knights and searched in every hut and cottage, but no one could find little Princess Ta Ta.

By afternoon, everyone in the castle was glum and gloomy. No minstrels sang or strummed their lutes or played their flutes. No jester jested, no tumbler tumbled and all the clowns wore frowns. Yes, all the castle was a melting, melancholy.

Except for two.

Oh, they both appeared sad outwardly, but for different reasons.

Griselle dabbed at her eyes with her handkerchief, but there were no tears in them.

And then there was Cha Cha. Remember what a smart little boy Cha Cha was? Everyone thought so. Especially Ta Ta. And when the castle had been thoroughly searched and searched again and there was no sign of his sister, Cha Cha had run to a battlement, the highest in the castle, and stared out into the distance all day. Everyone thought he was looking for Princess Ta Ta. But he wasn't, for he knew he wouldn't see her. Instead, he had gone up there to hide his tears. Tears for what he was afraid might have happened to his sister. But also, tears for being betrayed.

For Cha Cha understood immediately. The castle was too well guarded for Ta Ta to sneak out on her own. Besides which, she would never do such a thing. She was such a goody-goody. The only way to sneak out was through the secret passage. He knew she didn't know about it, for if she had known she would immediately have blabbed it to their parents. That was a given. That was why he'd never told her about it. Only one other person knew.

Griselle.

He felt like such a complete fool. He'd made everyone's life miserable, made an ass of himself and humiliated his parents, and the whole kingdom knew of it.

Slowly, the tears began to dry. Now what was he going to do? A very intelligent and observant child, born into a royal court, had better also have the genetic material known as survival instinct. As everyone had observed, he had the makings of a great king, but first, he must live long enough. As it was, his instincts told him that whatever Griselle was up to, she was not stupid enough to move alone. She knew that he knew she knew about the secret passageways. She and her henchmen would be watching closely to see what he did.

Of course, he could make a big show of going to her and throwing himself into her arms for comfort. But, unlike Ta Ta, he didn't believe he'd be able to match wits with an adult, especially one as cold and ruthless as he now knew Griselle to be. So, he stayed on the battlement desperately trying to out think a murderess. How long could he stay there before she saw through what he was doing? Even now, he had the feeling he was being watched.

The obvious thing was to go to his parents, reveal the secret passage, and tell them what he was sure must have happened. But, he faced the same problem Ta Ta faced—he was a child. Would they believe him?

More disturbing, he now realized something that had been bothering him for a long time, but he hadn't been able to put his finger on it. His father always seemed to have Griselle by his side anymore. She would be whispering into his ear, while his mother stared resolutely in the other direction. If he told his suspicions, his mother would probably take his side, but she was only the Queen, and his father was the King. If Griselle's hold was strong enough, and Cha Cha suspected it was, she could keep the King from acting until it was too late. Another thought—what if she was already strong enough to launch a coup? He had to be sure before he acted.

And one final thought grew stronger and larger in his mind. Griselle would never allow him to live long enough to see either the King or the Queen.

He knew now what he had to do.

***

"There, Tanya. I think you're ready for bed now."

Tanya murmured softly and smiled drowsily up at Father who stood up and carried her to the hall.

"Goodnight, Charles," he said softly. "Don't forget your prayers."

Chapter 4
The Two Dreamers

After he said his prayers, Charles lay on his back and stared at the ceiling for a long time. He tried to make out the patterns in the ceiling formed by the interplay of the spackling on the ceiling with the moonlight that came through the window. If he stared long enough, he could see cowboys, or space ships, or ghosts or whatever he wanted to see. But, however long he stared, he could not see why his parents wouldn't tell him what was wrong with his sister.

He thought about asking them, but he wondered if he really wanted to know. Maybe that was why they didn't tell him. Maybe they knew he didn't want to know.

He slowly dozed off to sleep and began his fitful dreaming.

They were flying beautiful kites, vivid against a bright blue sky. They ran across the long green grass. His sister stopped running, and so he stopped too. He looked at his sister who stared into his eyes. Then she turned and pointed at her kite. It now seemed impossibly small, just the tiniest white dot against the blue. Then Charles saw that she was letting the last of the kite string slip through her fingers.

"No, Tanya," he yelled at her. "You'll lose your kite."

Tanya said nothing, but let the last of the string play out gently through her fingers.

Her kite disappeared, swallowed up in an immense, blue vastness.

In her room, Tanya ignored the knocking, scratching and growling from her closet. Instead of the knife, she was holding a little, toy nativity scene in her hands. It was enclosed in a tiny, glass bubble. Her mother had bought it for her on their visit to the city. She supposed her mother had bought it for her to somehow make her feel better, or maybe, because mother didn't think she would see another Christmas.

It was very pretty, Tanya thought, but it really didn't make her feel any different. She knew that when you died it was just like going to sleep, only without the dreaming.

She'd been taught different, of course, but none of it made any sense. How could there be anything else? All the stories they had taught her seemed so made-up. Made-up to make people feel better. Just like her mother had bought this to make her feel better. Or maybe mother really bought it to make herself feel better.

She turned it upside down and then right-side up and watched the fake snowflakes drift down. It was pretty.

But, it wasn't real.

She put the toy on her nightstand, picked up the steak knife with her right hand and struggled vainly to stay awake.

Once again she joined the beautiful procession of fair-

ies glowing in the twilight headed up to the castle. This time, as she approached, she tried to steer herself. As her flight became faster, she tried to guide herself to a different window, any different window. She strained with her entire strength and will.

It was useless.

Some force pulled her away, as if she were a toy boat on a raging current and hurled her up before the great black window. She tried to tear away, to retreat, but was held there against her will. She hovered there, captured, as though in a net.

Something wanted to claim her! What was this thing that pulled at her? She felt herself beginning to suffocate and choke.

She woke up sweating. Again, she heard the knocking and scratching noise from her closet. She picked up her knife and tried to stay awake.

The next day was bad. Tanya stayed in her room all day. By lunch, Charles had tired of the depressing atmosphere and went out into the woods. He found his tree, crawled inside and curled up with a couple of comic books. He got halfway through one, then threw it aside and, for the first time in his life, went into a serious reverie about what he wanted to be when he grew up. He thought about being a firefighter or a policeman, and finally, he thought for a long time about being a doctor.

That evening there was no story because Tanya was sleeping. Father offered to tell him another story, but Charles said he would rather not. Charles noticed that Father seemed relieved. Later, while Charles was trying to read another comic book, he noticed that his parents were having a very long, low-voiced conversation in the kitchen.

The next morning Charles awoke feeling tired. The first thing he heard was the sound of his sister laughing in the kitchen. Curious, he got dressed and went down into the kitchen. His sister was making sandwiches, while his mother was hurriedly putting on a coat.

"What are you doing," he asked Tanya, drowsily.

"What does it look like?" she laughed.

"It's too early for sandwiches. It's breakfast time."

"We're going on a picnic," she answered.

"All of us?"

"No, just you two," his mother said. It was the first time she'd spoken since he'd entered the kitchen. Charles saw that, despite his sister's cheerfulness, his mother still looked tired and depressed. "I have to take some things into town."

"Where are we going?" he asked his sister.

"Anywhere you want to," she said.

"Stay away from the lake," his mother snapped.

"Sure, Mom."

"I mean it! Don't take advantage of your sister and drag her down to the lake. I've told Mrs. Johnson to keep a sharp eye on you. It she tells me you went to the lake, I'll tan your hide when I get home."

"Okay, Mom."

His mother picked up her purse and a small canvas bag. She pulled a cell phone out of her purse and handed it to Tanya.

"You keep this with you all day. You hear? If anything goes wrong or you feel the least little bit weird, you call me right away. Charles, you know how to use this phone, don't you?"

"You know I do, Mom." Charles felt himself wanting to cry.

His mother nodded to him and gave Tanya a long hug.

"Mommy loves you, Tanya."

Then she slung the bag over her shoulder and kissed Charles on the top of his head. This time she spoke very softly to him.

"Charles, you be good to your sister today. Don't give her any trouble, and do what she tells you. Okay?"

"Sure, Mom."

He watched his mother go out the door and get into her car and drive away. He still wondered if he was going to cry when Tanya spoke up.

"So. Where do you want to go?"

He turned to her, glad to have something to talk about.

"I found a real neat tree cave."

"A tree cave. What's that?"

"I'll show you. It's really cool. You'll like it."

They finished packing the lunch in silence. They both knew that as little as a week ago Charles would never have given up such a treasure so easily. He would have hinted and hinted until Tanya's curiosity got the better of her, and she took the bait. Then he would have teased her unmercifully until she coaxed, wheedled and bullied the truth out of him. But things were different now.

They took a roundabout way to the new discovery. On the way they stopped to turn over rocks, look under logs, and watch squirrels and birds. Tanya seemed to notice every flower and blade of grass as they went and would wait patiently while Charles chucked rocks at the squirrels and birds. Through all of this, they never mentioned the thing that was foremost in their minds.

Finally, he showed her the tree cave. She liked it and oohed and aahed just as he had when he first saw it, although she thought it needed more cleaning. Charles insisted it was plenty clean just the way it was but, perhaps defensively, scraped out a bit of debris with the side of his foot. They sat in the cave and talked awhile avoiding what was really on their minds until Charles could stand it no longer.

"What's wrong with you anyway?" he blurted.

"I'm sick."

"How sick?"

"Pretty sick."

"How sick is that?"

"The doctor said they have to do some more tests, and I might have to go away for awhile."

"Is it cancer?"

Tanya shook her head.

"I don't think so. It's something new. He didn't tell me the name."

Charles didn't want to ask, but he knew he'd never be able to talk to his sister again if he didn't.

"Are you going to die?"

Tanya felt a surge of relief that everything was now out on the table. She was tired of all the half-truths and evasions, but she realized it was important that she choose her words carefully.

"The doctor didn't say that, but from the way Mom looks at me, I think I probably will."

Charles felt a huge surge of gratitude to his sister for telling the truth, though he was not surprised. He too, had read his mother's looks at Tanya the same way. He also felt an impulse of anger. He felt he should say something.

"Maybe Mom's just real sad because being sick hurts a lot."

He instantly regretted bringing up pain.

"Sometimes," he added.

Tanya didn't wince.

"Maybe. But..."she hesitated, "I don't know how to

describe it, but I don't see any hope in her eyes."

"Sometimes, people get well all by themselves, or the doctor's find new cures."

"It's alright, Charles, I don't mind."

"What do you mean, you don't mind? Of course, you mind."

"I did before. Before I knew. But now, I feel free. What happens, happens."

"Don't talk like that. Don't give up."

They both fell silent. Tanya studied her brother. It was useless to try and explain, she felt. No one could understand. Not even grown-ups. Especially grown-ups. Especially their mother and father. This new feeling she had that every day was a gift. That no matter what happened it would never happen again, at least not quite in the same way, with the same weather, the same light or temperature, or the same emotions. It all went so fast and it was always so new. Each day was an adventure, each day was it's own lesson in something grand and wonderful and mysterious, and she had never known that before. And no one else around her knew that, and she didn't know how to explain it to any of them. She looked at Charles and studied him in detail.

I see the freckles on your nose, Charles, she thought to herself. How they seem like a fine powder except the three or four big ones on the bridge of your nose like specks of red dust. I see how the light makes your blonde hair almost yellow in the late afternoon as it comes through the hole in the tree trunk and lights up the side of your head from the back. How the blue in your left eye has a little, tiny spot of gray on the right side of your iris and how your eyes are always darting around and always noticing things you keep to yourself. Things you don't like to talk about. Why is that, Charles? Are you afraid you'll be laughed at or hurt if you talk about things? Or are you afraid you'll hurt others? I see how the dust in the air catches the light and makes your face glow as if you'd just been running. I see how it floats behind you and looks like a halo. I never thought of you as having a halo before. But, maybe you do. Maybe we all do, if we only knew it. And I see you trying to understand what I can't explain, what nobody can explain, and what no one can understand until it's time to understand.

She closed her eyes and tried to memorize every detail of Charles' face. She wanted to hold on to this particular gift. To be able to take it out later and examine it and treasure it in every detail. But it was no good. The more she tried to hold on to it the more it faded away. Funny, she thought. All gifts were like that. So strange and novel when you first opened them. But the more you played with them or used them the less special and wonderful they were. And that, she supposed, was her mysterious lesson for the day. Just take the day and enjoy each moment as it was given to you, complete and entire of itself.

"What are you doing?" Charles asked.

"Just thinking."

"About what?"

She opened her eyes, not wanting to lie, but not wanting to attempt to explain what she knew she couldn't.

"I'm hungry," she evaded. "Are you?"

"Not really."

"Well, I am." She smiled and reached with pretended gusto for the picnic basket. She wasn't really hungry, but she was tired of everybody feeling sorry for her. Besides, something told her it would be better to make others happy rather than sad. So, she put on a good act, and before long, she had Charles laughing, eating and mimicking, he was an excellent mimic, the different teachers at school.

Before Charles realized it, the light was beginning to fade, and they packed up and headed for home. Charles felt so good that he began to convince himself that maybe the doctor had it all wrong--maybe Tanya wasn't so sick after all. He even allowed himself one guilty moment when he thought that maybe she was taking advantage a little bit and playing for sympathy, but he generously brushed that notion aside.

Chapter 5

To Rescue a Sister

That night Tanya snuggled securely in Father's arms, Charles sat in his bed, and Father picked up the story where he had left off two nights before.

***

The rest of the day, after discerning Griselle's treachery, Prince Cha Cha contrived various ways to avoid her presence without being too conspicuous. He made no attempt to see the King and Queen. He knew they were too busy organizing searches for Ta Ta. He wanted to go back to his room and think, but of course, one of the secret passages opened directly into his room. Griselle would come to see him, and he was sure he would not be able to conceal his true thoughts, so that was too risky.

Instead he went down to the courtyard and began to practice his archery. He plied away at it all afternoon until supper time. If anyone asked him why he wasn't looking for his sister he would reply, with as haughty an expression as he could muster, that tomorrow morning he would personally lead a detachment of knights in a search and would have his silly sister home safe in time for supper. This response brought the desired contemptuous glares. For the time being, the last thing Cha Cha wanted was to be taken seriously. Even so, he still felt a prickly sensation of being watched by hostile eyes. He ignored it and kept shooting, concentrating on the target.

He had heard from his father that one of the secrets of hunting was to not let your quarry see your eyes, but to watch them out of the side of your eyes until they looked the other way. Then you could look at them and take your shot. So, he would focus intently on the target, and when he went to retrieve his arrows and pulled them out of the target and marched back to his shooting spot, he made sure not to steal glances to the side or around the courtyard. All the while, all he saw out of his side vision seemed to be the natural courtyard traffic and movement. But finally, he gradually became aware of something out of the ordinary, a shape in the shadows that was unfamiliar. It was unmoving, yet lifelike, but unnaturally still.

Cha Cha continued with his practice, taking more care than ever to place his arrows accurately. Still, the figure in the shadows did not move. "Patience is everything in hunting," his father had told him. "Your game must never be aware that you are there."

Well, thought Cha Cha, I am aware that you are there.

"Wait until the quarry becomes careless," he remembered his father saying, "and begins to move and look away. Then you can move."

Finally, the shadow began to shift about.

Good. He's getting tired, thought Cha Cha. Now, if he'll just move more into my line of vision, maybe I'll recognize him. Then I'll know who at least one of Griselle's spies is. Suddenly, Cha Cha had an inspiration. He turned away from the figure in the shadow and walked to the side of the courtyard where the water bucket was. He took a long draught of water. Then he sprinkled some on his face and neck. I have the advantage, he thought. I can move and he can't. I can make myself comfortable and he can't. Cha Cha stretched his arms, and he rubbed his shoulders as if they ached from all the archery practice. You've been standing there for ever so long, thought Cha Cha. Wouldn't you like to stretch too? Cha Cha picked up his bow and started back to his shooting spot, resisting the temptation to steal a glance at the figure which was still motionless.

He began to shoot again. He aimed as carefully as possible, seemingly oblivious to everything else. As the shadows began to lengthen, he sensed that the figure had reached the end of its patience. It began to stir and shift about, obviously uncomfortable. If only he would lean forward a bit. Just enough to reveal his face. Cha Cha had another inspiration. As he drew back his bowstring, he stopped in mid-draw and looked ahead at the ground as if he saw something interesting. He let his string go slack, stepped up half a step and leaned forward, peering intently at a spot on the ground. His heart began to beat faster as the figure stirred, its fatigue and boredom eager to be relieved by this bit of novelty. The figure leaned forward a bit, and the hood on its head slipped back. Out of the corner of his eye, Cha Cha saw a bald, red scarred pate with a fringe of wooly, black hair. His heart beat still faster. It was the Royal Huntsman. How easy it would be for him to arrange an "accident" on a hunt. How cleverly Griselle spun her web.

Cha Cha waited until the beating in his heart subsided, then shrugged his shoulders as if he hadn't seen anything interesting after all and resumed his archery practice. He paid no more attention to the figure. He knew he was safe in the courtyard. His mind was now preoccupied with his parents' safety, his own plans to escape and how to find his sister and rescue her if she was still alive.

When it became too dark to shoot he went to the armory. He returned his bow and arrows to the armorer, a large, stout, slow moving man who kept careful count of all weapons, including the Prince's. There would be no chance to take any of these weapons back to his room. Instead, he headed to the kitchen. The cooks and servers eyed him warily, afraid he might throw one of those tantrums for which he had become so famous of late. Instead, to their immense relief, he quietly helped himself to a generous portion of stew. He was not hungry, but he forced himself to eat as much as he could. He knew he would need all the strength he could muster for the ordeal ahead. Finished, he stuffed his pockets with apples, nuts and pears. Then, he wrapped up a large portion of meat, grabbed a loaf of bread and stuffed them both under his shirt. When he was sure that no one was looking, he also hid a long kitchen knife up his sleeve. He would much rather have his sword, but there was no way to get it back. The knife would have to do. Finished, he made his way back to his room.

Once in his room, Cha Cha made sure there was no one hiding behind the tapestries or in the closets. Fortunately, the designer of the secret passages had fashioned the doors so they opened into the rooms and not out. He took a stool and, using the kitchen knife, cut off some wedge shaped pieces and jammed some of them into the cracks under the door. He hammered them in as far as he could with the stool and then tried to open the door. It stayed firmly in place. Next, he hid all his food and the knife under the bed and the stool in a closet. All that done, he pulled on a bell rope to summon Nana.

Nana came in, bringing a tray of cakes and a pitcher of milk. Setting the tray on a night table, she turned and began turning down the bed covers. Cha Cha noticed how silent she was and sadly realized she was afraid of sparking one of his famous tantrums. Guiltily, he remembered that he had treated her horribly of late. One more victim of Griselle's work. He wanted to tell her everything, but he bit his lip and kept silent. Even if Nana believed him, she would be no match for Griselle. Nana wore her emotions on her sleeve, and Griselle would immediately know what was up and do something horrible to her. So, he ate his cake in silence, while Nana prepared his bed. As she was about to leave, he could contain himself no longer and hurled himself into her arms.

"Nana, I love you," he said.

Nana beamed with pleasant surprise and held him close.

"Of course you do, dear."

"Nana, I'm sorry I've been so mean lately."

She patted his head.

"There, there, dear. I always knew you would be."

"Nana, I promise, no matter what, everything I do from now on will be good."

"I'm glad to hear that. Now, it's been a trying day. Let's get you to bed."

Abruptly, the Prince pulled back from Nana and looked her in the eyes. The look was so stern it took Nana's breath away. It was exactly the look the King had when he was giving orders of the most serious nature.

"Nana, promise me that you'll remember what I said. That everything I'm going to do will be good. Promise me!"

Stunned, it took a moment before she could respond. Then Nana did something she had never done before, and which she had believed she would not do for many years yet; she curtsied to Cha Cha and said, "Yes, your highness." With that, she whirled and left the room, her heart bursting with pride and love.

As soon as she left, Cha Cha took the remaining wedges and shoved them under the hallway door to his room. He tested the door and the wedges held firm. He went to the closet and took out a hunting outfit. It was not the bright, resplendent type used for a royal hunt with hundreds of beaters, which was really more pageant than hunt. This was sturdy, colored a dusky brown and green that blended well with the forest and field. It was heavy and sturdy enough to withstand branch and bramble and had a large hood, to shield one's head from the rain and hide one's face in the shadows.

"I want my son to be a real king, and a real king is a real hunter, not a popinjay!" his father had roared, and the Royal Tailor had made this outfit for the Prince.

As he put it on, he remembered how Griselle had told him he was too fine to wear such a lowly costume. And, like a fool, he had believed her. Quickly, he took the knife from under the bed and cut off one of the tapestries from the wall. Then he cut it up in strips and tied the strips end to end. When he felt he had enough, he blew out all the candles and went to the window with his makeshift rope.

He looked out the window and surveyed the scene below. His part of the castle wall was protected by a steep, rocky descent of about 40 or 50 feet. At the bottom of the descent lay a broad, green meadow. On the other side of the meadow were woods and forest. It was peacetime and some scrub trees had been allowed to take hold beneath his window. He guessed it was about 30 feet to the top of the trees.

He tossed the end of the rope out the window, and it fell almost to the top of a tree directly below. He pulled it back up and added another length of tapestry. Then he went to the door to the secret passage and listened carefully. He could hear some shuffling noises on the other side and the muffled sound of two male voices.

So, they were taking their time. They were waiting until he was well asleep before they made their move. Noiselessly, he moved back to his bed, retrieved his food, put it in a leather pouch, which he slung around his shoulder, and headed for the window. He tied one end of the rope around a heavy chest and threw the other out the window. He let himself out the window. As he did so, he heard the sound of the secret door straining against the wedges he'd placed.

Hand under hand, he let himself down as quickly as he could go, not knowing how long his wedges would hold against the strength of full grown men. He tried to imagine what was happening on the other side of the door. Was Griselle with them?

If not, then surely they would go to her first for orders. Perhaps, they would think he was only protecting himself while he slept, and they wouldn't want to risk waking him and having him sound the alarm. If Griselle was with them she might think the same thing. Time. He needed time. They might go to the hallway door and try that. Maybe, his absence wouldn't be discovered until morning, by which time he would be long gone.

He heard a loud scraping noise above. Inwardly, he groaned. Hurry, he told himself. Hurry! He let himself slide down the tapestry rope now, ignoring the burning in his hands. The tree top was just below his feet. He stopped, looking for a firm footing in the tree. He tested the branches with his feet. They were too light to support his weight. He had no more rope. What was he going to do?

Suddenly, he felt the rope being pulled up. He looked above and saw the bald, scarred pate of the Royal Huntsman and his two huge arms above him, pulling the rope up. He looked down at the tree which was receding at alarming speed.

Without hesitating, he let go of the rope and turned his body face down as he fell and aimed for the center of the tree. There was a brief moment when he held his breath, and then, he was crashing through the tree top, his hands clutching desperately for a hand hold. His leg caught on something, and for a moment he was upside down. His right hand found a branch and grabbed it. Then his leg broke free, and he was hanging by both hands. He looked about and found another, lower, branch and then another and another until he quickly lowered himself to the ground.

He took off at a run. He had hoped for more time. Now, the only thing to do was to put as much distance between himself and the castle as possible. They would have to come all the way down to the courtyard level. Then, they would have to pursue him on foot or come up with a suitable pretext for leaving the castle on a midnight ride. Next, they must saddle the horses and wait until they were a decent distance out of the castle before they put their horses to the gallop. If he moved quickly, he could still escape. He scrambled recklessly down the steep rocky slope that fronted his side of the castle. Once at the bottom, he ran full speed through the open meadow to the woods beyond.

In the woods, he worked his way very quickly through the undergrowth to a game trail he had discovered in one of his forays outside the castle. He was encouraged by the sound of swiftly running water. He was gasping for air now, but it was not the time to rest. His blood pounded in his temples, but he kept running. He rounded a bend and saw a small, fast river. He splashed through the shallows where the water boiled and bubbled as it headed for the deeper currents. He would rather have moved quietly along the banks, but he couldn't be sure they hadn't caught his trail yet. When he reached the deeper water, he plunged in headlong and began to move swiftly downstream, swimming with the current. The water was cold, but it was bracing, and he was able to get his breath back. Ahead, he heard the sound of water moving over rocks. Quickly, he angled to the shore. There, he slipped swiftly past the rocks and boulders, past the rapids to where the water deepened again and plunged back in.

He began to breathe easier. This was a long stretch of deep water, and he was making excellent progress. The current was doing most of the work for him, and he did not have to do much more than float. He heard a whizzing noise above his head. He recognized it immediately, and he began to swim hard. He berated himself as he went. Was there no end to his stupidity? First, trusting Griselle. Then tonight, under a full moon, running straight through the tall meadow grass. In the moonlight, the beaten grass would point like an arrow, straight to where he had entered the woods. From there, the Royal Huntsman would certainly go to the first game trail, which he would surely know about. Probably, he had believed no one would be stupid enough to use this trail. Certainly, he must have thought Cha Cha would try to cover his trail—which he had not. No, he'd run full speed down the trail, his feet no doubt digging deep marks in the soft dirt. How hard would it be for the Royal Huntsman to send a couple of horsemen down the straight, main road, to set up an ambush, if he were so silly as to go out on the open river? He heard another whizzing noise over his head, then a splash somewhere in front of him. He paddled harder still, digging his head into the water, trying to present the smallest target possible. Another arrow splashed a little behind him to his left. The deflection of the water pushed the arrow in his direction, and he felt it slide smoothly under him. From the sound of their voices, he guessed there were two men shooting at him. He waited a moment, to give them time to notch their arrows and take aim, then sharply veered to his right. One arrow fell way to his left and the other well ahead. He waited a moment again, then cut to his left. Two arrows sailed close over his head. He veered right and paddled hard at a slight angle to the current, hoping to put more distance between himself and them. An arrow skipped off the water and passed harmlessly overhead. Then, another hit his food pouch but did not penetrate all the way through.

He heard yelps of glee from the pair at the shore. He kept paddling. There was a curse from the shore, then silence. Dolt! He berated himself. Why didn't you play dead? They thought they had you. While they were celebrating, the current would have carried you to safety. Now, they were renotching for another try. He dug in and paddled as hard as he could. He noticed the current was swiftening and he heard the ominous sound of white water ahead. Another arrow splashed nearby. Then, there was a searing pain in his left shoulder and he screamed. He lost control now and the current swept him into the swiftest part of the river. Like a broken branch he was hurled about and smashed against a rock, then swept under the raging torrent and back up again. A huge roaring noise drowned out all other senses. His mouth filled with water. A light exploded in his eyes as he slammed into another rock. There was a moment of dizziness and then a feeling of falling into a cavern with walls of sound before blackness engulfed him.

"Meanwhile, Princess Ta Ta…"

"Daddy, what happened to Prince Cha Cha?"

"Yeah, Dad, what?"

"I'm going to tell you that in just a little bit, but you won't understand it unless you know about Princess Ta Ta."

"But, Daddy, I want to know what happened to Prince Cha Cha."

"Sweetheart, don't you want to know what Typhus the rat did to Princess Ta Ta?"

"What did he do, Dad?"

"That is what I am about to tell you."

Chapter 6

A Different Kingdom

When Ta Ta led the wizard out of the woods he was beside himself. First, he looked about to make sure no one had seen them come out, embarrassed at being led out by a little girl, princess or not. Now that he felt safe, his irascible temper was reasserting itself and he inexplicably blamed TaTa for his embarrassment. He had a good mind to just use the horse himself and let her walk. But then he thought, what if some eligible young maiden saw him being so ungallant? His reputation would be toast for sure. No, better to play the gracious host. He insisted upon her riding while he walked. Ta Ta, of course, suggested that he ride too, but no, he was firm, for he was a gracious and gallant wizard and would fain have a young damsel be forced to share a saddle with such a lowly servant as himself.

In truth, Ta Ta found this little speech rather pleasing and, not knowing the wizard very well, thought he might actually be nice after all. So they proceeded on the road back to the wizard's kingdom, but as they went along, she noticed the wizard kept tripping. This startled her, of course, but he seemed to pay it no mind. At first, she was touched, thinking he had some physical affliction. But after awhile, she remembered how he had tripped in the woods and realized it was just because of those outlandish, curled up toes on his shoes that he was tripping. This amused her. But as they traveled on, the constant tripping began to grate on her. It came at irregular, unpredictable moments, and she could soon focus on nothing else—not the beautiful green grass, nor the gaily singing birds, nor the soft glow of the setting sun. There was just that glaring, bright red robe plodding along until…until…there, he tripped again…and yet again, two in a row. Now, watch, watch, watch, maybe he's getting the hang of it, maybe he won't—there, he tripped again. Of all the ridiculous exhibitions, Ta Ta fumed. Turn him loose on a kingdom with a book of spells, and it would be a miracle if the kingdom were still standing a week later.

Slowly, Ta Ta worked her way through amusement, contempt, disgust, pity, back to contempt again and, finally, to blazing, white anger. Nevertheless, she told herself, she was a princess of the Seventh Higher Kingdom, the highest of all the kingdoms. Therefore, she must speak softly, politely and as sweetly persuasively as she could. She strove to make her voice as lady like and musical as possible.

"Oh, excuse me, kind wizard, sir."

"Huh?" the wizard grunted. He was very tired, and while normally the sound of such a voice would have moved him to frantic efforts to please, right now, he barely heard it.

"Kind wizard, sir."

"What?" he whined.

She coughed discretely to clear her throat.

"Are you aware that you trip sometimes when you walk?"

"What? Oh, that's all right. I don't mind."

Ta Ta was incredulous. Didn't mind? How could he not be bothered? Then, her heart softened. Of course. It was obvious. It was some sort of penance for some wrong he had committed. Or perhaps, and she liked this explanation much better, it was a humiliation he willingly suffered to prove his love for some lady. How could she have been so unthinking, so judgmental?

"It's all right," she said. "I understand."

"What?" In irritation, the wizard half turned around as he walked. What the deuce was she going on about now? "Understand what?"

"Your shoes. I realize why you wear shoes that make you trip so much."

"I said I don't mind."

"I understand."

"Understand what?"

"Why you don't mind."

"Really!" He stood stock still and turned around to face her. "And why, pray, don't I mind?"

She leaned forward and, though there was none to hear but the horse, whispered confidentially in his ear, "It's for your lady love, isn't it?"

The mention of the wizard's sore spot sent him into a rage. His arms went rigid by his sides, his fists clenched and, without realizing it, he bounced up and down on the balls of his feet so fast his curled toes again quivered in a red blur. Ta Ta put her fist in her mouth again to keep from laughing.

"What business is it of yours what's for my lady love and what isn't?"

"But, I only…"

"For your information, I happen to like these shoes. Look at them."

He stuck out his feet one at a time and wiggled the shoes this way and that to show them off. He was smirking with satisfaction as he did this, but Ta Ta's nose wrinkled in distaste. Still, she was a lady and felt the need for tact.

"Kind wizard, the color…it doesn't quite work, does it?"

"What!"

"I mean, it doesn't really match the robe at all."

"The shoes are red. The robe is red."

"Red is very hard to match. You see, your shades don't go together."

"Well, what does that have to do with it?"

"It has everything to do with it! They don't match. At all!" Tanya could hear the lady like tone of her voice beginning to slip.

The wizard was sputtering with indignation. "Well of all the…of all the…of all the nerve!"

Ta Ta could stand it no more and her words came out in a torrent.

"They're ridiculous! They're grotesque and ghastly and wretched and horrid and they don't match and they make you trip."

The wizard stood, staring up at Ta Ta in disbelief, a little, black cloud forming in his mind. Let a woman in your life, he fumed, no matter her age or size, and within five minutes she will start trying to change you. And just who was riding on whose horse anyhow? You'd think it was the other way around. The black cloud began to turn into a gray rain cloud. It was all so unfair. He couldn't make her walk. How would it look? He was trapped between two bad alternatives. Like always. Always him. No matter how hard he tried. Why was life so unfair?

"You ride!" said Ta Ta.

"What?" Now what was this witch in training up to, the wizard wondered.

"You get up and ride."

"But…but…"

"I'm not going to let you humiliate me. I'm a princess. How do you think it looks for me to be introduced into a new kingdom being led by a circus clown?"

"Clown? I am a great wizard. The greatest of them all. I am not a clown."

"Get on the horse or I'll scream!" Ta Ta screamed.

The wizard caved. He was tired. It had been a long and humiliating day, and it would be so good to just ride the rest of the way back to the castle.

"Oh, all right," he said and climbed onto the horse. Ta Ta sat behind him on the rump of the mount and put her arms around his waist to keep from falling off. The wizard was still smarting from the criticism of his shoes and couldn't refrain from grumbling.

"Wizard of Fandon. Fat lot of good that'll do you. I've done a few tricks that wizard's never done."

Of course, the wizard was dying to tell her about changing a rat into a man, but if he told anyone then he wouldn't be able to use him for a spy, so he really couldn't tell her, and she'd go on thinking he wasn't really a great wizard. He sighed. Life was so unfair.

"What tricks?"

"Tricks better than you could imagine."

"Like what?"

"Secret tricks," he said pompously. "I can't tell them."

"If you say so."

The wizard ground his teeth. He heard the smirk in her voice. In his mind he could just see that smug, little smirk pointed at his back. And it wasn't fair. He was a great wizard. Typhus proved it. Unfair! Unfair! Unfair! He had a good mind to knock her off his horse. But what if someone saw them? How would that look? Instead, he changed tactics. How would she like it if he pried into her life?

"So, just why do you want to see the Wizard of Fandon?"

"Because he is the greatest wizard of all."

"Assuming that to be true, and it isn't, why do you need to see 'the greatest wizard of all?'"

He put a sarcastic sneer into "the greatest wizard of all," but Ta Ta didn't seem to notice.

"Because my troubles are so great that only the greatest wizard can possibly solve them."

"But, you're just a little girl."

"That's just it. Because I'm a little girl no one will believe me, and I can't talk to my parents because they'll never take me seriously."

Her words tumbled out and her tone was passionate. It intrigued the wizard. He thought he knew what the matter was.

"Perhaps there is some handsome knight in your father's court? Perhaps he ignores you because of the difference in your age?"

"You want to make me a love potion?"

Ta Ta was outraged, but the wizard mistook it for enthusiasm.

"No, no, my dear," he said over his shoulder. "A

clumsy wizard, like the Wizard of Fandon might. But, not I. No. This is where I show my true genius, for I will make you a potion that will make him wait for you. A magical elixir that will make him lose interest in ladies altogether until you are old enough, which won't be as long as you think, and then, I'll make you the love potion to win his heart. Of course, in the meantime, he might seem, well, a little lethargic. But, not to worry—once you slip him the old love potion he'll be like a dog after a bone."

The wizard was rubbing his hands with glee. It had been so long since he'd had a client. He heard nothing from Ta Ta in response and imagined that she was dumbstruck at her good fortune.

"Well, what do you think, Princess? How soon do you want a potion?"

"You monster! You brute!" Ta Ta pounded on his back as she railed at him. "You're just like all the rest. Why won't anyone take me seriously? It's because I'm just a little princess."

The wizard was amazed by the outburst, then irritated, then dismayed. Women! Was there no pleasing them?

"But I do take you seriously. Love is a very serious business. At any age. It's the most serious business of all."

"You don't understand at all," she sobbed.

He started to protest, but they rounded a bend in the trail, and as they came out from behind some trees, the castle of his kingdom loomed into sight.

"Oh, listen," he said, bewildered and dismayed to find himself touched by her sobbing, "do dry your tears now. It doesn't do for a princess to show tears, you know. In a little while, you'll be surrounded by the ladies of the court, and you'll have a nice bath, and they'll brush out your hair and put you in a nice, soft, feather bed. Only just dry your tears, and hold your chin up and smile. You're a princess, and you have to behave like one. There now, chin up."

The princess did as she was bid and slipped one leg over the rump of the horse and rearranged herself in side saddle position. She put one hand on the rear of the saddle to brace herself and composed the other hand on a knee. Then she squared her shoulders, sat stiffly erect and put on her broadest smile. In a few moments they were at the castle gate, and a guard came forward to challenge them. He saw Princess Ta Ta who turned her smile in his direction and nodded her head ever so slightly at him. Despite her plain clothing and bedraggled appearance, he instinctively saluted, bowed his head and said "M' lady."

Somehow, word had already spread of a newcomer's approach, and a small crowd of nobility and peasants was forming in the courtyard, which was lit by the flickering light of torches. The ladies pushed forward first. A plump one, with hair pulled back too tight and a pasty face, bulled her way to the front. She ignored the wizard and inspected Princess Ta Ta and, by her smile, seemed to be favorably impressed. Some other women, dressed in the finery of ladies of a royal court, crowded up closely behind her. The peasants stayed discretely in the background but watched with interest.

The pasty faced lady addressed herself to Ta Ta.

"Child, who might you be?"

Ta Ta broadened her smile until it hurt, and said, "I am Princess Ta Ta of the Seventh Higher Kingdom."

Etiquette demanded that the ladies should curtsey, and the nobles should bow, to her rank, notwithstanding her age, and they all did so. There would be time to check her credentials later, and she would pay dearly if she was lying. But her bearing certainly looked regal, and most sensed that she was telling the truth.

"I am the Duchess of Dendora, Princess Ta Ta. Please step down and accept the hospitality of our court."

Princess Ta Ta bowed her head in gracious acceptance, and two noblemen stepped forward to assist her down. A groom appeared out of the darkness and placed a little portable stairway in front of her. Each nobleman took one of her hands, and she slid graciously off the horse and stepped daintily down the stairway to the cobblestones of the courtyard.

"And what brings you to the Fourth Kingdom, Princess?"

It was one of the noblemen who helped her down who asked. He was tall, strong looking and had a shiny, black goatee.

The princess had already rehearsed her answer. She knew no one would believe her if she told the truth. But, she must still find a way to contact the Wizard of Fandon. So, she fudged.

"I became lost. I was out for a ride and became separated from everyone and became more and more lost."

Everyone clucked their tongues in sympathy.

"Well it's all right now, dear," said the pasty faced lady. "We'll get you home safe and sound. But, right now, you're probably very hungry."

Ta Ta noticed that everyone had quite neglected the wizard, including herself. Etiquette was etiquette, and as unpleasant as she had found his company, she must still thank him properly. She turned to him and found that he was already slinking away on his horse, his shoulders sagging, his countenance crestfallen.

"Where is he going?" she murmured.

It had been a long, long while since anyone had been afraid of the wizard.

"Rigirus? Who cares?" one lady said.

"Yes," piped another. "I'm sorry he's the one you found to give you a ride."

"Yes," a pompous noble thundered. "Don't judge the rest of us by the likes of him."

"Don't worry," the goateed nobleman whispered in a voice loud enough for everyone to hear. "We'll make sure he doesn't bother you again."

Princess Ta Ta stamped her foot. This was unbearable. Something was dreadfully wrong here. She felt as if a cold hand was running up and down her spine.

"Wizard!"

She barked the word out like an order, which it was. If any had doubted she was a princess before, none did now. The wizard's horse stopped dead in its tracks as if it had been spoken to personally. The wizard turned his head to her with a shocked expression.

"Come back here," she commanded.

Nervously, the wizard did as he was told. When he stopped his horse in front of the Princess, she put on her most gentle demeanor.

"You have not allowed me to thank you for rescuing me. That is a breach of etiquette. Would you let the court think that I am ungracious?"

In the background she heard voices mumbling in surprise.

"Rigirus? Rescue someone?"

"Impossible."

The wizard cringed. He just knew he was being set up. She was going to tell how he had found her by accident, and how it had been her that led them out because he had lost his head because he was tired and sweaty and confused.

Princess Ta Ta turned to the crowd, which had grown

considerably, and smiled sweetly.

"Please understand, I had wandered into Dark Wilde Forest and was lost and without hope. I was sure it was my end. Then somehow, as if by some great magic, my rescuer appeared in the woods, unarmed and alone. He made his way to me in Dark Wilde Forest and then led me out. What manner of wizard is this that can penetrate forests with his thoughts and rescue the distressed?"

The crowd, having long experience with the wizard, remained skeptical.

"Rigirus?"

"Rescue?"

"Penetrate Dark Wilde Forest?"

"He couldn't penetrate an open door."

The wizard was terribly pleased and grateful to the Princess, but he tried to appear nonchalant.

"Oh, it was really nothing," he said, waving a hand dismissively.

"You have saved the life of a princess," Ta Ta corrected. "That is hardly nothing."

"Yes, that's all well and good," the pasty faced Duchess interjected. "Now, run along, Rigirus. Princess, come along. We will care for you and feast you tonight."

Something in Ta Ta rebelled. As much as she had longed all afternoon for just this, to be in a royal court, bathed, dined and pampered, somewhere deep inside, something recoiled from these people. She looked around at the smug, self satisfied faces that surrounded her and felt a knot in her stomach. As much as she detested the wizard's constant caviling, she now felt that it was better to stay with him. Somehow, it seemed safer.

"I'm sorry, good Duchess, but I believe it is the rule throughout all the Seven Higher Kingdoms that the rescuer has first right of hospitality, does he not?"

"Why, yes, but he's only Rigirus. He lives in a tower and doesn't have any suitable quarters."

Ta Ta turned calmly back to the wizard whose face was displaying a kaleidoscope of emotions from anger, to embarrassment, to panic and back to anger again.

"Wizard, you have the right of hospitality as rescuer. Do you invoke it?"

The wizard was flummoxed. The Duchess was right, of course. His miserable quarters were absolutely no place for any woman, not even the lowest servant, let alone a princess. But, oh, how he longed to snap his fingers at the court. How he wanted to walk away with the Princess while they stewed. But the embarrassment of having the Princess see his quarters, which he now realized, as if for the first time, were dreadfully substandard, filled him with horror. Better to politely beg off.

"I'm sorry, Princess, but a wizard has many, many pressing responsibilities. My quarters are, perhaps, slightly less tidy than an august personage such as yourself might…"

Princess Ta Ta cut him off in mid sentence.

"Do you mean to tell me that a 'great wizard' such as yourself can't secure suitable quarters for a princess?"

It was the slight curl of her lip as she said "great wizard," the little snicker that ran through the crowd as she said it, that got him. The anger in him flared up, and he forgot to think ahead.

"Of course, I can. I am Rigirus, the greatest of all the wizards in the Seven Higher Kingdoms."

Just as quickly, the anger was replaced by a sinking feeling that he had over committed, and he began to backtrack.

"But, of course, a great princess, such as yourself, would no doubt…"

Princess Ta Ta interrupted him again. She was becoming impatient. Why couldn't this simpleton see what she was getting at?

"Do you mean to tell me that you refuse to provide suitable quarters for the Princess of the Seventh Higher Kingdom? Is this a deliberate provocation?"

The crowd gasped. Was Rigirus trying to start a war? An angry rumble began to run through the courtyard, and the wizard became very confused.

"But, no, of course not. It's just that…"

"Then, I accept," said Princess Ta Ta with a peremptory wave of her hand. She turned to the Duchess and said, "Torch bearers, please."

The Duchess beamed with pleasure. Ta Ta noticed the whole crowd seemed delighted with the way she'd put Rigirus in his place. This was good. She had escaped their company without offending them.

"Torch bearers! Torch bearers!" the Duchess yelled in a shrill voice. "Get up here this instant. The Princess needs you."

Two young torch bearers hustled to the side of Princess Ta Ta. She noted with dissatisfaction that their clothes were tattered, and they looked underfed. Her father would never have allowed his nobles to get as fat as the ones here while the servants were this thin. She waved a hand, and the torch bearers went forward to light the way for her and Rigirus.

"I shall be at the Queen's disposal," she called over her shoulder to the Duchess.

As they went to his quarters, the wizard steamed. To be publicly manipulated like this, he saw it clearly now that it was over, by a little girl. Even if she was a princess. As if he couldn't see he was being maneuvered into giving up his privacy. Naturally, those fools in the court lapped it right up. Well, he'd put things back in their proper place. And thus he occupied his mind all the way back up to his chambers.

Ta Ta, for her part, was appalled. The torch bearers led the way to the dingiest part of the castle. They left the wizard's horse in an unpleasant, seedy stable, then entered into a smelly, narrow, little lane. They walked through rubble and refuse and, finally, entered a splintered, creaky, little door and began to climb up a narrow, crumbling, stone staircase made up of ever so many tiny, little steps. The walls were devoid of any color or art or even candles and, even in the torchlight, looked as if they hadn't been washed since the day they were built. How could the wizard possibly let himself live like this, she wondered.

The stairway wound upward and upward in an increasingly tighter circle, becoming ever more unsteady and treacherous as they climbed. One of the torch bearers nearly fell to his death when a piece of stairway gave way under his feet. The higher they climbed the damper the walls became, and the air was increasingly chilly. Ta Ta began to shiver from the cold. At last, they came to a small, plain wooden door that looked as if it were about to fall off its hinges. The lead torch bearer squeezed himself up against one wall of the narrow passageway, and the wizard wriggled past and pushed the door open. It creaked loudly enough to hurt Ta Ta's ears. The wizard bent slightly and entered, followed by the lead torch bearer, followed by Ta Ta, who was followed by the second torch bearer.

Once inside, she shook her head in dismay. How could

the wizard possibly live like this, she asked herself again. The walls turned increasingly black as they rose, and the ceiling was pitch black. Opposite the door was a small fireplace with the fire out and a black cauldron sitting in the middle. The cauldron was caked with various colors on the side. Obviously, it had boiled over many times, and just as obviously, it had never been cleaned. There was a small table to the side of the fireplace that was piled to the ceiling with a tottering stack of books and scrolls that looked as if it would topple over soon, if the table didn't collapse under the weight first. On the table, in front of the books, sat a few malodorous, dirty pots and jars. Along the wall to the right of the table was a crude wooden shelf, built of rocks and rough planks, that was crammed with jars, pots and vials and, between them, still more books and parchment scrolls. To the left of the fireplace was the wizard's bed. It was only a few wooden planks topped by a musty, straw mattress. There was no sheeting, but two moth eaten blankets were crumpled up at one end. Above the bed, fastened to the wall, was a collection of soot covered charts and diagrams. Here and there on the charts were smears, where the wizard had apparently tried to wipe away enough soot to read the charts.

It looked hopeless, but Ta Ta spied a small door, about half the size of a normal door, in the wall opposite the wizard's bed.

"Where does that door lead to?" she asked the wizard. The wizard had been watching the disapproving gaze of the Princess as she surveyed his room and had gone into one of his internal rants. How dare she, he raged. Does she have any idea of what's involved in being a wizard? The study? The long hours? The discipline!

But he bit his tongue. When they were alone he'd set

this child straight. Princess or no princess. So, he just said, "The door goes no place really. Just to a small attic."

"Open it," she said to the lead torch bearer.

He bent down, shoved the door open, and stuck his torch in far enough to illuminate the space. Ta Ta leaned over and also looked in. It was dirty, filled with cobwebs and insects that scurried away from the light. It was long and narrow and just high enough for a man to walk in if he were bent over double.

"This will do nicely," she said, and stood up.

The wizard was stunned. Was she actually going to stay in there?

The Princess turned to the second torch bearer and said, "Run downstairs and fetch a dozen of your most industrious servants. I know the hour is late, but tell them Princess Ta Ta commands it. And be sure to tell them the wizard will reward them handsomely for their efforts."

The wizard sucked in a huge breath. He was going to reward them handsomely? He wanted to throw everybody out of the room. But, how would it look? He saw the torch bearers approving looks at the mention of a reward and decided it wouldn't do to set the servants' tongues wagging about his miserliness. So, he bit his lip and decided to wait. After all, he consoled himself, the princess was going to stay in that tiny attic. That should be amusing.

Before long, the torchbearer returned with a dozen very eager servants and a message from the Queen that Rigirus was to ensure that the accommodations for the Princess were befitting the standards of royalty. That irked Rigirus enough, but what irked him even more was when he found that Princess Ta Ta had no intention of living in the attic. That, it seemed, was for him, for after a perfunctory sweeping out, she ordered all of his goods moved into the attic.

The wizard howled in protest, but Princess Ta Ta suggested the Queen would not think the attic was suitable for royalty. And besides, she told him, he should never have insisted upon invoking the right of hospitality if he was not going to be generous.

The wizard fumed and steamed but did as he was ordered. He moved the cauldron himself, lest some clumsy servant might spill one precious drop of his latest recipe for turning Typhus into a human. And he moved a few jars of the ingredients he was using in his attempt to recreate the formula. After that, he sat in a corner and sulked.

The work went on until just before dawn. After the room had been cleared of every last vestige of the wizard's belongings and bedding, the walls and ceilings had to be completely washed. Buckets and buckets of water were carried up the stairs. The grime was so thick it seemed it would never be cleaned up. Even the Princess took a scrub brush in hand and scrubbed. The wizard sneered at her for this, but the servants beamed and worked all the harder. At last, it was all washed. The door was mended and reset on its hinges. Tapestries were brought up and hung on the walls. Sturdy shutters, gaily and brightly painted with flowers, birds, and dancing peasants, were mounted upon the window. Thick, heavy rugs were hauled up and placed on the floor. Fresh flowers were placed on the mantle.

Next, a huge, heavy wooden bed was hoisted up by pullies and placed in a corner. A fluffy, feather bed was placed on the bed frame, and even fluffier feather pillows were placed on the fluffy feather bed. The bed was then made up with pink, silk sheets, soft thick blankets and a fluffy feather comforter. Two gold inlaid wooden chairs and a small, silver trimmed table were added to the room's furnishings. Then, a partition of brocaded silk was put around the bed, chairs and table for privacy. Lastly, a roaring fire was built so the predawn chill would not discomfort the Princess.

At last, everything was finished to the Princess's satisfaction and she said, "The wizard will reward you now."

The wizard hemmed and hawed but grudgingly produced a purse from beneath the folds of his robe, as the servants eagerly lined up. He tried to pay off with small copper coins, but the Princess glared at him, and so, he paid off each servant with a thick gold piece, much to their delight.

At last, the last servant was rewarded and out of the room. The wizard closed the door with satisfaction. His moment had finally come. Now to give this princess a piece of his mind. You do not trifle with the greatest of wizards, and if she thought for one second that he was going so sleep in that attic, she was in for a very rude awakening. He whirled with a look of triumph which was quickly replaced by consternation when he saw her starting to enter the attic.

"What are you doing?" he howled.

The Princess turned to face him.

"Going to my room."

"But, this is your room."

"Did you really think I'd kick you out of your room and put you in the attic? This," she waved an arm at the newly decorated chamber, "was for show. This is what your people expect of a Princess. Now, if you please, I'm very tired and must sleep. Good night."

And with that, Princess Ta Ta turned away and, stooping a little bit, went through the tiny door and shut it firmly behind her.

The wizard stared after her, stunned. Then, he realized

that he too was very sleepy. He looked at the huge feather bed that had been prepared for the Princess. It looked so inviting. But he thought of the Princess sleeping on his own musty mattress in the dirty attic, and much to his own surprise, he curled up on the rug in front of the fireplace and went to sleep.

***

"And speaking of sleep," said Father, "I see you're both starting to nod off yourselves." He stood up with Tanya in his arms and headed for her room. "Good night, Charles."

Chapter 7

Grown--Ups

After they were gone, Charles turned off the light, got down on his knees, and prayed really, really hard for the first time in his life.

"Please, God, it isn't fair. It isn't right. Make her well, God," he prayed over and over, as the deep anger he'd felt that afternoon began to stir in him again.

He had been mulling over what his sister had said all day. While his father's fairy tale had engrossed him and provided welcome relief, the enormity of his sister's revelation was back upon him, full force. A life without his sister, whom he had so often wished gone and never born, who hitherto seemed such an impediment to his schemes and projects, now seemed like a life without an arm or a leg. Only, worse. Without an arm or a leg, life went on, however imperfectly. But this was a permanent emptiness. And, back of that, was an overwhelming sense of unfairness, a sense that his sister had done nothing to deserve this. Yet, he knew that God was supposed to be mysterious, and that you were supposed to pray for those in need. So, he prayed hard and intently for his sister, until he could barely keep his eyes open. Then he got in bed and went to sleep.

In her room, Tanya huddled in her bed, listening to the noise from the closet. Whatever was in there scuffled and nosed about. Night by night, the growling became louder. It now sounded like it was scraping at the bottom of the door. She wondered how much longer it would be before it burst through. Wearily, she tried to stay awake, but finally, she fell asleep.

Once again she had been through the valley of the fairies. Again, it had been beautiful and serene up to that last headlong rush to the window she dreaded. Now she was trapped again, as though in a net, waiting, wondering why this thing did not consume her. It had the power, yet it didn't.

She fought back the feeling of suffocation. She looked about the darkness. As she calmed, she noticed how restful, how peaceful it seemed.

She looked back at the valley of fairies. It was beautiful. But there was no finality to it. This, the darkness, looked like an ending, a place to stay.

She floated in the window, waiting, looking deep into the dark. Why was she here? Why wouldn't she go in? It wanted to draw her forward, but she pushed it back. Why?

What did this blackness offer? She felt an urge to go in--explore it, touch and taste of it. But something inside herself checked her. She wouldn't enter yet. Not until a time of her own choosing. The blackness, the castle and the valley all gradually dissolved.

The next morning, Charles got up early and dressed in a wondering mood. Sometime during the night something had happened, he mused. But what? He stopped dressing and sat on the edge of the bed. Was it his imagination? He shook his head. The feeling wouldn't go away. Then, it hit him. Something had woken him up during the night. He was sure of it. He tried to recall it, but it kept slipping away from him. He seemed to remember rolling over and sitting up and opening his eyes. Or was it a dream? He wanted to think about it until it came back to him, but his hunger intruded upon him, and he got up, finished dressing and went down to the kitchen for breakfast.

In the kitchen, he noticed his mother's eyes were red. She made him some cereal for breakfast which he ate in silence. He had hoped his sister would be able to go to the tree with him again, but the sound of her coughing told him she would be resting all day. He looked at his mother and could see her hands ball up into fists every time his sister began to cough. Silently, he finished his meal and left the house, headed for his tree cave.

He walked slowly, head down, hands jammed into his pockets. It kept eating at him, now that his hunger was sated. He didn't notice the sunshine or the slight breeze. All he felt was a dull anger and a sense of helplessness. That he could do nothing, when he so very much wanted to do everything, overwhelmed him. He began to rail within himself against grown-ups. How could they not be able to manage something so simple as making his sister well? He began to daydream of becoming a scientist or doctor and curing his sister. He carried on with his fantasizing until he reached the tree. There, he buried himself within it, pressed his back into its curved interior and, pulling his knees tight up against his chest, wrapped his arms around his knees. Suddenly, he plunged his face to his knees as it hit him, full force, that his sister would never live long enough for him to grow up and become a doctor and make her well. The realization made the dull anger within him sharpen and focus. He began to sniffle and his eyes began to tear and that made him angrier still.

Stupid grown-ups, he thought. They shouldn't let kids get sick. Mentally, he tried to exclude his parents from this. It's not their fault, he reasoned. They're not doctors. Still, you'd think all the grown-ups would get together and do something. Uncomfortably, his thoughts began to shift in another direction. He fought it back but the question kept coming to him.

Who was the biggest grown-up of all? It was God, of course. Everything, Charles remembered being told, happened because God made it happen or let it happen. So, why would God let this happen? It didn't make any sense. Tanya had never hurt anybody. All the petty annoyances of the past, the teasing, the snitching, the bullying(as Charles perceived it), had melted away in importance. Indeed, when he remembered his annoyance he felt guilty and small. So, why didn't God do something about it? He thought about this until he finally hit upon the only possible answer.

He wasn't praying hard enough.

He got upon his knees and began to pray with his eyes shut. He prayed until his knees hurt and then resumed his sitting position against the inside of the tree trunk. He stopped praying and waited for an answer. That too, he remembered. When you pray, you're supposed to wait for an answer. So, he sat and waited for an answer. After awhile, his mind began to roam. It moved restlessly about the memories of his life, of his sister and of his parents, when suddenly, out of the blue, it happened. He remembered. What woke him up.

It was a growling noise.

Chapter 8

The Slither Hither and Thithers

That evening, Tanya was feeling better and her coughing had stopped. Despite the new, stronger medicine she had been given to stop her coughing, she seemed alert and lively, so Father assumed his place in the easy chair, Tanya assumed her place in his lap, and Charles sat expectantly at the foot of the bed.

Father looked up at the ceiling a long moment, thinking, then smiled at them and said, “Well, now, where shall we begin? Or, to put it another way, where did we leave off?”

“The Princess, Daddy. She went to sleep in the attic.”

“Why, so she did. I'd nearly forgotten.”

“What about Cha Cha, Dad? What happened to him?”

“Oh, Cha Cha. Right, let's see.”

“Did the arrow that hit him kill him? Did he drown after he blacked out?” Charles asked, his voice beginning to rise in anxiety.

Father stroked his chin and looked back up at the ceiling again.

"Well, now, just what did happen to Cha Cha? As I recall, it went something like this."

***

Prince Cha Cha was dimly aware of the sound of rushing water. His head hurt, right behind his eyes, with a splitting pain. It almost made him not notice the horrible burning in his shoulder. Slowly, he gathered his wits and tried to remember what had happened to him. He fought down the urge to throw up. He tried to understand why he was in so much pain. It started to come back to him. He was trying to find Ta Ta and rescue her. If she was still alive. Suddenly, it all flooded back into his awareness; Griselle, his escape from the castle, the pursuit by her henchmen, the arrow hitting his shoulder, banging his head on the rock and, then, unconsciousness. But, why was he still alive? Why hadn't he drowned? Before he had a chance to think of the answer, a certain noise blocked all thoughts, including the pain he felt, out of his head.

He heard a slithering sound.

Ever so slowly, he opened the eye closest to the noise the merest of slits. In a dim haze he saw a series of green teeth only a few inches from his stomach. He tried not to breathe. It was a slither hither and thither. The creature let out a bellow and, despite himself, Cha Cha flinched, for which he quickly berated himself. His father had always said a good king must anticipate everything. He should have collected his wits fully before opening his eye. But the creature did not seem to notice his movement. Instead, it hurried rapidly away from him on its four bottom legs, scraping noisily against the ground as it did so. It seemed to be terribly angry about something. While its back was turned Cha Cha felt stealthily for the knife he'd taken from the kitchen. With horror he realized it was gone.

He heard another slithering noise, this time just to his right. He felt a hot, fetid breath upon his face. In alarm, he rolled away, springing to his feet as he did so. He backed up quickly until he was stopped by the rocks behind him. The scene before his eyes horrified him. Slither hither and thithers of all sizes covered the ground in front of him. He saw he was in a cavern that was apparently the den of these loathsome creatures. A waterfall roared over the front of the cavern. It was obvious they had found him before he'd had a chance to drown and brought him here. But why hadn't they eaten him already? In fact, why didn't they eat him now?

They seemed hungry. They roared and bellowed and shook their heads from side to side. Their mouths hung open as they looked at him, and their tongues lolled about and dripped saliva on the slimy cavern floor. But they didn't eat him. The biggest one, apparently the head of the clan, came forward and lunged at him repeatedly, coming to within an inch of his face. But every time he was about to strike Cha Cha his head would snap back as though on a leash. Cha Cha was terribly frightened but, remembering the lessons his father had implanted, took a deep breath and forced all the fear from his face. Then, as he seemed to be in no immediate danger, he sat down. To calm himself, he began to scan his eyes about the cavern and make escape plans. First, he counted the creatures. There seemed to be about forty of them, at least that he could see. Besides the obvious way out, straight through the repulsive creatures and through the water fall, there seemed to be an exit through some rocks to his left, about twenty feet away. To his right, about the same distance away, there seemed to be a little trail which led away and upward. He saw no sign of his knife lying about. He looked for sharp edged rocks. He saw one, with a jagged edge, just about the right size to fit in the palm of his hand. Getting to it was the problem, for it sat directly in front of a thin, hungry looking slither hither and thither.

Why didn't they attack? As long as they held back there was hope. He continued to scan the cavern.

He heard a noise. Something was coming down the trail to his right. It didn't make a slithering noise. It sounded like human footsteps. But they weren't being stealthy enough. It must be a search party from the castle! Perhaps, his father was at the head. He must warn them. But would it break the spell? Would the beasts turn and rend him? It didn't matter. He must take the chance and warn his father the King, and give the soldiers a chance to defend themselves.

"To arms! To arms!" he cried as loudly as he could. "The cavern is full of slitherer hither and thithers."

The green scaly monsters looked at him, as if startled. Then they turned away from him and all faced the trail. The sound of the footsteps stopped. Prince Cha Cha braced himself. They were preparing to rush. In a moment there would be a large shout, a rush of feet, and his father and his soldiers would burst upon the slither hither and thithers and destroy them all. He braced his feet against the wall, ready to lunge for the jagged edged rock at the right moment.

The footsteps resumed. He realized there was only a single step, and the tread was too light for a man. His heart sank. What if they belonged to…

Griselle strode triumphantly down the trail onto the cavern floor. She strode straight past the slither hither and thithers as if they weren't even there, straight to Prince Cha Cha. She stopped in front of him and smiled down at him. But the pretense was gone now, and it was her real smile, the gloating smile she must have smiled every time she left his bedroom by the secret passageway.

"So, my little prince. Did you really think you could get away from me?"

Cha Cha wanted to speak, but something told him to be silent. He was a prince. Time to act the part. He stepped slowly away from the rock, folded his arms, looked up with a steady gaze and said nothing.

Griselle, however, saw through his game. She too folded her arms and stood still and eyed him with a steadfast gaze. But she did speak.

"Very good, little Prince Cha Cha. Make me speak first. Maybe, I'll give something away. Let's see, what might I mistakenly reveal? That you can't escape from me? No. You already know that. That you are completely within my power? That if I give the word these beautiful creatures will devour you? Why, I do believe you know these things too."

She bent forward and shook her head as if sad.

"So quick for your age. Oh, Cha Cha, you will make a great king. Under my tutelage, of course."

"My father will teach me to be a king."

Her face seemed to become even sadder, and she shook her head back and forth.

"But how can he? So trusting, so naive. It's the common failing of your family. All his ability squandered. But, don't worry, my little prince. I won't let your abilities be squandered."

She straightened up, smiled brightly, and held up her index finger.

"First lesson," she said. "Trust no one. But trust me. Trust no one but me."

"You tried to kill me!"

"No, no, no," she crooned, shaking her head side to side and wagging her finger. "That was strictly against orders."

She stood beside him and put an arm around his shoulder. Cha Cha wanted to pull away but forced himself to show no emotion.

"You are much too valuable to me. In fact, you are very necessary to my plans. Look over there if you don't believe me," she crooned and pointed to a dark part of the cavern Cha Cha hadn't noticed before.

Cha Cha followed her outstretched hand to where it pointed. At the edge of the cavern he saw a pile of human bones that had been picked clean. Almost. A couple of the beasts were gnawing at the last bits of red flesh that clung to them. Cha Cha fought down the sickness inside him and also fought down the urge to fling himself wildly at Griselle, kicking and flailing, trying to do anything to wipe that insufferable smirk off her face.

Griselle arched her eyebrow in feigned surprise.

"Oh, my little prince, aren't you happy with how I protect you? I do everything with your father in mind. You see what I do to people who don't obey me? If only your father knew how to instill fear in his people. What could he not accomplish? But, your father won't take my advice. However, those who do obey me," she waved an arm at the slither hither and thithers, "they eat well, do they not? And you shall learn to obey me. I promise. And then you will not only eat well, you shall rule."

"I am going to rule anyway. I am going to be king."

"Ah, yes. But only of one kingdom. With my guidance you shall come to rule all the Seven Higher Kingdoms. We shall have power. We shall be treated as gods. All it takes is to instill fear."

"I'm not afraid of you."

"Posh. Of course you are. It's only natural. You needn't be ashamed. You're so very young. Life still has so much to offer you. You want to experience it all, don't you?"

"Not with you running it."

Griselle's expression fell as if in sad surprise.

"Oh, didn't anyone tell you? Even a king does not get everything he wants. He must learn, as you must learn to…what's the best word?" She pretended to hesitate, as if searching for the right word, then snapped her finger and said, "Oh, yes, compromise, that's the word, the very best word. Don't use nasty words, like grovel, or cringe, or fawn, or toady, or surrender, or even obey, if they offend you. Just call it a compromise. It's quite all right. The very best people do it all the time."

"I won't let you use me."

"No? Not even for your father?"

"No. Not even for him."

"Not even for your mother?"

"No!"

Griselle pretended to be puzzled. Then she acted as if she'd just thought of something.

"I know. How about for your sister, then?"

Cha Cha's composure snapped. He whirled on Griselle, fists up, ready to strike her.

"What have you done with her?" he screamed.

Instantly, he regretted it. Griselle's face lit up as if she had just eaten a piece of candy. He realized she was testing him, finding his limits, already fastening the bands of control upon him. Her eyebrows arched up in mock surprise again.

"Done with her? Why, I've taken her somewhere she'll be safe. Isn't that what you want? I'd never hurt either one of you. You should know that by now. Would you like to see her?"

He held his silence, searching for a neutral answer, then said the safest thing he could think of.

"Is she nearby?"

Griselle acted disappointed.

"Alas. Her safety required her to remove two days journey from the Seventh Kingdom. Don't worry. You'll see her soon enough. Now, let us leave this damp, uncomfortable place. I have a much drier abode not far away. There, I shall begin to instruct you in how a real king acts. Not like some sentimental fool. Someday, you will thank me Cha Cha. Someday, when you realize that a real king rules by blood and for blood. Let us go."

She put a vise like hand on his wounded shoulder. Immediately, his knees buckled, and beads of sweat appeared on his lip and forehead. Her surprise seemed genuine this time.

"You are hurt worse than I thought. No matter. A king must learn to live with pain. The sooner the better." She squeezed harder and, once again, Cha Cha became unconscious.

Meanwhile, in the Fourth Kingdom, Ta Ta had gone to sleep just before the sun came up. Typhus had been watching her while she slept. He had been on one of his forays down into the rat world and had returned just before she went to bed. He watched until she was fast asleep, then scurried back down his rat hole. He ran about the castle, gathering all the gossip, from the servants' quarters to the royal chambers. None of this he told to the wizard. The wizard still considered him too slow witted to do a proper job of spying. For the time being, that suited Typhus's purposes well. Once he was convinced he knew everything of importance concerning the princess, he came back to the wizard's chambers and took a quick nap. When he was refreshed he helped himself to some formula and became human. He dressed himself and prepared breakfast. He took the wizard's silver plate, (the one that he had inherited, and never used, just as he never used the gold he'd inherited) set the breakfast on it, let himself into the attic and watched the Princess while she slept.

What a strange child he thought to himself. She sleeps so restfully. She's in the greatest danger, but she sleeps as soundly as if nothing could harm her. He knew she was in danger for the higher your station the greater your danger. That was true for humans as well as rats. She slept with her arm curled under her head for a pillow, disdaining to use the wizard's dirty, straw tick pillow. So very curious. He had heard her refuse the wizard's splendidly refurbished room. Why? Rank was rank in all the world. It was to be used. Yet, she had chosen this dirty, cramped, bug ridden attic. Perhaps, he mused, there was some secret, tactical advantage she sought. Humans were so hidden in their motives. Rats operated on force and instinct. They fought for primacy, for food and to protect their young. But this princess had given up her rightful primacy, had not complained about food and was younger than the wizard. There had to be some hidden tactical plan. But, she was so young. Could humans really be so cunning, so forward looking at such an early age? Then again, she was a princess. The same families dominated, generation after generation, among both rats and humans, he observed. He shuddered. What monsters these royal families were. How cunning this little one must be. He regarded her as he would a sleeping snake. He was sure the wizard, whom he had come to detest as a simpleton, wouldn't stand a chance against her.

As he watched, something uncomfortable stirred within him. He fought against it, but he could not help feeling a softening within his breast. She looked small and helpless. He realized that the natural instinct to protect the species was stirring within him. As a rat he felt the urge to protect the young of that species, and as a human he felt the urge to protect that species. That was the trouble. He continually fought down attractions--to protect children, to talk to young maidens, to belong. What was it about humans? They could destroy the young of their own species, either quickly in war, or slowly, through starvation, neglect and deprivation. And they had this institution called marriage, which was supposed to make them happy, but from what humans told him, it only made them miserable, and yet they pushed their own offspring into it with celebration and fan-fare.

Certainly, he was miserable. What was he now? A rat or a human? If he had to choose, which would be better—the open terror and brute force, experienced through a minuscule intelligence, of the life of a rat or the hidden terror and implied force, experienced with full intellectual awareness, of human existence? Moreover, what happened when the formula was used up? Could he really stand to slowly sink back to the dim, instinctual existence of a rat?

For some time now, he had been trying to duplicate the formula of the wizard. Though he'd done very well at controlling dosages, the original formula eluded him, as it did the wizard. He knew he was making progress. But how much longer? Would his own formula hold out until he made his breakthrough? Besides, there was the other reason.

His life was a hellish nightmare. When he returned to his rat clan he would always carry choice morsels of food with him, and the instinctual warmth of the clan would give him some comfort. But as his intellectual capacities grew the barriers grew also. How much he wanted to tell them, to somehow communicate everything he was experiencing and living to them. It was impossible, of course. And how long before the barrier grew so large that they would no longer recognize him and turn and rend him to pieces? And how long before the humans discovered his secret? If they did, he was sure they too would rend him to pieces.

He mused about the formula. Maybe, if he tried another way of heating the formula. It had been very cold in the room that night. Maybe the difference between surface temperature and internal temperature affected the workings of the recipe. But the Princess began to stir, and Typhus put his musings to one side.

Ta Ta was startled to awake with Typhus staring at her. She sat up rapidly, pulling the stained bedcover in front of her as she did so.

"Who are you?" she asked.

"I am Typhus, the cousin of Rigirus, the wizard. Here is some breakfast for you."

Ta Ta looked at the man with curiosity. He was bent over because of the low clearance of the attic, but he moved about effortlessly, not seeming to mind at all. In fact, he seemed quite comfortable. Then she looked to the breakfast as her appetite stirred.

"Yes, I'd like that. I'm quite hungry."

"I thought you would be. I heard about your adventures

yesterday. Being in the woods for a day gives one an appetite."

Typhus decided not to smile as he spoke. He never quite knew when to smile around humans. It was so easy to get in trouble if you smiled at the wrong time. He put the silver tray with its silver cups and ware on a little table he had procured and put by the sleeping princess. The wizard never used the silverware himself. He had some money from inheritance, but he was far too miserly to spend it or even to use the silverware. Instead, he lived in the cheapest quarters he could procure and ate off cheap, broken crockery. All of which caused Typhus to reflect, not for the first time, on how a human could waste something as valuable as a human lifetime.

It was a simple breakfast. Milk, water mixed with wine, porridge mixed with peaches and pears, a loaf of bread and a small tub of butter. He attended to the Princess closely while she ate, not because she really needed his help, but because he wanted to continue watching her. Ta Ta ate her breakfast with enthusiasm. As her hunger eased, she began to notice something odd about her server. In a way he was handsome. He seemed very energetic, quick and sure. His hair was sleek and thick, but his nose was a little long and pointed. His eyes, also, seemed too small and very dark. He was very polite, but somehow it seemed strange, as if he weren't really used to it.

"You'll have to move back into the main room after breakfast," Typhus said. "You have an invitation to see the queen this evening. The maids-in-waiting will be here shortly to prepare you. They'll have to think you slept in the other room, of course." Typhus said all this as he was buttering a slice of bread for the Princess.

"Thank you," she said, accepting the buttered bread that

was handed to her. "I shall be done eating in a moment."

Ta Ta was surprised at the matter of fact tone of the wizard's cousin. He seemed like such an odd companion for the wizard. So competent and orderly and quick. He also seemed to understand completely about the sleeping arrangements. Suddenly, she saw him throw his left hand over his nose.

"Oh, my," he said, in a voice that sounded strangely high pitched. "I must have a runny nose." With that, he snatched the tray and everything on it with his right hand and hustled out the door.

Ta Ta stared after him, frozen in total surprise. All she had left was the remaining fragment of buttered bread which she held suspended before her mouth. What a most peculiar cousin the wizard had.

That afternoon was frantic. The maids-in-waiting bathed her, brushed and scented her hair, insisted upon powdering and rouging her face, dressed her in a white silk gown with gold trim and put gold slippers, perfectly made by the Royal Cobbler, upon her feet. Then they plaited and braided her hair and piled it high upon her head. The maids-in-waiting fussed and preened over her and tried their best to get in her good graces.

The wizard, of course, had been chased out of the room and, to his surprise, was promptly accosted by the Court Tailor. Regrettably, said the Court Tailor, court custom and etiquette demanded that the wizard, as host of the Princess, must accompany the Princess to the royal reception that evening. Happily, said the Court Tailor, Her Majesty was not going to allow the wizard to make a mockery of the proceedings by dressing however he pleased. The Court Tailor then waved his hand, and abruptly, the wizard was seized by a gang of valets and hauled to another part of the castle. There, he was given a good scrubbing, his hair and beard were washed, brushed and trimmed, and he was given a new, bright red robe, which pleased him tremendously. Then they tried to replace his shoes, and the fight began.

"No! I won't have it," the wizard howled. "These are my favorite shoes. No one else in the kingdom has shoes like this."

This remark brought diverse snorts and snickers from the pages, tailors and valets which the wizard put off to jealousy. The issue was finally settled when a message came from the King informing the wizard he would be beheaded if he set foot inside the royal court wearing his old shoes. After some grumbling, the wizard finally decided this was a sign that the King was hurt by his refusal to accept the gift of a pair of shoes to such a distinguished wizard as himself and was a sure sign of his rising status in the world. This brightened him up considerably, and he began to be anxious about what sort of speech he should give if the King asked him to give a speech.

Back in the wizard's room, at last, all was in readiness for the grand moment. The light was beginning to fade and candles and tapers were lit. The maids-in-waiting were flushed and beaming with pleasure and exchanged looks of satisfaction over their handiwork. After a few last pats and tidying of strands of hair they pronounced Ta Ta ready for the grand event—the reception of royalty by royalty.

They led her to the door and opened it to allow the wizard and his entourage to enter. Ta Ta was impressed. With his hair and beard trimmed, washed and brushed, with a resplendent new robe, and with shoes that matched and didn't make him trip (she noticed his shoes immediately), he stood erect and imposing, a figure to be reckoned with. He graciously offered her his arm, and with a gracious smile, she accepted it. All present glowed with pleasure and relief. Maybe the evening wouldn't be a total disaster after all.

The Princess smiled at the attendants and nodded her head at them to indicate her approval. Then, she took one last glance up at the wizard and froze in puzzlement. Did his hair just move?

Yes. His hair definitely seemed to be rising and falling like an ocean wave. She looked at the attendants and maids-in-waiting. Surely, they saw it too. But, they seemed to take no notice at all. She felt her jaw beginning to drop. This wouldn't do at all. She tightened her face up and tried to smile at the same time. When she felt she had regained control of her expression, she again looked up at the wizard.

She definitely saw a lump in his hair. And, peering at her through the strands of hair, two tiny, beady black eyes.

She screamed and all the attendants, pages and maids-in-waiting jumped back in fright. She dropped the wizard's arm and pointed at his head.

"There's a rat in your hair!"

A vast sigh of relief swept through the tiny, crowded chamber, except for the wizard, who's face reddened.

"Oh, that's all right," said one of the pages.

"Rigirus always has that rat in his hair," said an attendant.

"It's what makes him special," said a maid-in-waiting.

Ta Ta looked around the room in disbelief, her composure forgotten. The people were all nodding their heads in agreement. What kind of people were these? She took in a deep breath, forced a smile upon her face and spoke as sweetly as she could.

"Would everyone be so kind as to allow me and the wizard, Rigirus, a moment to talk, please? If you will wait upon the stairs and the landing we shall join you presently."

The crowd, somewhat confused, exited the room as she bade them. When the last person had left the room and the door was firmly shut Ta Ta whirled upon the wizard.

"A rat in your hair!"

The wizard was beside himself with perplexity. On the one hand, he was sick of the rat in his hair. On the other, it was his trademark, and obviously the people expected it. Besides which, who was this upstart, princess or not, to object? And, besides which, he felt the need to defend himself.

"It's my trademark." He had meant to say it with a grand, airy demeanor, but as usual, it came out sounding like a whine. "You heard them. It's what makes me special."

He would have said more, but the sight of the Princess, with her jaw gaping, her eyes wide, her shoulders hunched, as if either to spring away in flight, or perhaps, to leap upon him and strangle him, left him speechless. Finally, the Princess shook her head and stamped her foot.

"Absolutely not," she said. "I will not be presented to the royal court by someone with a rat in their hair. Never! Take it out and throw it in the fire."

"But it's what sets me apart."

"Never!" shouted Ta Ta and she grabbed a handy broom and swung it at the lump in the wizard's hair. The wizard threw up his arms and the lump began moving frantically about as the two whirled around the room--Ta Ta trying to hit the lump, the wizard trying to keep from being hit, and the lump moving all about the wizard's head until, finally, Typhus the rat exploded out of the hair, bounced off a wall, hit the floor and scurried into the nearest rat hole.

Out of breath, Ta Ta put down the broom.

"There," she said, and sat down heavily on a stool. "Now we can go to the royal court."

Chapter 9
The Sinister Kingdom

Meanwhile, Cha Cha was in despair. When he regained consciousness, he found he was blindfolded and trussed. He was on horseback on some sort of journey. How long they'd been traveling he had no idea. After he came to, the journey continued for a long time, partly by horseback and lastly by walking. Blindfolded, he stumbled often and was prodded cruelly and jeered at by what sounded like two of Griselle's henchmen. Finally, they halted and the blindfold was removed.

As his eyes adjusted, Cha Cha looked around, searching desperately for some sort of landmark, but found nothing he recognized. All he saw were trees and brush and more brush and trees on every side. The trees were so thick that above he could see no sky. They stood in a small, gloomy clearing in which the light of day barely penetrated. He was the captive of two henchmen, both of which he recognized as lowly servants in his father's castle. One, a short, stout, greasy fellow with a bushy, black beard, held a dirty rag, which Cha Cha took to be his blindfold. The man wiped his face with the rag, then stuffed it into a pouch that was slung over his shoulder.

"This is as far as we go," he said. "What's to come of you now is unbeknownst to us. If you see your sister, say hello for us."

At that, the two henchmen laughed and shoved Cha Cha face down on the ground. He struggled back up, which was difficult as his hands were still tied behind his back, and his arms were bound tightly to his sides. When he was on his feet, he turned around and saw he was alone. He searched the edge of the small clearing for some sign of a break or trail in the brush. He saw nothing, so he used all the tricks the huntsmen and his father had taught him. He looked for footprints, bent blades of grass, broken twigs, small threads of clothing and strands of hair, but there was no trace of how they had left.

Convinced that there were no visible signs, he sat down and asked himself what father would do. "Always keep your head," he remembered his father saying. "Give no sign of your dismay."

Cha Cha sat down on the grass, took a deep breath, closed his eyes and tried to think.

Let's see, he began to himself. I am lost deep in a forest. Probably, it is Dark Wilde. I am helpless. If I am discovered by a wild animal I shall be eaten. He felt a stirring of panic rising within him and fought the urge to hurl himself headlong into the brush.

"Keep your head," his father's voice thundered in his memory. "Give no sign of your dismay."

Cha Cha forced himself to take some more deep breaths and began to reason again. Let's see, he began. Noise, motion and scent attract animals. So, I must sit here and not move or make any noise. No crying or yelling, stay out of the wind, and try not to sweat. And think. There must be a way out. Think.

He sat there and closed his eyes to help himself concentrate, but think as he might, he could think of no way out. Unless…unless, he could break off a sturdy branch with his foot. That would leave a sharp point. He could cut free his hands and then his arms with that. Once free, he could fashion a club on one end and a spear point on the other. Then, somehow, he could find the trail out and begin to make his way to some familiar landmark. He was just about to begin when he heard a noise.

He opened his eyes and saw a strange sight. A large, black tree in front of him appeared to be splitting in two. It was a dark, gnarled tree with thick, twisted, black branches and a heavily burled, knotted trunk. But a crack of light seemed to be coming out of the trunk. As the crack of light grew wider, he realized that there was a door in the trunk which was slowly opening with a loud, slow, creaking noise. He held his breath and expected the worst.

The door fully opened and light filled the clearing. From down inside the tree he could hear a loud, raucous music, composed of a discordant banging on drums, a shrill of tin whistles and reed pipes, all out of key, all trying to play the same tune but not succeeding. A thin smell of food wafted out of the tree trunk, but it didn't make him hungry, even though he hadn't eaten for ages now. At first, he thought the food smelt burnt, but no, that wasn't it. It didn't really smell burnt, but something else about it killed his appetite. A shadow filled the light in the doorway and out of it emerged Griselle's voice.

"So, my little Prince, you have disappointed me."

Cha Cha was too curious about what was down inside the tree to be annoyed.

So he simply asked, "How have I disappointed you?"

"You have just been sitting here. A king must fight back. This is one of the things I will teach you."

Cha Cha felt a surge of hope. Was she really that blind? Couldn't she see that he'd done the most prudent, kingly thing he could under the circumstances? Then, his survival instinct warned him to play dumb.

"What else could I do? It was hopeless."

"Yes, but a real king would never give up so easy. You will learn to fight. You'll see. I will teach you."

Cha Cha sensed it was best to divert her attention away from himself before she figured out what he was up to.

"You wait till my father finds out what you've done. Then he'll be the one teaching you."

Griselle threw her head back and cackled loudly.

"Your father? Soon, I'll have him completely under my power. But, enough! Come visit my kingdom."

At the word kingdom, Cha Cha noticed with a start that Griselle was wearing a crown. She walked over to him and drew a long, thin dagger from the folds of her sleeve and deftly cut his bonds. He did not bother to attempt to run away. He had no doubt he would be quickly caught, and his muscles were still too stiff and sore to be of much use. Instead, he judged it better to learn as much as he could about Griselle's "kingdom" and try his escape later when opportunity offered better chance of success. So, rubbing his hands and swinging his arms to restore circulation, he allowed himself to be prodded by Griselle with the tip of the dagger to the doorway in the tree. There, the raucous music became a din which tore at his ears. A dirty smoke within began to hurt his eyes, and the smell of the food grew ever more offensive to his nostrils. Griselle shoved him in the middle of the back, and he slowly descended the wooden steps into an underground world.

His eyes bleary from the smoke, he tried to take in the scene. The hall at first appeared large, but he quickly realized, by noting the distance between the ceiling beams and counting the number of beams, it was designed to appear larger than it was. As his ears grew accustomed to the music, he noted that its chaotic nature also had the effect of making the hall seem larger.

It was an odious place. The walls were dirty with grime and grease. The torches were of poor quality, giving off too much smoke and a sputtering, flickering light. Tapestries on the wall displayed horrific scenes of cruelty and torture. A clumsy juggler dropped his balls and props in the center of the hall. The crowd jeered and booed the juggler and hurled bits of food at him. He picked up his balls and ineptly began again to loud laughter. Table after table filled the hall. People of every rank and occupation ate together, tearing at the peculiar smelling food as if they could never be filled. They laughed unpleasant laughs, grunts really, and shoved and jostled each other as if afraid their food would be stolen by another. Bats hung from the ceiling. The floor was littered with bones and spilled food which a roaming herd of pigs devoured. At the head of the hall was a raised platform on which was a table covered with a black table cloth. Nobody was sitting at that table, but there were two empty chairs, one of which resembled a throne with a high, black back. The table was piled high with steaming food. As they approached the table, Griselle motioned for Cha Cha to sit in the smaller chair while she sat in the larger, black one at the center of the table.

Cha Cha sat where he was bid and noticed, to his surprise, that although the food was steaming it was cold. However, it looked like normal castle fare. Roast duck, pheasant, wild boar, deer, rabbit and assorted vegetables and legumes. But it was all covered with a slight, yellowish tinge. Without a word, Griselle threw herself into it and ate insatiably. Silently, she ate everything with her fingers. Cha Cha watched, fascinated and appalled, as she hunched over her food, elbows on the table, both hands shoveling in the food, a drumstick in one hand, a rib in the other, taking a bite of one, then the other. She ate them faster and faster, until finally, she held both to her mouth and gnawed on them at the same time, while suet and fat ran over her hands and out of her mouth and down the side of her chin. After she finished those, she ate dish after dish of food, her mouth unsmiling, her eyes glazed and unseeing. As he gazed about the room, Cha Cha, saw that others ate in the same fashion, but none as intently as her.

Finally, Griselle had consumed the piles of food in front of her. Gradually, she became aware that the food was gone. She leaned languidly back against the chair and stared into space, her mouth hanging open. She made no effort to wipe the grease off her face or hands. Cha Cha watched as the entire assemblage finished every last scrap of food on the tables. When they finished, they all stared into nothingness. Cha Cha leaned back and fought the feelings of disgust and despair that welled up inside him. With effort, he rallied himself and began to scan the room, looking for escape routes and possible weapons. Of weapons there was no shortage. Knives lay all over, and every man in the room appeared to carry at least a sword and a dirk. There appeared to be several exits, all of which were guarded by soldiers leaning against the wall in the same dazed state as everyone else. Now seemed as good a time as any to try his escape.

Stealthily, he began to slip out of his chair. Inch by inch, he began to move and was almost off the chair when Griselle's talon-like grasp fastened on his injured shoulder causing him to writhe in pain.

"Leaving us so soon, my little Prince?"

The voice came out like a croak and chilled Cha Cha's heart. He looked up and saw Griselle looking at him, her eyes red, but still with a faraway look. Sluggishly, she focused on him, and the faraway gaze disappeared. She shook her head three times to clear it, became her normal self, and released her grip.

She stood up and clapped her hands loudly three times. The crowd began to stir, shaking their heads and looking around as if they had all just awoken from a deep sleep.

"My loyal subjects, hear me and rejoice. Tonight a bright new star joins the heaven of our kingdom."

She lifted Cha Cha up by his injured shoulder.

"Look! The Prince and heir to the throne of the Seventh Higher Kingdom joins us tonight!"

There was a sustained round of applause, but despite his pain, Cha Cha realized there was no joy in the applause.

Then, Griselle summoned a servant who brought a large silver goblet of wine and sat it in front of them. Other waiters brought out similar goblets and sat them in front of all the diners. This done, Griselle poured a full goblet of wine for Cha Cha and placed it in front of him. Then, with a grand sweep of her arm, she addressed the crowd.

"And now, our guest of honor will drink of the cup of cheer and join my kingdom."

Cha Cha refused, of course, and sat down. This seemed to surprise no one and none seemed concerned.

"Oh, very well, little Prince," Griselle crooned. "You

are minding your manners and letting the grown-ups drink first. I'll have to teach you ever so much about how a real king behaves. But, never mind. When you change your mind, you can have a sip."

She lifted her own cup high and turned to the crowd.

"Drink well of the cup of good cheer, and let the festivities begin."

She downed a huge draught, wiped her lips with the back of her hand, and sat down in her chair again. The crowd also drank, but they didn't sit down. Standing, they drank cup after cup of wine. As they drank the music started up again, louder and more chaotic than even before. Cha Cha noted the drinking with pleasure, especially when he saw the guards joining in. At the rate they were going, he felt sure everyone would be falling down drunk before morning, and he could effect an escape.

But, as time wore on, he noticed no one was getting drunk. The more they drank the more animated they became. They began dancing, but not like anything he'd ever seen. Not the stately, planned movements of the court, nor the rollicking, good natured dancing of the peasants, but a frantic jumble of arms and legs. They hopped, swayed and shouted. No one made any effort to match their movements to the music, which was undoable anyway, so unmusical it was. The music progressively worsened, ever louder and more confused, more out of pitch and out of tune, until it finally became just spontaneous noise with no effort made to play together. And all the time, the smoke burning at his eyes and throat and the flickering torchlight and jumble of movements and the ache in his shoulder all combined until his head was splitting with pain. The room was starting to sway and rock, and it seemed even to revolve before his eyes. He wanted to close his eyes and sleep, to go back to his bed and Nana and wake up safe and sound. He felt the cold touch of metal to his lips, and he tried to pull back, but he could feel the soothing presence of sweet liquid just below his parched lips. Dimly, he sensed that they would not make him drink, that Griselle wanted him to assent to it. He tried to turn away, but his throat was so dry. When had he last had a drink?

"Drink. Drink. Just a little drop," Griselle's voice crooned.

"No," he said. "No."

"Drink, drink," Griselle crooned and the crowd began to pickup the chant.

"Drink! Drink!" they roared.

"Just a little drop," Griselle whispered in his ear.

"Drink!" the crowd roared as the room swirled before Cha Cha.

No, Cha Cha thought. But I'm so thirsty. Just one little drop.

Without knowing how it happened, he felt cold, sweet liquid flowing over his cracked, parched lips and down his burning throat.

What have I done, he groaned to himself.

Now, there was another banquet in the Fourth Kingdom, about this same time. In the Fourth Kingdom, the Royal Reception had ended. The Royal Reception was horrid. Ta Ta had striven throughout the evening to keep her smile and had waited for an opening to explain the plight of her kingdom and to beg for an escort to the wizard of Fandon, but she'd never had a chance. The entire court, including the King and Queen, drank too much, ate too much and talked too loudly. Nowhere had she seen a truly trustworthy or sympathetic face. And, when they did ask about her kingdom, they asked probing, seemingly casual, offhand questions that she instinctively sensed to be of treacherous intent. So, she played her part of an innocent, simple, little princess and deflected the questions with inane, vapid replies which, she quickly realized, were all they really expected of her. Amazingly, the only person who really earned her respect was the wizard. He nursed his one cup of wine carefully throughout the evening, said little, and seemed to Ta Ta to notice everything. Indeed, after one of her silly, misleading replies to one of the king's sly, probing questions, she glanced at the wizard, who was staring into his cup and seemingly nodding his head in approval.

When at last the evening drew to a close, and the court was too drunk to care, she made a graceful exit. This time, only one torchbearer was provided to light their return to the wizard's room, and when she took the wizard's arm she really did use it for support.

At last, they came to his room. The torchbearer was dismissed with a gold coin from the wizard, which he gave without any prompting from Ta Ta. They both sighed with relief when he left and turned and entered the room. Then, the wizard leapt back and pointed in horror. Startled, Ta Ta looked to where the wizard was pointing, expecting to see some deadly intruder. Instead, sitting in front of the fireplace, she saw Typhus and a comely young lass, gazing into each other's eyes and holding hands. She looked at the wizard to see his face contorted as he endeavored to speak, but could not.

Amazed that the wizard was so overwrought, she looked at the couple more closely. Typhus was staring at the wizard unconcernedly, but the girl seemed very nervous, even frightened. Then, Ta Ta noticed she bore a strange resemblance to Typhus. In fact, had it not been for the way they were gazing at each other, she would have thought they were related, for she too had a peculiarly long, slightly pointed nose and small, strangely dark eyes.

"Typhus, what have you done?" the wizard roared.

Ta Ta saw the wizard's whole body was shaking with emotion.

Typhus stood and, facing the wizard, calmly answered, "I have done what I must do to make myself more useful to you."

Now, that was a strange answer, thought Ta Ta. How does romancing make him more useful to the wizard? Quickly, her defenses went up. Something most peculiar was going on between the wizard and his cousin.

The wizard sputtered with indignation.

"How dare you? What gives you the right? The very nerve…All my work. You fool! Do you have any idea what you are playing with?"

"Did you?"

Typhus's answer stopped the wizard in his tracks. His outstretched arm dropped to his side.

"I think not," Typhus continued, advancing slowly toward the wizard. "No, you have never asked yourself if you knew what you were playing with. Such as the lives of others."

"You ingrate!" the wizard hissed. "You insolent wretch. After what I gave you?"

Ta Ta could restrain her curiosity no longer.

"What did you give him?"

The wizard looked at her in confusion.

Typhus raised both hands in the air with his fists balled, a snarl on his lips.

"Yes, Rigirus," Typhus gloated. "What did you give me? Go ahead. Tell us. Tell us all. What did you give me?"

Stunned and crestfallen, the wizard shuddered and his shoulders sagged. He staggered across the room and dropped into a chair. He buried his face in his hands.

"This isn't fair," he moaned. "It just isn't fair. My greatest achievement."

Ta Ta felt moved to pity.

"What isn't fair?"

"I can't tell you. It's too important. It's a secret."

Ta Ta shook her head in perplexity.

"What isn't fair?"

She turned to Typhus.

"What's he talking about? What's his greatest achievement?"

"Oh, hasn't he told you? Well…"

"TYPHUS!"

The wizard's commanding shout startled everybody. Typhus flinched and the strange girl shrank back by the fireplace. The wizard stood to his full, imposing height and fixed Typhus with a glare that frightened Ta Ta.

"I made you, Typhus, and I can unmake you. Don't you dare trifle with me. I can unmake you in the most horrid and wretched ways. Don't forget just how powerful my wizardry can be. Use your imagination, Typhus. Imagination is a very powerful tool for humans. Maybe you should cultivate it."

Typhus had seemed to grow steadily smaller as the wizard spoke. His face had turned sullen, then spiteful, then bitter. Now, totally defeated, he went back to his stool in front of the fireplace and sat. He slumped forward, his wrists on his knees, his hands dangling. Staring into nothing, he wept.

Ta Ta felt overwhelmed. What was going on?

"Will somebody please tell me what this is all about? Please!"

The wizard stared at Typhus and shook his head sadly.

"I have made some very poor choices it seems. Choices made for the wrong reasons and the wrong ends. Do you know, Princess, I've been thinking ever since last night when, you left me in my own room, and you went into the attic to sleep? You said all this," he waved his arm around his newly refurbished room, "'show' you called it, was what my people demanded. 'What did she mean?' I asked myself. Of course, I knew, but I didn't want to know. Then, at dinner tonight, I was so proud and full of myself. So happy to be in the Royal Court and escorting a princess, no less. At last, Rigirus, I thought, you're getting your due. Recognition at last."

He shook his head ruefully at the memory, then continued.

"Then, I saw the place truly for the first time, as it really is. I've spent a lifetime trying to impress them. And they aren't worth impressing. And you. So simple, so honest, so direct. But, when they tried to find out secrets of your father's kingdom, how easily you put them off the track. And it didn't make you angry—it just made you sad. Your father, he must be a wonderful king."

Ta Ta felt tears welling up in her eyes.

"He is. He is a most wonderful king."

"And your mother?"

"A most fitting queen, for a most wonderful king."

The wizard smiled gently at her, then walked over to Typhus and put his arm around his shoulder.

"There, there, Typhus, no more tears. I've been unspeakably cruel. Please forgive me. I promise, I'll make it up to you. Whatever is in my power to grant, I will grant."

Typhus seemed to come back to life and looked at the wizard with a devoted look that Ta Ta found strangely disconcerting.

"But first, Typhus, we have a serious situation on our hands. We are both playing with explosive forces, and we must plan our moves very carefully to make sure we don't blow ourselves up. Yes, the cat's out of the bag now."

"Where!" shrieked the girl and ran to a corner of the room and cringed. Ta Ta's eyes went wide with astonishment.

"I'm sorry, my dear," the wizard said soothingly. "There is no cat. It's just a figure of speech. Do you know what a figure of speech is?"

But the girl ignored the wizard and pointed a trembling finger at Ta Ta and said, "Is that the one? Is that the one that wants to throw rats into the fire?"

Ta Ta nodded bewildered. The girl screamed.

"But it was a big, ugly rat," Ta Ta tried to explain.

"It was just a figure of speech," the wizard soothed and, placing himself between the two girls, gently put his hands on the shoulders of Typhus's friend.

"But it was a huge, huge…" Ta Ta's protest trailed off when she saw the wizard turn and give her a very stern look. Tired and confused she sat down. This was the strangest group of people she had ever seen, and while she knew she was still very young, she was sure it would be hard to find stranger.

"Now, Typhus, introduce us to your friend," the wizard said.

"Well, everybody," Typhus stood up and put an arm around the girl's waist, "this is Water Guarder."

Typhus quickly realized his mistake and uncertainly

tried to cover it by saying, "At least, that's what we called her back home."

"Water Guarder! What kind of name is that?" said Ta Ta.

"Wattergarner," said the wizard. "Wattergarner."

"Oh, Wattergarner," said Ta Ta. "What's the first name?"

"First name?" said Typhus, beginning to panic.

"I am a wizard," Rigirus intervened. "Let me see if I can tell it. Silence now!"

The wizard put his hand to his forehead and closed his eyes as if in a deep trance, then muttered something that sounded like an incantation. Suddenly, his eyes popped open and he smiled.

"Is it Emily?" he asked.

"Why, just so," said Typhus, looking relieved.

"Then properly present her to the Princess and me."

"Of course," said Typhus.

He took his arm from around her waist, took her hand and nodded at the wizard and said, "Dear, Rigirus," and he made a slow, deep bow to Ta Ta, "and Princess Ta Ta. Please allow me the honor of presenting my dearest friend to you, Emily Wattergarner."

Emily hesitated for but a moment, then made a quick curtsey to the wizard, then turned to Ta Ta and made a full, slow curtsey that would have done credit to any woman in the royal court. Princess Ta Ta nodded her pleasure and Emily abruptly shot back upright and gave Typhus a startled, questioning look. Perplexed, Ta Ta opened her mouth to speak but the wizard spoke first.

"My dear," he said to Emily, "is this your first visit to our kingdom?"

"Yes, sire."

"Ah, then. I remember Typhus's first visit. Do you remember how tired you were?"

"Very well."

"How about you, Emily?" the wizard said. "Do you need to rest now?"

"Oh, yes, please. Very much, sire." She seemed very relieved at the offer of rest.

"Very well, then. Off with you two now. You've made suitable accommodations for her, Typhus?"

Typhus assured him he had, and the two left, looking very relieved. Then the wizard turned to Ta Ta.

"Now, tell me again, just why you need to see the Wizard of Fandon."

Before, Ta Ta had been reluctant to trust the wizard with so great a confidence. But now, after her disappointment with the royal court, she was desperate to tell another person why she had to find someone, anyone, to help her reach the Wizard of Fandon. More importantly, she realized that something very profound had changed in the wizard. Therefore, she told the wizard about her plight; how a traitoress had entered the royal court and corrupted her brother and was corrupting her father. How the traitoress had already placed spies and fellow conspirators within the castle to help her, and how she must be stopped before she destroyed the kingdom. When Ta Ta finished, the wizard looked at her very gravely and spoke quietly.

"This is a very serious business, indeed. You did the right thing in escaping and looking for help."

Ta Ta was overjoyed.

"Then you'll help me find the Wizard of Fandon?"

The wizard looked deeply into the fire. He seemed very troubled. At last, he whispered, "You never mentioned the name of this traitoress. What is her name?"

"Griselle."

A deep shudder ran through the wizard's body, a shudder so violent that he had to put one hand on the fireplace to keep from falling. When he recovered himself he turned to Ta Ta with a burning gaze.

"It is as I feared," he groaned in a hoarse voice.

"What?" Ta Ta said in wonder.

"Princess Ta Ta, Griselle is the Wizard of Fandon."

***

Charles and Tanya both opened their half shut eyes in amazement.

"Dad, how can a wizard be a girl? I thought all wizards were men."

"Well you might, Charles. For the word originally comes from wis-ard, which meant wise-man. And Princess Ta Ta asked the same question, as you shall find out in our next installment."

"Daddy, can't we hear the rest of the story now?"

"No, sweetheart, you're both just about to fall asleep. And if you do that, you might miss something. You don't want that, do you?"

Both children quickly agreed they didn't. So, Father took Tanya to her bedroom and tucked her in. Meanwhile, Charles prayed, getting down on his knees again by the side of his bed. As he did so, the temporarily forgotten miseries of his sister's illness came flooding back to him. With them, no matter how hard he prayed, came feelings of bitterness, despair and resentment.

"Come on, God," he prayed. "This is so easy for you to fix. You cure plenty of people. So, why don't you cure my sister? She never hurt anybody."

He went on and on like this, and as he did, he felt something very hard and dark welling up inside him until his praying hands closed into fists.

Wait!

There it was again.

Chapter 10

Behind the Closet Door

He was sure of it. How could he have forgotten? The growling noise. He didn't just dream it. It was growling now.

He forgot all about his prayers and listened very carefully in the dark. What was that he just heard? It was a new noise. It sounded like scratching. Yes, there it was again. A frantic, trapped scratching, like a rat scratching at wood. Then there was some more growling and then scratching and growling at the same time. But where was it coming from?

He listened very quietly. There was a long period of silence, then suddenly the scratching began again, faster and louder. Was it in his closet? Of course. He reached under his bed, grabbed a baseball bat and advanced stealthily on the closet. As he approached, the growling and scratching became louder and more frantic. He put his hand on the doorknob, then paused and held his breath as second thoughts began to form. Maybe he should get Mom and Dad. What if this thing was really dangerous? Maybe it was a badger, or a wolverine or a bobcat or something. Was a baseball bat really enough? He wanted to go get his parents, but something told him not to do it. Besides, he thought how cool it would be to kill a bobcat all by himself. So, he turned the knob as quietly as he could, took a last deep breath, and with his bat held high in his right arm, yanked the door open.

There was nothing there.

Just clothes, shoes, magazines and toys. And silence.

How could that be? He was certain he'd heard growling and scratching. He couldn't have been imagining it.

Cautiously, he poked around in the darker recesses of his closet with his bat. He found nothing. Feeling both relieved and disappointed, he relaxed and was about to go back to bed when the scratching and growling began again.

He wasn't imagining it! He began poking around with the bat again when it hit him. It wasn't coming from his closet at all. It was coming from his sister's closet on the other side of the wall.

But how could that be? Couldn't she hear that thing? It was loud. It wasn't like her not to tell Mom and Dad. He was seized with a horrible fear that his sister might be in immediate and grave danger. Clutching his bat in one hand, he ran out of his room and down to his sister's door. Without hesitating he burst into her room.

To his great surprise she wasn't being eaten alive or cowering in a corner in fear. Rather, she was sitting up in bed, leaning back against the headboard, a steak knife lying in the palm of her right hand. The noise from the closet became very loud and Charles quickly shut the door rather than let the noise escape the room and wake his parents.

The fact that his sister too had not told them made Charles want to investigate this before he decided what to do.

He went over to his sister and prodded her gently. Quickly, her eyes flashed open wide, and the knife went up in her hand poised to strike. Charles quickly stepped back.

"It's only me, Tanya."

A look of recognition came into her eyes.

"What are you doing in here?"

"What's that noise in your closet? It sounds terrible."

A look of fear came into her eyes.

"Don't tell Mommy and Daddy, please. They won't understand."

"Understand what?"

Tanya was thunderstruck. Yes, understand what? Why didn't she tell them about this? It made no sense. Yet, she knew she couldn't. Somehow, if she did, only bad things would happen. She turned the question around on Charles.

"Why did you come in here? Why didn't you just run down the hallway and tell them?"

Charles knew what she meant. She hadn't told them and neither had he. Why not? What was there about this that held them silent?

"How long has this been going on?" he demanded.

"I don't know. It started before I got sick."

"Aren't you scared?"

"Of course. Why do you think I have this knife?"

Charles shook his head, duly impressed. This wasn't like his sister at all.

"What is it?" he asked.

"I don't know."

"Well, what does it look like?"

"How should I know?"

Charles was incredulous.

"You mean you haven't looked?"

"Are you crazy? Suppose it's a monster."

Charles shook his head.

"You know that's silly. You don't even believe in the Loch Ness monster. Let's take a look."

He turned toward the closet, but his sister quickly leaned forward and grabbed his arm.

"No! You don't even know what's in there."

"That's why I want to look."

"No, Charles, you might get hurt."

Charles frowned in disgust.

"It's probably just a big, old rat."

"He might try to bite you."

"That's why I've got a baseball bat."

Charles would have started for the door then and there, but something in his sister's eyes stopped him. They were moist and afraid. She was shaking her head.

"It's not a rat," she said.

Charles now felt uncertain.

"Sure it is," he said, but his voice wavered.

"Do you really think it's a rat?"

"Well, if it's not, what is it then?"

"I don't know," she sobbed, "but I know it's no rat."

"How can you stand not knowing what it is?"

"I can't." Tears ran down her cheeks. "Oh, Charles, I'm so glad you found out. I've felt so alone. It's just awful listening to that noise every night. I can't stand it anymore."

Charles understood. There were always things you wanted to tell people but didn't know whether it was a good idea or not. So you just kept it to yourself. But this was really serious and something had to be done.

"We've got to look," he said.

"No, Charles, it's too dangerous. I know it is."

"Then, I'm going to tell Mom and Dad."

"No. Don't. I don't know why but that's not the answer."

Charles hesitated. Anything else, anywhere near this important, and he would have told them. So would Tanya. But something kept insisting to him that this was meant for the two of them to work out. At any rate, he was tired of arguing about it, and he knew there was no way he was going to leave his sister alone in the dark with this thing until he knew what it was.

So, he turned away from his sister and advanced quietly upon the closet door. As he did, he could hear the growling and scratching subsiding in intensity. Behind him, he heard his sister sliding off her bed. Then, he heard her close behind him as he neared the door. When he reached the door there was complete silence within the closet, but there was a more palpable sense of something alive and dangerous on the other side. There was a clammy, wet stickiness in the air, and his pajamas clung damply to him. He grasped the door knob, but it was so cold he couldn't hold it. He pulled his pajama top out of his waistband and, using it to protect his hand, grasped the door knob. He waited a moment. He felt his sister's hands lightly upon his shoulders.

"Go ahead," she whispered. "Open it."

He tore the door open with his left hand, his right hand holding the bat ready to strike. They both gasped.

A glowing, gaseous, pulsating globular light floated in the bottom of the closet. It was dark red at the center, but the rest of it was a smoky gray. Though it was a cloud, it was perfectly round. They both had the eerie feeling it had been expecting them.

"I don't like this," said Charles.

"What is it?" Tanya whispered.

"I don't know. Stand back."

"What?"

"I said stand back," Charles whispered, both angry and afraid, not quite believing the rashness of what he was going to do. Frightened by his intensity, Tanya stepped back. She watched in horror as Charles pulled the bat back over his head, and swung it down full force upon the globe of pulsating light as if he were chopping wood.

To their amazement, the bat bounced off the gaseous globe as if it had hit a rubber ball. The globe did not change appearance at all.

Charles stared, dumbfounded, at his bat. Then, he noticed a slight discoloration on the bat where it had struck the globe. He leaned close to inspect the bat, and his nose wrinkled in disgust. He held it out to Tanya.

"Here. Smell this."

Tanya hesitantly put her nose close to the bat and grimaced.

"It smells like rotten eggs. What is it?"

Charles leaned the bat against the wall in a corner of the room and thought. This didn't resemble anything he'd ever seen or heard about. A surprising notion came to him.

"Maybe it's hungry," he said.

"How can it be hungry? It doesn't even have a mouth."

Charles turned to his sister.

"Sit on the bed. Don't go into the closet. If anything happens, yell real loud. I'll be right back."

Charles ran off to the garage where he had seen a spider web that morning. Quickly, he emptied a jar of loose nuts and bolts and, using the jar, captured the spider and two of its victims that were entangled in the web. All the time, he kept an ear open for his sister's voice. He screwed the jar shut and ran back to his sister's room. She was still sitting on the bed staring at the closet. He shut the bedroom door behind him and went to the closet.

"Has it moved?" he asked.

He heard his sister slip off the bed and come up behind him.

"No, it hasn't moved at all."

Charles nodded his head and uncapped the jar. He drew out one of the flies, recapped the jar, opened the closet door, and held the fly over the globe. The globe seemed to quiver. He let the fly go, and when it fell into the globe there was a tiny, red flame and it was gone. He dropped in the next fly, and the same thing happened.

"The spider's alive, Charles. See what happens when you put something alive in it."

Charles nodded. He looked into the jar and noticed that the spider had positioned itself as far away from the globe as possible. Even if it was only a spider, it was so obviously afraid that Charles felt a little guilty. But they had to know what they were up against. Charles shook the jar vigorously, knocking the spider back to the bottom so it wouldn't escape when he took off the cap. Then he removed the cap, turned the jar upside down over the globe, gave it a couple of shakes, and the spider tumbled into the globe. Instead of disappearing instantly in a red flame, like the flies, it tumbled slowly, over and over, down into the center, through the gray, smoky cloud and into the dark red center. There it writhed for a moment, then was thrust back to the surface again. Then, back down again. This happened over and over as the children watched, spellbound. Finally, the spider disappeared into the red center as though a door had closed over it. The globe hovered before them, entirely motionless.

Charles shut the closet door. He told his sister, "Get in bed. I'll be right back."

Normally, Tanya would never have let Charles order her about, but these were not normal times. Besides, she was sick, and so glad to have someone to share her secret with that she did as she was told. Within a few moments, Charles was back in the room, carrying a pillow and blanket and with his wrist watch on his wrist.

"What are you doing?" she asked.

"You're nuts if you think I'm letting you sleep in here alone with that thing."

"Mommy and Daddy will wonder why you slept in here."

"I've set the alarm on my watch. I'll be back in my room before they're up."

"Couldn't we just move into your room?"

Charles stared at the closet door and shook his head.

"Why? It'll just follow us into my closet."

"You don't know that."

"Yes, I do. Now shut up and go to sleep will you? I'm trying to think. And keep your feet out of my face."

Charles had laid his pillow and blanket at the foot of the bed, placing himself between the closet and his sister. Tanya looked at him fondly. Of course, she knew he'd be helpless to protect her if that thing came out of the closet. But, she felt much better having him there. Without realizing it, she drifted off to sleep.

Charles, however, lay there for a long time, staring at the closet door as his mind raced furiously. He was asking himself many questions and devising many theories to explain the presence of the creature, and none of them made him feel any better, especially the one he really believed. But, at last, he also fell asleep.

Next morning, Charles's alarm woke him up. When he got out of bed he saw his sister was sleeping peacefully but was covered with a thin film of sweat. Impulsively, he leaned over and kissed her forehead. She smiled in her sleep, and for some reason this embarrassed him. He hurried back to his room and was in bed a quarter hour before his parents woke up. Once there, he did not go back to sleep. His mind picked up where it had left off when he fell asleep the night before.

What was this thing and where did it come from? And did it have anything to do with his sister's illness? He heard his sister cough in the next room. That meant she was waking up. Yesterday, she had coughed up blood for the first time. He wondered if she was coughing up blood now. Why couldn't the stupid doctors do anything? He listened to his mother help Tanya get up and get washed and also to the sound of his father dressing and, finally, departing for work. Eventually, he too got up, washed, dressed and fixed himself a bowl of cereal for breakfast. He was almost finished eating when his sister appeared, dressed, looking thin and drawn but, strangely it seemed to him, happy. As he heard his mother leaving out the front door, Tanya noticed his questioning look.

"Mother says she has to go see someone. I think she's going to see a new doctor."

Charles had lost all faith in doctors so he just shrugged and offered her some cereal. Tanya declined the cereal and ate an orange instead. It seemed to him she was forcing herself to eat.

"Mother says I can go with you today if you want to go out."

Charles was surprised.

"You were coughing pretty loud this morning."

"She said the doctor said I needed fresh air and mild exercise. But I can't do any running."

Charles was happy to have her company. They had plenty to talk about, but he wanted to get to the tree before they did. He felt things were somehow clearer there. They left the house, and it was quickly apparent it was going to be a slow walk. Tanya frequently had to stop and catch her breath. Charles became alarmed and wanted to go back. But Tanya insisted on going ahead, and after sitting and resting they would walk some more. Of course, she had their mother's cell phone or Charles would have made them go home. Once she coughed and went over to some bushes and spit something out. Using her foot, she covered it with dirt before he could see what it was.

At last, they arrived at the tree and they sat in it, Charles with his back jammed against the trunk and Tanya next to him. She waited patiently for him. She knew his mind was working, and it was important for him to speak. Charles stared at his feet for a long time and finally said, "I don't think it's going to come out of the closet."

Tanya was puzzled.

"Why not?"

"If it wanted to come out, it could have done it last night. I couldn't have stopped it."

Tanya stared at Charles.

"Then we have to tell Mother and Father. Let them see it."

"Is it there during the day?"

"Of course not. I'd never be able to get dressed."

"If Mom and Dad come to see, I bet it'll go away until they're gone. Then, they'll just think we're nuts."

Tanya didn't say anything. She thought about it, and she supposed maybe that was why she'd never said anything to their parents. Because, inside, she'd known all along that was what the creature would do. Still, that left another question.

"How come it didn't disappear when you showed up?"

"I think it wants me too."

"So, it's not going to come out of the closet?"

"No," Charles said. "I think it wants us to come in."

Chapter II

Strange Journeys

That evening, Charles and Tanya were both beside themselves. They had tried all day to think of what to do about the strange creature. They couldn't kill it, they were sure they couldn't scare or drive it away, they didn't know what it was, and they couldn't tell their parents. By supper time they were both irritable and tired.

Father noticed their mood and said, "Maybe, we should skip the story tonight. You both seem like you need a rest."

This brought a storm of protest. Both Charles and Tanya suddenly realized how much they needed something to take their minds off everything that was bothering them. Besides, there was something about the story that compelled them. So, later that evening, all three of them were gathered in Charles's room and Father picked up the story.

"Let's see, now. Where were we? I can't quite remember."

"The wizard, Daddy, she was the Wizard of Fandon. It was Griselle."

"Yeah, Dad. How can a girl be a wizard?"

"Oh, that's right. And that's a very good question with a very good answer. But, first…"

"Awwh, Dad!"

"But, first, where do you suppose Cha Cha was by now? Was he in the belly of a slither hither and thither or something even worse, as if that were possible? Well, after he drank from the cup of wine, what do you suppose happened?"

***

Cha Cha was no longer in the secret lair of Griselle, the great and powerful Wizard of Fandon, the most powerful wizard of the Seven Higher Kingdoms. He had been kept there for awhile, he had no idea how long, for he was underground where there was no day or night. Moreover, the partying and feasting seemingly went on without letup, and it was always the same awful music, the same steaming food that was cold and never satisfied, and the wine that didn't make one drunk or satisfy the thirst. Not that he minded. He no longer cared. The wine had that effect. You didn't mind the music, or the food, or the nonstop activity. There was no joy or happiness in it. No matter how much you ate or drank or danced you were never satisfied. It was all appetite and no satiety. But it didn't matter. It just was.

Still, it was not for nothing that Ta Ta, and everyone else in the Seventh Higher Kingdom, thought Cha Cha would make a great king. For while he'd ceased to mind, there was one little part of his mind that, it didn't mind either, mind you, but it was just, well, not about to give up. Give up on what, it couldn't remember, but though it didn't really mind, and it didn't really seem to matter, it kept gnawing away at the problem. What was the problem? It couldn't say because nothing really mattered, including the gnawing away, and so it gnawed away, if only for want of anything better to do. And why not? After all, it didn't really matter.

And then, at some point, it didn't really matter when, Griselle's henchmen blindfolded him again, and after much traveling and stumbling around they took the blindfold off, and he was standing in front of his father's castle.

And, oh, such a hoopala and hollering and tears of joy and hugs and scoldings. And when they asked him where he'd been, he saw Griselle staring at him, and he knew exactly what to say.

"I was lost in the woods."

And, oh, another round of hoopala and hollering and three cheers for the Prince, and his mother swept him up in her arms, and his father cuffed him a good one on the side of the head for being so stupid as to be lost and then laughed and took him in his arms and hugged and kissed him, and the whole kingdom wept for joy. Except for Griselle and her followers who only pretended to weep for joy.

But the cuffing on the side of the head had a salutary effect beyond what the king had intended, although he was a great believer in admonitory cuffings and would not have been surprised had he known the result. For, it clued the gnawing part of Cha Cha's mind. Yes, it was father. Something he had said. What was it? And, for want of anything better to do, the gnawing part of his mind went to work on it, even though it really didn't matter.

The rest of his mind was numb. Not pleasantly numb. Just numb. After the celebration of his return died down, he was quickly and politely back into his routine of lessons, fencing and archery. Griselle no longer egged him on into open defiance of the rules. Indeed, his outward behavior was so pleasantly changed that everyone in the castle was exchanging winks, nods and nudges, saying that being lost in the woods had taught him his lesson. Taught him a little humility and respect. Made him realize how really good he had it in life. He must have shed many a tear in the forest and made many a promise to be good if only, if only, he could once more see his dear kingdom and his bed. So said all in the kingdom, save Griselle and her followers who knew better. And save Nana, who would look at Cha Cha curiously, remember how he had commanded her to remember that from now on all he would do would be good, shake her head uncertainly, and go quietly about her business

The Prince was aware of all the gossip, but of course, it didn't really matter. He noticed, without really caring, that now that he was one of Griselle's subjects he could spot all the other subjects, and there were many of them, without difficulty. There was just something in their slightly dull, slightly lifeless gaze that revealed them all to each other. Except Griselle. Nothing in her public demeanor betrayed her. Not her eyes, nor her speech, nor a slight listlessness. Only when the Prince reported, like a dutiful little puppet, to the nightly feast down below, via the secret passageways, did he see the other side of Griselle. There, gorged with the food that didn't satisfy, she would sit in a stupor, eyes vacant and unfixed, staring into nothing, while grease and bits of food dribbled down her chin from her slack, open mouth. He also noticed, not that it mattered, that her mind, unlike her body, was far from being in a stupor. No.

It was very alive, sending slithering, little tentacles into the minds of everyone present. The tentacles would grasp, the Prince felt this very clearly, on stray, useful thoughts and bits of information, squeezing them in their grasp and withdrawing them back to her. Every once in a while, he thought he saw someone attempt to resist. Then a sudden grimace of horrible pain would mar their countenance, the struggle would cease, and they would slump forward on the table exhausted, sometimes even unconscious.

And, since he saw that resistance was futile and it didn't really matter, when those little, slithering tentacles entered his mind he allowed them free access. Except for the gnawing part of his mind which somehow always shut down when those tentacles entered. But for the rest of the time, when Griselle wasn't around, which was a lot now that she had him under her control, the gnawing went on and on.

Then, one day, Nana showed him her very own miniature of his sister that she'd had painted with her very own money. That's right. He'd meant to rescue her. It didn't really matter, of course, nothing did, but why hadn't he done that? But it made no difference, so he went about his business while the gnawing part of his mind gnawed away on that one.

And it gnawed and gnawed until a couple of days later, when, right in the middle of archery practice, his instructor, frustrated by his sudden mediocrity in archery ever since his return, asked him sharply, "Lad, what's the most important advice your father ever gave you?"

He was referring, of course, to the most important archery advice the Prince's father ever gave him. But the gnawing part of the Prince's mind ignored that and bit through to the marrow of the matter.

A sudden image of his father, stern, terrible and wise all at once, standing in front of the fire, looking down at him, hands clasped behind his back, appeared and said, “Always remember this, the Duty of Love and the Love of Duty are what make one a good king. If you always remember that you will be a good king.”

Not that it mattered, but what did that mean? “The Duty of Love and the Love of Duty?” And the gnawing part of his brain moved to another part of the bone looking for more marrow.

Otherwise, the Prince went about his duties and did what he was told by Griselle and everyone else. And why not? It didn’t matter. And besides, there was no point in resisting.

Just yet.

Now, back in the Fourth Kingdom, on the same night that the wizard gave Ta Ta the awful news that the Wizard of Fandon was actually Griselle, she asked the wizard, “How can a woman be a wizard?”

The wizard poked at the fire to stir it up, then stared at the end of the poker.

“Most wizards are male, but there is no hard and fast rule they have to be. Have you ever heard of anyone seeing the Wizard of Fandon? Has anyone ever said what ‘he’ looked like. For that matter, did I ever refer to the Wizard of Fandon as ‘he?’”

“No. I was always told no one had ever seen him, I mean her. But I just assumed it was a he. Everybody did. You never said it wasn’t so.”

“Guilty as charged. Even so, never assume. It’s a bad habit for anyone. For royalty it is fatal. I didn’t tell you the truth about the Wizard of Fandon, because I had no idea how serious a business you were about. If I had, I would have corrected you."

"But how can a wizard be a woman?"

"A wizard is not a male witch. That's a warlock. Many witches and warlocks get their power from contact with spirit entities. No matter how good the witch's own intentions may be, the entities may have evil intentions of their own. A wizard, however, gets his power from bending natural elements, herbs, seasons, tides, animals, but, if he is a proper wizard, never from spirit entities. And even then, it is still a very dicey business, with much potential for mischief. As I have recently found out to my own dismay."

"But you use incantations, don't you."

"At the risk of oversimplifying, there are words whose vibration's natural effects on other vibrations in nature can produce desired results when used in conjunction with other, carefully controlled, circumstances. Say the wrong thing or say it in the wrong way and it may produce undesirable effects. But, never does a true wizard use incantations to summon entities, good or otherwise."

Ta Ta watched and listened as the wizard paced in front of the fire. This was all very confusing.

"So, wizards never do evil?"

"I didn't say that." The wizard waved his hands in frustration and paced faster. "It's all a matter of intention. Evil intentions produce evil results. And, sometimes, even good intentions produce evil results. As Typhus may soon find out. Oh, I wish he'd just consulted with me first. But, never mind that. The point is, most wizards are male, but it's not mandatory. And the Wizard of Fandon, Griselle, oh yes, she's the best by far. The very best."

"Then, what shall I do? I can't go back to my kingdom."

The wizard looked at her, surprised, and said, "But you are the Princess. It is your duty to warn your kingdom."

"But how? I'm just a little princess. No one will ever listen to me, and I have no one to help me get back, and how will I ever confront Griselle if she is a great wizard?"

The wizard sat down on a short three legged stool by the fireplace and leaned back against the wall. With his hands on his knees he closed his eyes and spoke in a weary voice.

"I wish I'd never become a wizard. It would be so very much easier to just work for a living. Much more profitable too, I dare say. Not nearly as dangerous either."

He opened his eyes, leaned forward and said, "All right, it's settled. I'll go with you. I'll help you."

"But, if she's so powerful, won't you be in great danger?"

"No more than you, Princess. Besides, if she succeeds in her designs, everyone in all the Seven Higher Kingdoms will be in great danger." He shrugged his shoulders, smiled and added, "Besides, if a wizard can't help his friends, what's the point in being a wizard?"

So, they went to their beds, Ta Ta vastly relieved at the offer of help but fully aware of, and troubled by, the danger they and the Seven Higher Kingdoms faced. This time, the wizard wouldn't hear of her using the attic. He went through the tiny door and shut it behind him, and she slept in the feather bed.

In the morning, Ta Ta and the wizard arose before dawn. They had a simple breakfast, served by Emily, while Typhus, at the wizard's instruction, began to pack for their journey. Typhus insisted upon bringing Emily with them, and the wizard, to Ta Ta's surprise, agreed without hesitation.

They left when the sun was still low above the horizon, and everything was still covered with dew. The wizard sat upon his own white steed while Ta Ta and Emily shared a gray mare, with Emily, being larger, in the saddle, and Ta Ta riding behind. Typhus was on foot, leading a donkey piled high with baggage. No one paid any attention to their leaving, indeed, scarcely anyone was up. The two sleepy guards at the gate did not even bother to salute the princess.

They rode out in silence. Emily seemed a little less nervous to Ta Ta than she had been the night before and strangely delighted to be upon a horse, looking down at every thing. She looked about every which way and gave little squeaks of pleasure at almost everything she saw. She struck Ta Ta as extremely restless, continually shifting her weight as if she wanted to scamper about the horse. Her two hands went up in front of her mouth whenever she became excited about something, which was almost continually. The only thing that seemed to calm her down were the many stern looks that Typhus shot at her.

After awhile, Ta Ta noticed that she did not recognize the road they were taking. It did not look at all like the way they came in. When she asked the wizard about it he replied, "Of course not. It was pure luck that we were able to leave Dark Wilde Forest unscathed." The wizard shuddered and added, "There is no way I will risk this expedition trying to find our way through. Even if we could find our way, Dark Wilde is full of bears and lions and wolves and, most dreadful of all, the slither hither and thithers."

All shuddered at the mention of the slither hither and thithers. They were, strangely enough, a new addition to the Seven Higher Kingdoms. No one knew where they had come from. Still, everyone did know that they were the deadliest and hardest to kill of all the creatures in the kingdoms. But, despite her personal fears, Princess Ta Ta had to think of her kingdom.

"But we must return as soon as possible. My parents, the King and Queen, must be warned."

"Of course, they must," the wizard said, turning in his saddle to look behind at Ta Ta. "But don't forget, I must face Griselle. And the longer way around will give me more time to prepare my spells and potions. I must have every advantage I can."

Ta Ta nodded. The wizard was right. She realized now how horribly dangerous Griselle was and how easy it must have been for her to corrupt her brother. And her father—how long before he too would be completely under her spell? And then what would become of her mother? And what would become of the happy people of the kingdom? Yes, they must get back as soon as possible. But, indeed, the wizard must have time to prepare.

And prepare he did. They had no sooner lost sight of the castle of the Fourth Higher Kingdom than the wizard became lost in thought, speaking to no one. Stroking his red beard, he muttered continuously, looking down at the top of his horse's head, seemingly oblivious to the surroundings, all the while shaking his head in discouragement. Occasionally his face would go bright with glee, and he would abruptly sit upright in his saddle. But then, just as quickly, he would shake his head, his shoulders would slump, and he would return a mournful gaze to the top of his horse's head. Then, he would resume stroking his beard, running his fingers through it, sometimes twisting, pulling and tearing nervously at it, then clenching it, and then stroking it smooth again, all the while muttering and muttering, and shaking and shaking his head.

Ta Ta found all this very disturbing, so she left off

watching the wizard and tried to concentrate on the scenery of their journey. As the sun rose, they passed along a broad trail through a long meadow of green grass and wildflowers of many types and colors. On their left was a forest of oak and maple and on their right was a forest of fir and pine. The meadow became pleasantly warm and the scents of the grass, flowers and trees soothed Ta Ta's heart. But, about half way through the meadow, the wizard stopped his horse. He put his right hand to his brow to shade his eyes and scanned the fir forest to his right very slowly, back and forth, muttering to himself all the while. At last, he saw what he was looking for and turned his horse in that direction. But, he looked no happier. If anything, he seemed even more disturbed.

They crossed the meadow and entered the forest by a narrow path that was imperceptible from the main trail. They went a little ways and the path began to twist and wind and descend. It became dark and damp. Emily and Ta Ta both pulled their cloaks tight about them. A thin mist began to permeate the air. As they descended, a fog began to grow around them. The mist turned into a drizzle. The drizzle was mild, hardly a rain at all, but it was unceasing. As they traveled down the narrow, winding trail the path alternated between sticky, clinging mud, which had to be periodically scraped off the animals' hooves by Typhus, and slippery, round rocks that forced everybody off their mounts for fear the creatures would stumble. The horses would become visibly nervous at times, but the wizard would mutter something into their ears that would calm them down enough to move over the patches of treacherous rocks. Down and down they went into the ever thickening fog, drizzle and gloom. Eventually, the drizzle soaked through all their clothes, and they were chilled to the bone.

The wizard spoke to them only once.

"Patience, patience. This is the only way. We must endure it."

At one point, while they were mounted on their horse, Ta Ta noticed that Emily was reaching her breaking point. Her head was darting from side to side, her hands were in front of her mouth, her breath was coming quickly, and she was starting to make strange, high pitched noises. The trail was exceptionally thin and slippery. The canyon fell away so steeply that only the tops of the trees were visible. The trail was too narrow for Typhus to come up and calm her or for them to dismount, and their horse was beginning to shake with the nervousness being communicated by Emily. Instinctively, Ta Ta put her arms around Emily and comforted her by hugging her. Immediately, Emily calmed down and pressed her back against Ta Ta's body. Emily wrapped her hands around Ta Ta's and pulled them tightly to herself sighing with relief. Her breathing suddenly became normal again, and her head slumped forward upon her breast, almost as if she were asleep.

Ta Ta was amazed at how quickly Emily had responded to such a simple gesture. As they rode on, she found that if she continued to touch Emily, stroking her arm or rubbing her back, Emily stayed quite calm.

During their descent, the sound of rushing water became gradually louder until they finally came to a small swift river and the bottom of the canyon. Here, the trail ended. The wizard looked anxiously across the swift, tumbling current which boiled over boulders and around fallen trees and logs. Ta Ta noticed his rapidly changing facial expressions. Hope would flicker, then exasperation, then despair, then anger, but at last, triumph.

"There it is!" he shouted and pointed a finger at the

solid, black, rock wall on the opposite shore. "Do you see it? Do you see it? I made that mark when I was just a little lad. Just a little tot, indeed."

The wizard was trembling with pleasure, and Ta Ta noted that it was the first time she'd ever seen him look joyous, and that his eyes were moist with tears. Then he got off his horse and, eyeing a spot on the opposite bank, began to carefully measure off his paces. Ta Ta exchanged glances with Emily and Typhus. It was apparent to her that none of them could see the "mark" the wizard was talking about. Was he already losing his mind?

"Here! Here is the way across." The wizard stamped his foot upon a spot on the ground and traced out an X in the dirt with his foot. "Have no fear. Follow me across the torrent."

The wizard stepped confidently into the swift current, pulling his mount, who balked and tried to pull back. But the wizard pulled hard on the reins, dragging his horse along. The wizard got three steps out into the stream when the current swept him off his feet. Had he not had such a tight grip on the reins he would have been lost to the torrent. But he held onto the reins, and with his horse backing away from the river and Typhus tugging on his robe, he was pulled back to safety. He climbed back on shore, dripping and shocked.

"This is impossible. I measured the distance very carefully. I was just a little boy, only six years old, but I knew how to count. And I burned the figure in my mind. I used a mnemonic device. Foolproof, mind you. Two plus three makes five. I have two hands, each with five fingers. Two from five makes three. Therefore, the correct number is 23. There, you see how it works? Absolutely foolproof."

Emily and Typhus must have looked as dumbfounded by the wizard's logic as Ta Ta for he suddenly exploded.

"Don't you fools know what a mnemonic device is? It's a way of using words in a pictorial fashion to help you remember something. Two fingers plus three fingers makes two hands of five fingers minus two hands leaves three. Twenty three, see?"

The wizard had used his hands to demonstrate by alternately holding up two clenched fists, then two open hands of five fingers, then one hand with two and the other with three fingers showing and looking at the rest of them all the time with an expectant smile.

Emily shook her head doubtfully.

"But, sire," she said, "two fingers plus three fingers makes one hand of five fingers. So, one hand plus five fingers makes six paces, or four paces, if you minus the one finger. Or," she brightened as if a light came upon her, "fifteen paces if you set the one in front of the five fingers like a regular number."

Then she looked uncertain again.

"Of course," she continued, "if you take the hand, which is more than a finger, and set if first, then it's 51 paces. It's most confusing, sire. But, it can't possibly be 23 paces."

The wizard gnashed his teeth, clenched his fists, stamped on the ground and said, "It's my mnemonic device, and it means exactly what I want it to mean, and it means there are 23 paces. No more, no less."

Emily remained undaunted and helpfully offered, "Two hands of five fingers is ten fingers. Minus two makes eight. Maybe it was 18?"

The wizard took a deep breath, as if to start explaining all over again, when Typhus coughed discretely.

"Perhaps," Typhus said, "it's not a matter of number but of size."

The wizard looked at Typhus blankly.

"Sire, I doubt if your steps were as large at the age of six as they are now."

The wizard blinked twice, then lit up with delight.

"Of course, of course. I was just a child. There are 23 child size paces."

"How big are those, sire?"

It was Emily that asked and this time her point was well taken. The wizard and Typhus began a long discussion of the proper method of measuring child steps as opposed to adult steps. It somehow turned into a matter of philosophical precepts and then Ta Ta spoke.

"I'm still a child."

All eyes turned to her with interest.

"True," said Typhus, "but you must be taller than Rigirus was at the age of six."

"I suppose I am. But I take dainty, little princess steps, not little boy strides. They should be about the same."

That sounded sensible, so the wizard lined Ta Ta up with his mark on the other bank and she stepped off 23 dainty, little princess steps and marked the last one with a large X with her dainty toe. Then the wizard stood on the X and eyed the opposite shore. He stroked his beard and hemmed and hawed. He leaned in the direction the Princess had walked and nodded his head. He took half a step in that direction and, then, a quarter step back the other way and made a new X with his toe. He took a large stick and probed the water in front of the X carefully. He moved another eighth of a step back the other way and made a new X with the stick just in front of the water's edge.

"This is it," he said with finality.

He led the way into the water. They crossed single file. The wizard led his horse, Emily held on to its tail with one hand and to Ta Ta's hand with the other, while Ta Ta's other hand led their horse. Behind Typhus held on to the tail of their horse while leading the donkey.

The passage was not nearly as bad as it looked. There was a flat rough bottom here, with a solid footing, between two lines of submerged boulders. So, while the surface boiled with activity, below Ta Ta's waist there was very little current. Moreover, the downstream line of boulders acted as a natural wall to keep one from being swept away.

When they crossed to the other side they were on a small sandy patch with no vegetation and no way out save the way they came. The wizard examined the cliff with care.

"There it is, see? The mark I made so many years ago as a boy."

He traced his finger upon the mark in the cliff side and all three realized they had seen it from the opposite shore but had taken if for a natural marking in the rock.

"Where is the entrance?" Ta Ta asked. All she saw was a black, cliff wall with no discernable opening.

"Oh, my," said the wizard. "It was right underneath the mark. A small door. But, it's all covered with sand and dirt. We didn't bring a shovel."

To Ta Ta's surprise Typhus and Emily smiled at each other and, without a word, fell to their knees where the wizard had pointed and began digging with their hands. The wizard did not seem surprised at all. The sand and dirt flew in great clouds and before too long a tiny wooden door with a round top appeared.

Typhus and the wizard were quite satisfied, but Emily looked at her torn nails and scratched hands and said in dismay, "Why, these hands are no good for digging at all."

"It's all right, darling," said Typhus, "they have many other uses."

Ta Ta thought that most strange but was eager to get through the door and pushed it with her foot. It didn't budge.

"This door seems to be locked," she said.

"It is locked," said the wizard.

"I don't see a keyhole," she said.

"There is none," he said.

"No matter," Emily gushed. "I can fix it."

Then Emily, who was still on her knees in front of the door, shocked Ta Ta by leaning forward and biting the door. Emily yelped in surprise and sat back on her knees, anxiously feeling her teeth with her fingers. Then, she looked up reproachfully at Typhus.

"Why, these teeth are no good at all," she said.

Typhus looked apologetic.

"I'm sorry. I forgot to tell you about that."

Emily felt her teeth again, then held up her scratched hands in front of Typhus's face.

"It seems to me, there's a lot you forgot to tell me about."

Typhus shook his head.

"You're just looking at the bad side. Try looking at the good side."

"Good side of what?" Ta Ta burst in.

"Not to worry, everyone," the wizard soothingly interjected. "There is a key to open the door."

The wizard reached up his sleeve and pulled out a red wand with a ruby tip.

"That's a key?" asked Ta Ta.

"For this door it is," he said.

He tapped his wand three times on the door, muttered something in a low voice, tapped once, muttered a little more, tapped three times again, and the door swung open.

Ta Ta was impressed. This was the first really wizardly thing she'd seen him do.

"That's very good. Do you have other tricks?"

The wizard put a hand in front of his mouth, lowered his eyes to the ground and coughed. Ta Ta saw Typhus and Emily exchanging amused, secret looks. She felt left out.

"Is there something going on I don't know about?" The wizard shrugged his shoulders and Typhus said, "Let's just say you don't know everything there is to know about our Rigirus."

"Not by a long sight," Emily added with a wink at the others.

Ta Ta opened her mouth to complain, but the wizard had already crawled through the door with Emily close behind. So, she followed them through the opening while Typhus stayed with the animals. Once inside, it was very dark. The wizard felt around and found a torch which he lit with the end of his wand by tapping it three times. It illuminated a round, damp chamber, the floor of which was covered with pools of water.

"Ooh, what a lovely place," Emily cooed. "I'm surprised there isn't anybody living here."

Ta Ta was becoming used to this sort of thing from Emily and paid it no mind. It was clear to her now that Emily was a half wit and Typhus had graciously chosen to love her anyway. The wizard undoubtedly tolerated her out of respect for Typhus. She found it all noble and inspiring, and it increased her fondness for her companions.

The wizard went to the wall opposite the entrance and found a palm size rock on a ledge which he slid to one side.

Behind Ta Ta and Emily a crack appeared in the cliff wall. It was just wide enough for Typhus to lead the animals through. Once the animals were through, the wizard slid the rock back to its original position, and the wall reclosed.

The wizard led them along a passage that wound and turned about. While it was hard to be sure, Ta Ta felt they were going up again. At any rate, although the cave was damp, at least they were out of the drizzle.

Finally, they came to a warm, dry chamber where the wizard told them to leave the animals. They stepped through a narrow door into another chamber that was cut out of the rock into a squared off shape. Four huge, square columns supported the large room. The wizard used his wand to light four torches, one on each column. In the center of the chamber was a large, raised, square fireplace, open on all sides. There was a large pile of logs on it which he struck with his wand. They blazed up and gave off a smokeless flame. Ta Ta stood by the fire, soaking up the warmth. She looked around the room. In the opposite wall beds had been cut out of the wall. They looked soft and inviting and were topped with fur blankets. On the wall to her right she saw an eating space with a table and benches carved out of the rock. The seats of the benches were covered with thick cushions. The wall to her left was filled with shelves lined with books, scrolls, beakers and bottles and reminded her of the wizard's room except that it was tidy, clean and well organized. She turned around to warm her back and saw that the wall next to the entry was covered with a large tapestry. The tapestry was covered with strange gold lettering and strange animals she didn't recognize and other animals she did recognize. There were still other creatures which she took to be sprites and fairies. In the center was a man who was as tall as the tapestry. He was holding a wand with his arms stretched out to his sides. All the animals and sprites and fairies were looking up to him as if in homage.

"Is this his place?" she asked the wizard.

"Indeed, it is."

"Who is he?"

"That was Sarnus, greatest of the great. The wizard of all wizards."

"I never heard of him."

The wizard chuckled and shook his head.

"No, I suppose you didn't. He wanted no fame. But all the wizards knew of him, I assure you."

Ta Ta gazed up at the tapestry. Sarnus's face radiated a humility, as if unaffected by the adulation of all the other creatures. She was curious about the sprites and fairies.

"Did he use the sprites and fairies in his magic?"

"No, he was their friend and they looked up to him, but his magic belonged to him alone."

"Is he dead?"

"Yes, for some time now."

"Who takes care of this place?"

The wizard shook his head in wonder.

"It takes care of itself. That was part of his wizardry."

"Were you a student of his?"

He sat down in one of the chairs by the fire and gazed forlornly at the tapestry.

"If only I had been. No, he gave up training wizards."

"But, you said you were here."

"I was lost in the woods. I was chasing a robin with my bow and arrow. I became lost and wandered into Drizzling Forest. As it was easier to walk down than back up that's what I did. When I realized how completely lost I was I began to cry. Well, some wood sprites heard me crying and told Sarnus who came up and fetched me here. That's how I learned the way. The next morning, I made a mark over the door while he was bustling about doing something else. If he knew about it he didn't say anything. Perhaps, he didn't know about it. Perhaps, he didn't care."

Ta Ta hung her cloak by the fire to dry.

"So, that was when you decided to become a wizard?"

"No, that was much later, when I realized I wasn't any good at anything else."

"But you knew how to open the door and how to use the wand."

He chuckled and nodded his head.

"Yes. I spent one night with him. I was well fed, but he fell asleep before me. He was getting on in years. Anyway, I started rummaging through his books. Well, I found one with lots of pictures, so I took it to bed with me. I assure you I had no intention of stealing it, but before I went to sleep I innocently put it in my cloak."

"Do you think he minded?"

The wizard steepled his fingers in front of his chin and peered more closely at the tapestry.

"I rather suspect now that he knew. Perhaps, he saw my future more clearly than I did. At any rate, when I turned to wizardry it was my first, and best, text book."

He shook his head regretfully.

"But there is so much in it I still don't understand. All the rest of the books I own are nonsense or mere child's play by comparison."

"Is that why we're here?"

"Yes. Somewhere in these jars and bottles, in these scrolls and books, may lie the answer to defeating Griselle."

"Princess, I have some dry clothes for you."

It was Emily, with a change of clothing for Ta Ta and a dry robe for the wizard. Ta Ta also noticed that she had not changed her own soaked clothing but was tending to her duties first. Ta Ta felt a surge of guilt that she had not told Emily to change first and made a mental note to reward Emily when she had the chance. In the background, she saw Typhus, also soaked, approaching with a large platter. On the platter were cheeses, bread and apples, two cups, a decanter of wine, and a large round of beef with a spit stuck through it.

"Here, sire. Something to refresh you while the meat cooks."

"Very good, Typhus. Princess, there is a room next to the beds. You may change in there. And you two," the wizard motioned at Typhus and Emily and said, much to Ta Ta's approval, "change into something dry also. Before you cook, Typhus. I don't want anybody taking sick. Do it right now, both of you. Princess, you don't mind dressing without the assistance of a maid-in-waiting, I trust?"

"Of course not. Quick, Emily, go get into something dry and warm."

Emily gave her one of her strangely perfect curtseys, and she and Typhus hurried off. As Ta Ta started to leave for the room to change, one last question occurred to her.

"Why did Sarnus stop training wizards?"

"His last pupil, his best and brightest, the crowning achievement of his career, the one into which he poured all his love and knowledge, betrayed him."

"Who was the pupil?"

Rigirus turned and stared into the hottest part of the fire.

"Griselle," he said.

Chapter 12

A Tasty Morsel

After Father left the room to put Tanya to bed, Charles stared at the ceiling for a long time. He listened to the growling and scratching next door and shook his head. He felt he should be afraid but he wasn't. The anger that had been building inside him for the last few days was beginning to focus into an energy, a determination. Maybe he couldn't protect his sister from her illness, and maybe God wouldn't protect her. But this was something he could do, this creature was something he could take on without having to wait for God or until he grew up. So, when he sensed his parents were asleep, he set the alarm on his wrist watch, grabbed his baseball bat and walked quietly to his sister's room. She seemed happy to see him enter.

"I thought you'd gone to sleep," she said.

"No way."

She looked at his baseball bat.

"Do you think that'll do any good?"

Charles shrugged.

"I don't know. I couldn't think of anything else."

Tanya turned the matter over in her mind.

"What about water?"

"Water?"

Tanya leaned forward.

"Why not?" she said. "Water killed the wicked witch in the Wizard of Oz. Get us some and we'll see what happens."

So Charles got a glass and went to the bathroom. He closed the door behind him and, as quietly as he could manage, slowly filled the glass out of the tap. Then he tiptoed back to Tanya's room. He shut the door softly behind him. When he turned, he saw she was sitting expectantly on the foot of the bed.

"What shall we do with it?" he asked.

"Let's pour a couple of drops on it and see what it does."

Charles nodded agreement and slowly moved to the closet listening to the growling and scratching which grew louder as he approached. Again, he felt the presence of his sister behind him, looking over his shoulder. He slowly opened the door and noticed the doorknob was not as cold this time. The growling subsided to an unpleasant buzz, like the sound of a yellow jacket next to the ear. Charles gulped, then said, "Here goes."

He sensed Tanya tensing up behind him as he wet his fingers in the glass. Then, he flicked his fingers at the globe. A few drops of water hit the pulsating, gaseous light and instantly turned into steam. The buzzing noise grew louder.

"I don't think he likes it," Tanya said.

"How do you know it's a he."

"It acts like a he."

Charles ignored the remark and flicked a few more drops of water on the globe. It began to pulsate more rapidly and the buzzing became louder and raspier.

"You're right," Charles said. "He doesn't like it. Tough for him."

He started to tip the whole glass over onto the creature.

"No!" Tanya whispered loudly.

He ignored her and dumped all the water onto the creature. There was no noise, but there was an explosion of energy nevertheless. One moment he saw the water splashing over the globe—the next thing he knew he was hurled through the air and he was on Tanya's bed staring up at the ceiling. He shook his head to clear it, sat up and looked about the room. Tanya! Where was Tanya?

"Tanya. Tanya, where are you?"

"Underneath you, you moron."

For a moment, he thought she meant underneath the bed, but then he felt her squirming around and realized he'd landed on top of her. Quickly, he rolled off her.

"Are you okay? Are you hurt?" he asked.

She sat up and shook her head a couple of times. She took a deep breath and said "I think I'm okay."

Then she punched him in the stomach.

"You little doof. What did you pour the whole glass on him for? You made him mad."

"Good! He makes me mad. Let him be mad."

"Suppose he gets real mad and comes out after us."

"He can't. I was right last night. If he could come out he would've come out when I poured the water on him. Look. He's still in there."

She looked at the closet. It was there, buzzing and

bouncing around, but it wouldn't leave the closet.

"Why won't it come out?" she whispered.

"Why is it here in the first place?" he whispered back.

They both stared at the closet, but the sphere did nothing to answer their question.

"Wait here," Charles said. It was an unnecessary thing to say as there was nowhere for Tanya to go. He padded swiftly to his parents' door. He listened carefully. How they could sleep through all this was beyond him. There was no sign of wakefulness or even restless sleep from their room. He hurried into his own room, reached under the bed and grabbed the jar he had hidden there that afternoon. Then he hurried back to Tanya's room and closed the door behind him.

"What've you got?" Tanya asked.

"A jar."

"I know that. What's in it?"

"A mouse."

"Charles, no! That's cruel."

"We've got to know more about that thing."

"No. It's wrong."

"It's just a dumb mouse."

Tanya looked at the mouse with a sad expression.

"He looks frightened."

"They only live a couple of months anyway."

"They live two years."

"Which may be a lot longer than we're gonna live if we don't figure out what that thing is."

That seemed to convince Tanya and, after another moment's hesitation, she nodded her assent.

Once again, Tanya followed close behind Charles as he approached the closet. As he advanced, the buzz changed to a soothing, almost purring, sound while the mouse became increasingly frantic with each forward step. When Charles stood before the sphere the red in it turned a pleasant rosy pink, but the mouse squealed in terror. Without hesitating, Charles turned the jar over and the mouse fell into the gaseous, round mist. Like the spider the night before it slowly descended and ascended in the globe again and again. The difference was the mouse had a visible face. It was only a tiny mouse but they could see shock, terror and even revulsion on its face. And agony. An agony not of body it seemed to both of them, but of internal struggle. And when that struggle was over, when it had surrendered to it, it too disappeared into the center as though through a door.

They both watched spellbound. When it was over, they were both trembling and sweating.

Abruptly, Tanya slapped him, hard, on the back of the head.

"You enjoyed that!" she said.

"Did not."

"You did too. I watched you."

"Baloney. I bet you didn't take your eyes off. Just like I didn't."

She stepped in front of him and shut the door. He felt oddly disappointed when it was gone from his sight. She stood between him and the door and looked him in the eye.

"I think it's your monster and not mine," she accused.

"What! He's in your closet."

"You're the one that feeds him."

"I was conducting an experiment."

"What are you going to experiment with next? Cats? How about Mrs. Johnson's dog?"

"Don't be ridiculous. Maybe a bat."

"Don't you dare!"

"I'm just trying to protect you."

"Then think of a way to get rid of it. Don't feed it so it has a reason to stay here."

She went back to her bed.

"I'm going to bed. I'm really tired. Are you going to sleep here?"

She tried to make the question sound as if she didn't care. But Charles heard the tension in her voice and knew she wanted him there.

"Sure," he said and curled up on the foot of her bed.

He lay there in silence, thinking. Finally, he said, "Maybe it's not like we think."

"Huh?"

"Maybe it's okay. Maybe it just wants to be our pet."

Tanya sat bolt upright.

"Are you crazy? You saw what it did to that mouse."

Charles shrugged and said, "Cats eat mice. Cats make good pets."

"They don't eat mice like that thing did."

"No, I guess not. You're probably right," he told her and she lay back down.

To himself he whispered, "It was just a dumb mouse."

The next morning Charles hustled back into his room before his parents awoke. The rest of the day was long and restless. Tanya was over exerted and had to stay in bed all day. Charles made the mistake of going in to see her, and she extracted his promise not to feed any more animals to the creature. Since his sister was really sick, he had no choice but to agree. Although, as he left the house, it occurred to him that the term, animal, was one that was open to interpretation.

Chapter 13

Conversations

That evening, the meal passed largely in silence. Tanya ate her special diet in her room. In the dining room, Charles noted Mother looked sad and pale and Father tired. Tanya had her coughing spells all day.

"I wonder if it's the story telling," Father mused. "Perhaps, they're too much for her."

"No," Mother answered. "The doctor thinks they're very good for her. In fact," Mother went on, "the doctor thinks they're the only thing that's doing her any good at all."

Charles watched as Father patted Mother's hand, and they exchanged tired smiles. At least, Charles thought, the story would continue.

And so that evening, Father carried Tanya into Charles's room and sat in the big red chair at the foot of his bed, and with Tanya bundled up and snuggled into his arms, he began again.

"Let's see," he mused, "how is Cha Cha doing in the castle?"

"He was under an evil spell, Daddy."

"That's right. And do you remember why?"

"Because he drank Griselle's wine," Charles said.

"That's right. But, remember he drank only because he wasn't strong enough to hold out against Griselle's pressure. That's very important. Never let anybody pressure you into doing something you know is wrong, or you'll be under their spell. And who knows when you'll ever get out from underneath it?"

Charles had an uncomfortable moment when he realized Tanya was staring at him during this little lecture, but the moment passed as Father continued.

***

And this was just the position Cha Cha was in. Still, even in his spell bound state, he could see that a dark gloom was descending upon the castle and kingdom. Everybody knew that something was wrong, but nobody could figure out what it was, besides Griselle and her subjects. The rest only knew that people did not sing as much, dance as much, or laugh as much in the evenings. The housewives no longer exchanged stories on their doorsteps, the children cried and fussed more, and the farmers in the field were no longer satisfied with their bountiful crops. In his tower, the King hung his head in despair and paced the floor endlessly. Griselle was now his most trusted advisor. His only real advisor in effect. At the official Meeting of Consuls, with his old advisors and his wife the Queen, he would listen perfunctorily then show them all out of the room and remain with Griselle and listen to her only.

Cha Cha heard of these goings on, and though it didn't really matter, he just happened to be in the area of the counsel room at the next appointed time. He arrived just in time to see his father hustling and bustling everyone out of the Counsel Chamber except Griselle. He noted the gray and crestfallen faces of the men whom his father had always trusted and who'd always trusted him. He saw his mother's face, red and humiliated, and he saw Griselle's triumphant smile as his father closed the door, shutting the others out.

Nothing really made any difference, so there was no reason not to go into an adjoining little supply room where they kept ink and parchment. There, he crawled out through a window onto a narrow little ledge. From this perch, as he looked down on the sharp, pointed rocks far below, he could hear his father and Griselle quite plainly through the open window of the adjacent room.

He heard that familiar, lulling croon of Griselle's drift into her sing-song delivery.

"It's not your fault, my King. No one could possibly do any more than you've done for your kingdom."

"Yes, I suppose that is true."

"Of course, it's true. And no one appreciates it anymore."

"No. Not at all."

"You should be more severe with these ungrateful wretches. Remind them you are their master."

"Yes, remind them. But my wife still appreciates me."

"Of course, but only…oh, it grieves me to say this. Is she not, at least a little, colder than formerly?"

"Why, no. Of course not."

"Oh, dear King, forgive me, but for the sake of your kingdom, for the sake of your beloved people…"

"I thought you said they were ungrateful wretches."

"And so they are, but you, out of your great, magnanimous spirit, still love them."

"Why, yes I do."

"Then, for their sake, please consider, is your wife still completely loyal to you, to the kingdom, to your beloved people?"

"The question is preposterous. She's completely loyal."

"Think, your glorious Majesty, my one and only King. Hasn't she said anything at all, even one slight, tiny, little thing that might make you suspicious? Just one?"

"Well, perhaps she did seem a little distant last night."

"Oh, your Majesty, you noticed it too?"

"You mean, you noticed it?"

"Oh, I thought she was sending daggers of ice straight into the loving furnace of your heart."

"That bad? Have I been that blind?"

"Do not be too hard on yourself, my beloved Majesty. If the flames of her love have cooled to treachery, your Majesty, surely it is only because she does not recognize true greatness when she sees it or, perhaps, realizing her own lack of your greatness, a spark of jealousy has unhappily sparked a conflagration within her breast."

"Treachery? Did you say treachery?"

"Treason? Did you say treason, your most glorious Majesty, my most august King? Nay, nay, say not treason. I would rather die than think my beloved Queen a traitor to you. Such a base accusation. Do not think it. Fight against that thought with all your might, and do not allow others to speak it. Not without proof."

"Proof?"

"Yes, proof. Demand proof if anyone should make

such a monstrous claim. And how can you even prove such a charge? It's impossible. Wait! I have it. Yes, we shall prove our beloved Queen innocent of all such accusations of treason. When is the next crescent moon?"

"A fortnight hence."

"That's just the time. I shall arrange a party. I shall host it myself."

"How shall you prove my wife's innocence?"

"We will set up a test. Simplicity itself."

"But, what?"

"We will only ask her to swear her undying loyalty and love."

"Is that all?"

"Three times.'"

"Three times?"

"And each time, she must bend her knee and curtsey."

"But, isn't that humiliating?"

"Humiliating? To prove her love and loyalty three times before the entire court? She loves you. She's loyal. She'll be proud of the chance to prove herself."

"I don't know. I'm not sure."

"Any loyal subject would do it. I would. That's it! Ask me to do it first. Then after I have, ask her. Then, there will be no question of humiliation. Her love for you will outweigh all other considerations. As does mine."

"I just don't know."

"Oh, my beloved Majesty, do not let our beloved Queen linger under this dark cloud of doubt. You must be certain she is not unjustly suspected of treason. Just a simple little act of loyalty on her part. Command it for your kingdom's sake. Silence the wagging tongues."

"What? Do others accuse her of this?"

"Not in front of me they don't! They don't dare. But,

your Majesty, I have ears that hear. I am the only one loyal enough to you and the Queen to tell you."

"Rumors like this cannot be tolerated."

"Then do it, my King. For the sake of your good name. For my Queen's sake. And for my sake."

"Then it's settled," said the King.

Cha Cha didn't listen to anymore. Griselle, of course, knew that his mother would never submit to so disgraceful a public humiliation. Her honesty and honor would prevent it. She would also realize that any such acquiescence would only be used by Griselle as a further pretext for exacting even more suspicion. Yes, his mother would see through the ruse, uphold her honor before the court and hope that justice would prevail. And if she did submit to the test, the court would despise both her and the king from then on. Griselle would exploit such an opening. It was a cunning, simple trap, and she won no matter what happened. But the most likely outcome, with Griselle there to pull the strings, was the Queen's refusal of the test and her instant death for treason. Cha Cha reasoned through all this without much caring, but he did see now why he'd been such an easy mark for Griselle. Even his father, the King, was putty in her hands. And, in a fortnight, his mother would probably lie dead on the banquet floor. Then, his father, in guilt and remorse for what he had done, would drink from Griselle's cup, and the Seventh Higher Kingdom would be completely under her sway. Oh well, in the long run one ruler was pretty much the same as another. The kingdom would get on somehow.

Casually, he let himself back into the supply room. Not much caring, he came out of the room, after making sure no one was in the hall, and went to his fencing lesson. On the way the gnawing part of his mind gnawed at a sack of juicy bones. The duty of love and the love of duty—the gnawer was getting closer and closer to the marrow, but it wasn't quite time to bite through.

How about this bone? Where was his sister? She'd never been found—not her body nor a scrap of clothing. It was possible Griselle had fed her to the slither hither and thithers, but he knew by now that Griselle was the gloating type. She would have let him know somehow. She said Ta Ta was being held someplace safe, but since then, she'd never mentioned her again, not even as a hostage. His sister could have been eaten by a wild animal, of course, but all those search parties and not one had found a trace of her remains. It was odd. He'd been told by Nana that his sister had always said he'd make a great king. What he'd never told Nana was that he'd always believed, that if anything ever happened to him, Princess Ta Ta would make a great queen. He was sure that was true. In fact, the gnawer inside him was counting on it.

And, one last bone to gnaw on. In a fortnight Griselle would execute her end game. Then, the kingdom would be hers.

That night, at Griselle's underground banquet, he sat by her side as always. After all, as the highest ranking of her subjects, he was "the guest of honor." That was the way she always introduced him. Of course, it was a slap in the face and an insult, and all her subjects laughed their hollow laughter to see him brought so low.

But not quite all. He noticed what he thought were tears in some of their eyes. And some of them resisted her mind tentacles, and the gnawing part of his brain noted these too. But that was not really important to the Prince. He left all these juicy bones to the gnawer and let it submerge happily beneath the surface of his consciousness to hunt for marrow. His surface personality took a rather small sip of his wine, for it didn't really matter how much he drank. And, when he felt the little exploratory, probing tentacles of Griselle's mind entering his mind, he let them enter. It really didn't matter, for there was nothing there to see.

At last, when Griselle had finished her meal and her mind probes, she arose from her stupor and left the room. After waiting a safe interval, Prince Cha Cha, not much caring, slowly scanned the room and noted again those whose eyes had bleared at his humiliation and those who had tried to resist the tentacles. Of course it didn't matter, for it would be impossible to communicate with them, because Griselle's mind probes would reveal any such communications to her. Oh well, eventually, all things came to the same end. So, he shoveled all these little bones into a heap and watched uninterested as the gnawer appeared briefly to snatch them and carry them back down into the darkest shadows of his mind.

Thus he passed his days, busy with his assigned tasks, watching the sun rise and set, not really caring, and waiting for the event or opening that didn't really matter and occasionally wondering how his sister was faring.

And his sister was faring, she thought, quite oddly. In fact, she found the wizard, Typhus and Emily the oddest crew she could ever have imagined. Nevertheless, they had spent three comfortable days and nights in the dwelling of Sarnus. The wizard and Typhus systematically worked their way through the entire stock of shelves of Sarnus's library and apothecary. Jar by jar, vial by vial and flask by flask, they took everything down and opened it. Gingerly, they sniffed at them, holding each vessel away from their nose and fanning the air above it with their hand to get a slight whiff of the odor. This precaution was necessary, for even the slightest scent of some would make them blanch or gag. But some would hold the most pleasant and intoxicating aromas while others were completely odorless. Carefully, they would read the labels on the containers. Then they would search through the scrolls and texts, reading all they could about the substance before them. Then, most carefully, they would taste minute quantities. All day they would do this, and late into the night they would read scroll after scroll and text after text. They took copious notes and conferred often and long in low, hushed tones. Ta Ta noted it was hard to tell whether Typhus was the cousin, servant, friend or fellow wizard of Rigirus.

Emily and Ta Ta were also busy. They left Typhus and the wizard alone, for they knew the success of their mission depended upon their ability to defeat Griselle, the Wizard of Fandon. In the morning, Ta Ta and Emily took the animals out across the river to forage and exercise. In the afternoon they came back and cooked and went through all the gear, mending it and reorganizing the hasty packing job that Typhus had done. In all this there was plenty of time to talk, and Emily was fascinated by the details of court life. Indeed, she asked question after question and would let Ta Ta talk of little else. But Emily would say nothing about her own life, or even her family, much to Ta Ta's surprise. The Princess did get her to answer one question, however.

"How come Typhus calls Rigirus sire? After all, they are cousins."

Emily looked away from her and said, "Their families come from very different stations in life."

Ta Ta thought she understood and asked no more about it.

Emily was also very concerned and nervous about the

progress of the experiments of the wizard and Typhus. Quite often she would steal a glance at Typhus who would shake his head in the negative. Then, she would turn away with a dejected look and bury herself in some menial task.

So, Ta Ta passed the three days patiently. She was anxious to return home but was aware that the wizard needed to prepare as carefully as possible for the coming struggle. Unfortunately, it did not seem to be going well. He seemed to be in increasing anxiety, even starting to yell at Typhus and Emily, and becoming more hurried and frantic in his rummaging through the scrolls and texts, sometimes even throwing them to the floor in disgust. Late on the third evening, he sat beside Ta Ta in front of the fire and spoke.

"I don't know what to do. There's some sort of grand theme to his work, but I can't discern it. There's some sort of linchpin, some magic ingredient or key that ties it all together, but I can't find it."

"Aren't you learning anything?"

"I'm learning a lot, but without the grand theme, a unifying principle, it's all basically parlor tricks."

"Surely, he must have written it down, Rigirus."

"There used to be a giant volume that sat in the place of honor in the center of the main shelf."

"Griselle?"

The wizard nodded his head sadly.

"That's my thought. If she has it, I don't know what we can do."

Emily was bustling about removing dinner plates and overheard them.

"Perhaps, he didn't write it down, sire."

"What makes you say that, Emily?" the wizard asked.

"But, sire, mightn't it be something very small or simple."

"The secret that unifies all the theories?"

"If it unifies everything, then it must be big, big as creation. But if it's secret then it must be small, small enough to hide in our hearts."

"That's a riddle, not an answer."

"Yes, sire, it is a riddle, but a very beautiful one."

"Beautiful or not, what we need is the answer."

"I know, sire, and I'm sure I know the answer, only I just can't think of it right now."

"If you do, be sure and tell us."

Emily paused and looked at the floor as if unsure she should speak. Without looking up she said, "One thing I do know, the answer is very simple. Beautiful things usually are. And the more beautiful they are, the simpler they are."

Then Emily meekly collected the plates and took them to the washing area. Ta Ta wondered if Emily had any idea at all what the wizard had been talking about.

"How long will we stay here, then?" she asked the wizard.

The wizard pointed at the fire. Ta Ta noticed that the fire, which had never needed replenishing, was not as bright as before.

"So far, Princess, this abode has been kind to us. We've had warmth and shelter, but now the fire and the torches are starting to dim. The abode wants us to leave."

"But, why? We've done nothing wrong."

He nodded his head eagerly, as if to convince himself of something.

"Just so. And that is what gives us cause for hope."

"Hope?"

"Yes, Princess. It is my belief that whatever I am supposed to find I have already found. That we are being expelled because my searching is complete. That I already have all I need."

Ta Ta nodded, as if in agreement, but interiorly she had doubts. Perhaps visitors were only granted three days sufferance. Perhaps, sadly, they had used up the last reserves of magic in Sarnus's abode. But, there seemed no reason to discourage the wizard, so she kept her reservations to herself.

Throughout the evening, the torches and fire slowly diminished, and the chambers began to cool. The wizard and Typhus continued their reading and note taking in a frenzy of activity. Ta Ta and Emily went through all the baggage one last time, inspecting and mending as they went along. Then they packed, trying to order all items that might be needed first for easy and quick retrieval, such as food, weapons and medicinals.

The wizard set aside certain selected potions to be taken with them. He insisted on taking only the smallest batches that might be necessary. He wanted to preserve Sarnus's abode as intact as possible. For the same reason, he would take no scrolls or books. Anything he decreed useful from them was copied by hand, either by himself or Typhus. These things he would not let Ta Ta or Emily pack. That was a last job he designated for himself. When Ta Ta and Emily went to sleep that night, the wizard and Typhus were still working frantically in the fading light.

In the morning, the chamber was cold for the first time since they'd entered. The fireplace was dark, but the torches still provided a dim twilight by which the wizard and Typhus were finishing their packing of the donkey and the saddling of the horses. From their somber expressions, Ta Ta inferred they were still unhappy with the fruits of their research.

Her thoughts were interrupted by Emily who brought

her a breakfast of bread, porridge and fruit. They were familiar enough by now that they ate together. Ta Ta ate everything, knowing the day would be a long one, except the bread, which had gone stale. Emily ate the stale bread with gusto, and Ta Ta thought that Emily must have had a very hard life. She also noticed that Emily seemed to have some sort of secret smile, for she kept hiding her mouth and looking away. Finally, Ta Ta could contain herself no longer.

"Emily, is there something going on?"

Emily smiled at her as if grateful to reveal her secret.

"I found the most wonderful thing last night."

"What?"

Emily reached into a pocket and pulled out a tiny little square of brass.

"Do you see how bright it is? I was up half the night polishing it."

She handed it to Ta Ta who inspected it closely. It was, indeed, highly polished, but it was nothing but a part of a horse's bridle. She was about to tell Emily this, but Emily was glowing with happiness and she thought better of it. After all, she reasoned, Emily was a half wit, and there was no point in depriving her of whatever small pleasures she got out of life. She spoke gently.

"It is very lovely."

"Do you really think so? Do you really like it?"

"Of course."

Ta Ta found Emily looking at her with an almost pathetic, but altogether touching eagerness. Emily's eyes shone as she leaned forward and her hand reached for Ta Ta's, but abruptly she withdrew it as she remembered her place. She turned away from Ta Ta, lowering her head and speaking with a low voice.

"I'm so very glad to hear you say that, Princess. I was hoping you might like it."

She paused for a moment as if gathering up her courage to speak.

"Would you like to have it?" she asked.

Princess Ta Ta didn't know what to say, and while she hesitated, searching for a response, she caught the fear of rejection in Emily's face. So, she answered with a kind evasion.

"I really couldn't. After all you found it. It wouldn't be fair. I already have so much."

Emily's face brightened and she turned back to Ta Ta.

"Princess, I have an idea, and…" she turned away, again uncertain. Clenching her fists, she bit her lip before saying, "Oh, I don't know how to explain it, Princess."

"Just do the best you can, Emily."

"Well, I was wondering if maybe we could…you see I may not be here for long."

"What?"

"Please, don't ask me to explain. I'm not wanting to keep a secret from you."

Suddenly, she grabbed the princess's hands in her own, which was an enormous breach of protocol, but her words came out in such a desperate rush, and she was so clearly on the verge of tears that Ta Ta ignored the breach.

"It's an awful secret, and I'm sorry I can't tell you. But it's just, you've been so very kind to me."

Ta Ta felt a twinge of guilt, for it seemed to her most of the kindness had been from Emily to her. But, she had no time to nourish this uncomfortable thought, for Emily's words continued to tumble out.

"You've been so very kind, and I want to remember you always, no matter what happens to me or what I become again. And I want you to remember me always. So, please take this. It's a wonderful, shiny thing and will look ever so lovely around your neck. And, maybe, if you was to be so minded, maybe you could give me a keepsake of your own."

Ta Ta felt disappointed. Was that her game?

"You mean, like one of my jewels, to wear around your neck?"

But Emily shook her head rapidly back and forth.

"No, no, Princess. Something really tiny. Something a really tiny person could carry about. That way, no matter what happened to them, they'd always be able to remember you."

Ta Ta felt ashamed of herself. She was touched by Emily's humility. Whatever her game was, she wasn't trying to trick her into giving up a jewel.

"Would you like this ring?"

She offered Emily a simple ring that Nana had given her. She was sure that Nana wouldn't mind under the circumstances.

"Oh, no, that's much too big."

"What would you like then?"

Emily pointed at a tiny brass button on Ta Ta's sleeve.

"But, Emily, that's nothing. It's only a button."

"If you please, Princess, I promise I'll always keep it nice and shiny. And no matter what, I'll always remember you."

Ta Ta plucked the tiny, brass button off her sleeve and gave it to Emily. Emily began to sniffle and ran a thread through the button and tied it to a strip of leather and hung it from her neck. Then, she handed Ta Ta another thin strip of leather and looked expectantly at her.

Ta Ta felt a little foolish, but she remembered her

mother had often told her, "A kindness done to the humblest is the greatest kindness you can do to yourself." She'd never understood it before, but now she did, and she strung the bridle piece on the leather strip and hung it about her neck. The gleam of delight in Emily's eyes told her that her mother was right.

"Thank you, Princess," Emily said and suddenly fell back into her role of servant. She gathered up the scraps of breakfast and bustled off.

Later, as they made ready to leave, the wizard noted the bridle piece upon Ta Ta's neck. He gave her a slightly startled look, studied it for a moment, smiled, then shook his head and went back to his business. Typhus, on the other hand, brightened with gratification when he saw it. Suddenly, she realized that Typhus had not really liked her, but now his whole demeanor, which had been correct but cold, changed. From here on his behavior was still correct but now underlaid with genuine warmth and devotion.

At last, they had cleaned out the living quarters and, following the wizard's directions, had put everything back as neat and orderly as they had found it, despite the handicap of the ever diminishing light. The wizard was the last to leave the living area, and as he left, the last torch sputtered out. As they made their way through the various chambers the torches in each extinguished themselves as the last person left the chamber. At last they stood outside. They waded across the river and turned for one last look.

"Look!" cried the wizard. "My mark is fading."

They all stared at the mark, which faded away before their eyes.

"Alas," the wizard said, with tears in his eyes, "so much

still to learn, so many questions I wanted answered, but now it will never be."

"Surely, you can find it again someday," Ta Ta said consolingly.

"No. It has yielded all it will to me. Its secrets are now reserved for others."

With that, the wizard turned his head resolutely away, and without ever looking back, led them up the trail out of the drizzly forest.

It wasn't until evening that they were out of the canyon, and they camped for the night by the forest edge. Late into the night, the wizard and Typhus carried on a hushed conversation. Every day thereafter, as they marched through forest, plain and desert, the wizard and Typhus would go up ahead, out of earshot, talking and gesticulating, poring over their notes as they went. Sometimes, the wizard would lean over in his saddle to listen to Typhus, his ear next to Typhus's mouth. At those moments Emily would tense up as if she was sure they were talking about her. Other times, the wizard would dismount and walk beside Typhus, and they would examine their notes together. At night, if they were in a wooded area, the wizard and Typhus would go somewhere they couldn't be seen from camp, make a clearing and light a fire. Soon, exotic smells would waft into camp; some were bitter, some sweet, some repulsive and others enticing. Ta Ta guessed they were working on potions and spells. But, on the nights when they were concealed from her sight, they would always call on Emily to bring them something they'd forgotten. Emily would disappear for a few moments, then return looking relieved, but also giving Ta Ta a furtive look as though she were hiding something. But this always happened late, when Ta Ta was already lying in her blanket, half asleep, so she gave it little thought.

One night, after they'd journeyed for several days, and Ta Ta was very tired, she'd lain down quickly and fell into a deep sleep. Suddenly, she sat straight up. Had she heard a scream? Then, she heard a piercing shriek. What she saw next horrified her so much that, for a moment, she thought she was still asleep and having a nightmare. A gigantic rat burst into the camp. Ta Ta screamed in fear. The rat stopped, looked at her with a terrified look, then ran away.

Immediately, Typhus and the wizard ran into the clearing. Ta Ta stood up, trembling and pointed in the direction the rat had gone.

"I saw a giant rat. It ran away over there."

Typhus shook his head.

"There's no such thing as a giant rat."

"But I just saw one. Over there."

Typhus shook his head again.

"Maybe it was a wild horse."

"It was a rat. It was huge. You should have seen the tail on that thing."

"Maybe it was a bear," Typhus offered.

"Bears don't have tails!"

"There, there," the wizard said, as he picked up Ta Ta's blanket and put it about her shoulders. "Don't catch cold now. Typhus, go out and find that big, bad rat and chase it off."

"Right away, sire," Typhus said and bounded off in the direction Ta Ta had pointed.

"But I did see a rat, Wizard, I did."

"Of course, you did, my dear. One can see anything in the dark. Or in a nightmare for that matter."

"Where's Emily? I want Emily. Emily!"

"Didn't you notice? She ran off in the same direction as Typhus."

Ta Ta started to sob.

"I did see a giant rat. It might kill Emily."

The wizard wrapped the blanket snugly around Ta Ta and gently nudged her to the ground. They sat there together, and he put an arm around her as she buried her head against his breast.

"I don't want anything bad to happen to Emily," she said through her tears.

"Yes, she's very sweet isn't she? I've become quite fond of her myself. Well, I promise you Typhus won't let any giant rat hurt her. Or any bear for that matter. As long as Typhus is around, Emily is quite safe, I assure you."

The assurance and easiness of the wizard's voice calmed Ta Ta and her sobs subsided.

"Isn't it a beautiful night, Princess? Look. So many stars. Like a fine powder in the sky."

She looked at the sky. It was beautiful, but she wondered what he was getting at.

"When I was a little boy, Princess, I used to go for long walks on nights like this. And I used to look at the stars and the moon, and I used to wonder what sort of secrets are out there. What a multitude of wonders. One thing after another to be discovered. And, then, one last thing—what holds all the secrets together? What is the secret of the secrets?"

"You thought all that when you were a little boy?"

"Yes, many times. From as young as I can remember. When I was even littler than you."

"That's why you became a wizard?"

"No. I became a wizard because I wasn't any good at anything else."

Ta Ta pulled away and shot the wizard a sternly regal look.

"Wizard. It is just as dangerous to underestimate yourself as it is to underestimate your enemies."

The wizard was somewhat taken aback by this sudden change of demeanor.

"Good heavens. Where did you learn that?"

"From my father."

He chuckled softly.

"Then I look forward to meeting your father."

"And I want him to meet you. When will you be ready?"

"In a little while, we'll be as ready as we'll ever be."

He shook his head ruefully.

"It would be helpful if I knew the secret of secrets. Especially, if Griselle has his book."

"Did Sarnus know the secret of secrets?"

"I'm sure he did. Pity he didn't let me in on it when he had the chance."

"Does Griselle know?"

"I don't know what the secret of secrets is. But, whatever it is, I am sure of one thing—if Griselle knew what it was, she wouldn't be Griselle."

The wizard saw Ta Ta was getting sleepy so he shifted his position to give her room to lie down and gently tucked her in.

"Now, sweet Princess, good night. And don't worry. I promise you, neither Typhus nor I will allow any harm to come to Emily."

As sleep overcame Ta Ta she was dimly aware of the wizard walking off in the direction that Typhus had gone.

The next morning, as they broke camp, Emily was gray, silent and withdrawn. When they were mounted and on their way, and the effects of sleep had worn off, Ta Ta asked Emily if she had see the rat last night. Emily seemed nervous when she answered.

"I didn't wake up until you screamed. Then I ran off to see what frightened you."

"I know it was a giant rat. And that was very foolish of you. It might have eaten us and bit off our heads."

"Please, Princess, I promise you, it could never harm you. If it were real I mean."

After that, Emily would say no more and they rode in silence. After awhile, Ta Ta noticed that Emily had her hands clasped around the button she had given her and was whispering something over and over to herself. Ta Ta leaned slightly forward until she could hear what it was.

"I will remember. I will remember. I will remember."

They journeyed on for days. Every night, Typhus and the wizard would disappear and work on their wizardry. It didn't seem to be going altogether well. Sometimes, there would even be loud explosions, and one of them would have singed hair and eyebrows the next day. As they marched ahead out of earshot during the day, they seemed to argue incessantly. Each morning, Emily seemed more depressed and fearful and would clutch her button as they rode. To comfort her, Ta Ta would put her arms around her which seemed to help, and by evening Emily would be herself again, cheerful, talkative and helpful. But, in the morning, her depression would mysteriously return.

They traveled by back roads and tiny paths through desert, swamp, forest and snowy passes, carefully avoiding all contact with others, for they had decided to return to the castle in secret.

"Better not to let Griselle know we're there until we know how matters stand," the wizard had said and Ta Ta agreed. She was sure that if she came in publicly, Griselle would find some means of preventing her from seeing her parents, or keep them from believing her story, even if she did reach them.

Then, one evening as it was growing dark, they stepped out of an obscure path in a forest, and there was the castle of the Seventh Higher Kingdom in the valley below them.

What do we do now, they all wondered.

***

Father ended the story at that point, even though the children wanted more. He was worried he might have overtaxed Tanya. So he put her to bed, kissed her good-night and shut off the light as he left.

Tanya huddled in her bed, waiting for her parents to go to sleep. In a little while Charles would come.

I'm afraid for you Charles, she thought. Why do you want the monster? Why does it want you?

In his bedroom, Charles wondered what he was going to do. The strange orb in his sister's closet was pulling at him. Initially, he'd been repulsed by the creature. But now, it was beginning to excite him. It was strange and unknown, yet it was undeniably dangerous. Just as a tiny part of him wanted to be dangerous. And it was cruel. He realized now his sister was right. Feeding the mouse to it had been cruel. That too, was part of the thrill of the creature. It was as if it beckoned to something hidden but very real and alive inside of him, something that he wanted to be but dared not admit to.

The thought frightened him, and he began to rationalize. Surely, this thing, this creature, if it could be used for cruelty could also be used for good, for mercy. If it could destroy why couldn't it create—or heal! That was it! That was why it was in his sister's closet. It was a force for good, not bad. It was just a matter of figuring how to use it. If he figured it out, he might be able to cure his sister. It was worth the risk. After all, it was to save his sister.

A delicious little shiver ran down his spine. It was okay to keep feeding the creature. He was going to make it his friend.

Why am I afraid of you, Charles, thought his sister, in her room. The monster doesn't frighten me now as much as you do. Why is that? Why?

Chapter 14

Home Sweet Home

"Ta Ta , the wizard, Typhus and Emily were in a pickle," Father began. "They had to get back in the castle, but they had to make sure of everything that was going on before they revealed their identities. So, they decided to disguise themselves. Ta Ta's disguise would be the hardest, of course. The wizard doubted if anyone would know him there as contact between the Fourth and Seventh kingdoms was very rare. Still, to be on the safe side, he too would assume a disguise."

But first, they must find a way into the castle. They worried about the main gate for they were sure Griselle would have her guards there who might recognize the Princess. There were a number of secondary gates but the wizard was sure Griselle would be careful enough to also put her spies there. The secret passageway, if they could find it, would certainly serve as a conduit for her people. They would be spotted instantly there. Finally, reluctantly, they decided the bold approach would be best and go in by the main gate and trust to their wits and their disguises to get them through.

The wizard disguised himself as a tradesman.

"What shall you be, Princess?" Emily asked Ta Ta.

"She shall be my son," said the wizard.

"A boy?" said Emily, incredulous.

"Yes. She'll be recognized instantly as a girl."

"But as a boy, I'll look almost like my brother," Ta Ta protested.

"True," answered the wizard. "Therefore, your face will be covered with a bandage, and your arm will be in a sling, the result of an unfortunate fall. We are coming to the castle to seek the aid of a physician. Emily will most tenderly cradle you in her arms. If anyone speaks to you, you will only moan in reply. This disguise you will maintain as long as is necessary to our mission."

When their costumes were complete they proceeded to the main gate of the castle. There, one of the guards wanted to wave them through after a perfunctory glance, but the other, sullen faced and suspicious, insisted on looking at them more closely. He poked at their baggage, and peered at each intently, and Ta Ta was glad that her face was heavily bandaged. Finally, he seemed satisfied and waved them through.

Once out of sight of the guards, Ta Ta and Emily took the lead, and Ta Ta guided them to a small stable where they left the horses. Continuing the masquerade, Typhus now carried her in his arms, and she whispered directions in his ear, guiding him through dark byways, until they came to a small doorway at the back of the king's palace. This was the outside doorway to the living quarters of Nana where she resided when not tending to her many duties.

Typhus knocked persistently but softly until they finally heard a stirring inside. A tiny peephole in the door opened and Ta Ta heard Nana's voice through the hole.

"What's the matter? Is Cha Cha ill?" Nana asked in a voice full of concern.

A rush of emotion filled Ta Ta. Home at last. She had not realized how lonely and frightened she'd been and how much she longed to be a little girl again. But now was not quite the time. She put her mouth in front of the peephole and put her index finger in front of it in a shushing gesture.

"Nana," she whispered, "say absolutely nothing. Nothing!"

There was a startled gasp on the other side of the door, followed by silence.

"Nana, blow out your candle, then quietly let us in."

Nana did as bid and quickly all four were inside, and once the door was shut, the peephole closed and the candle relit, Ta Ta's reserve broke. Tearing off her bandages, she threw herself into Nana's arms. They held each other tight, and tears flowed down their cheeks.

"Child, we all gave you up for dead. Where have you been?" Nana stroked Ta Ta's hair as she spoke.

"Griselle," Ta Ta whispered.

"I knew it!" Nana said, her face flushing with anger. "That woman's behind all the deviltry in this castle."

"What deviltry is that?" the wizard asked softly, but with authority.

Nana seemed to notice Ta Ta's three companions for the first time. She and Ta Ta broke their embrace, Nana picked up her candle off a table, and holding it aloft, she slowly and suspiciously scanned all three of them.

"And who are you?"

"Friends of the royal family," replied the wizard.

At the mention of the royal family, Emily abruptly gave a full, formal, perfect curtsey which so startled Nana that she nearly dropped her candle.

"For the present, our names do not matter. But we are here at the behest of Princess Ta Ta to aid your King and Queen."

The wizard would have continued, but Emily had abruptly curtsied again at the mention of the King and Queen. When she came up, she saw Nana staring at her in amazement, and she became nervous.

"Didn't I do it right?" she asked in a plaintive, high pitched voice.

Ta Ta, in what by now had become an automatic reflex, grabbed Emily's hand to calm her and said, "It was a beautiful curtsey, Emily."

"Then, why is she staring at me so?"

Ta Ta patted her hand and said, "I'll explain it all to you tonight."

It was all too much for Nana who sat down heavily in a chair.

Ta Ta kneeled down in front of Nana and, after apologizing profusely and tearfully for all the anguish she had caused by her disappearance, told her the entire story of all that had happened. When she had finished, the wizard pulled up a stool and sat in front of Nana and enfolded her hands in his.

"And now, good woman, by your love for the royal family," here Emily started to curtsey again, but Ta Ta's hand restrained her, "tell us everything that is going on in the castle. What is Griselle up to? Who do you suspect or know to be her spies? What are the rumors? The intrigues? Who are you sure is brave, steadfast, stalwart and true? We must lay our plans carefully. The fate of the kingdom hangs by a thread."

Nana started slowly, organizing her thoughts first, then answering his questions, point by point, without further prompting from the wizard. He and the others listened carefully, all aware of the stakes. Nevertheless, one part of him marveled as he listened. What a shrewd choice of a governess. A fountain of maternal love, but also practical, observant and wise.

Thoroughly, she went through the events of the last three weeks, detailing the increasing, unspoken tension in the castle. Name by name, she went through the personages in the castle, from the court to the scullery to the stable. She listed the certain, the doubtful and the probable and her reasons for her beliefs. She did not ramble nor stumble but moved methodically to the end.

No, the wizard thought, this was not a chance choice. The King and Queen knew what they were about. And only a wizard of Griselle's power could have sown so much confusion in them.

Lastly, Nana told of the King and Queen, the growing distance between them, the growing hold of Griselle on the King and the inevitable splitting of the court into two factions. When she had finished, Rigirus released her hands, and she folded them quietly in her lap and bowed her head.

Ta Ta, like the others, had listened intently. The wizard, as she expected, grasped everything and, to her surprise, Typhus seemed to take it all in also. How exceptionally intelligent he is, she noted. What is his real story? Emily, of course, was hopelessly confused but, Ta Ta noted with approval, had never given up, listening to the end, struggling to do the best she could. Emily, Ta Ta decided, would always have a place in their castle if she so desired. But, there had been one glaring omission in Nana's report. The wizard also noticed it.

"And Prince Cha Cha," he asked softly, "what of him?"

"Yes, Nana, what of Cha Cha?" Ta Ta asked, again kneeling in front of Nana.

Nana did not look at her but stared ahead into space with a puzzled frown and shook her head.

"Now, somehow, he's different."

"How is he different? Think carefully. We must know exactly," the wizard said, leaning closer and closing his eyes. Then he steepled his fingers and held them to his lips, and everybody waited in expectant silence for Nana's answer.

Speaking just above a whisper Nana said, "He's there, but he's not there. He listens, he's perfectly obedient, he answers when you speak, he goes about his daily routine, but it's almost as if it were a charade, a private game. His eyes, they're like shuttered windows. For a moment the shutters swing open, and there's a light inside. Then, it's as if he knows you see the light, and he bangs the shutters shut again."

"As if he's hiding the light?" the wizard asked, also whispering, his eyes still shut, his steepled fingers still at his lips.

"Yes, that's it exactly. Like he's hiding the light."

"Ooh, that's very bad, sire," said Emily.

The wizard opened his eyes, dropped his hands to his knees and gazed thoughtfully at the others.

"No, that's very good. It's better than I could have hoped."

He fixed his gaze upon Ta Ta.

"Princess, you must find a way to see your brother."

"When?" she asked eagerly.

"Tonight. The sooner the better. I think Griselle is moving into her endgame, and we must rearrange the pieces on the board as quickly as possible."

Swiftly, they decided upon another disguise. There was no question of using the secret passages as they were under the control of Griselle. So, they cut Ta Ta's hair to page boy length, which brought tears to Nana's eyes. Then, Nana made a quick trip to the laundry where she got a fresh pile of laundry. These were loaded into Ta Ta's arms until they piled high above her head with just a little space made in the middle so she could half see where she was going. Then, she and Nana set out for the Prince's quarters, Ta Ta barely able to see and being steered by her governess.

They were stopped once by a guard.

"It's late to be totin' laundry, ain't it?"

"It's for the banquet tomorrow," Nana said. "I'm going to arrange the Prince's wardrobe tonight. I want him to look his best. It's me everyone's going to blame if he doesn't look splendid and regal like. You have it easy. Me, I'm busy all day and all night. Worry, worry, worry. No one cares how you do your job, but me, I have to answer to the king, the queen, the whole royal court. Oh, how I envy you oafs your lot. Just stand around all day without a care in the world."

The guard, of course, quickly tired of this tirade.

"Be off with you, and take this ragamuffin with you or I'll box his ears."

"Well," sniffed Nana, "some people have no care for other people's problems it seems."

With that, she put a hand on Ta Ta's shoulders and guided her down the hallway away from the guard.

They passed without further incident to Cha Cha's

room. Nana knocked softly on his door. After a moment, it opened and Cha Cha appeared, still dressed for dinner, even at this late hour. Through the pile of clothing, Ta Ta could see his eyes. There was a dull, uncaring blankness about them, but at the sight of the laundry and her eyes the blankness, for the briefest of moments, lifted and then abruptly came back as if, as Nana had observed, he had banged the shutters shut again.

"See, Cha Cha," Nana said, "we brought some finery for you to try on for tomorrow night's banquet. You should try it on now. Are you alone?"

"Quite alone, Nana. But please go down to the hall pantry and see if I accidentally left my dancing slippers there. I can't find them and it's so important everything be just right."

The Prince spoke in an indifferent tone, but Ta Ta realized that the pantry, only a few paces away, would leave Nana perfectly positioned to intercept anyone coming to his door.

Once inside, the Prince seemed indifferent to her and pulled the night curtain around one side of the bed to shield it from the secret entrance to his chamber. Then, he led her around to the side of the bed. He sat at the head of the bed, and still showing no emotion, motioned for her to place the bundle on the bed. Ta Ta, of course knew about the secret passage ways and had no doubt one entered his room. She knew he was guarding against a surprise entrance by Griselle or one of her lackeys. Still, when she put down the bundle she expected a tearful reunion, but he only looked at her without interest and spoke in a flat voice as he examined the fresh clothing.

"Very good, page. Except this doublet. Yellow? Too showy. Here, hold it next to you."

Even though she'd been forewarned, Ta Ta felt hurt, rebuffed by this coldness, and part of her wanted to cry. The little girl in the Princess had so wanted a tearful, warm reunion, at least for a moment. Then, her brother, as he surveyed the doublet she held next to herself, said something that sent a royal thrill up and down her spine.

"You know, page, if your hair were cropped a little closer, I don't think anyone could tell us apart at first glance."

He threw the yellow doublet on the bed and selected a blue one.

"I have another one identical to this except for the white piping. I'll be wearing this one. When you're at the banquet tomorrow night the King and Queen are going to be the center of attention. I expect you to watch them and me closely, page, and be ready to do whatever needs doing."

Princess Ta Ta stifled a gasp at the mention of her parents. It was obvious they were in great danger from the guarded way Prince Cha Cha talked. She wanted to ask a hundred questions, but he was already piling clothing into her arms.

"Here, I shan't need this or this or this. Here's something extra for the laundry and this blanket needs washing."

When the pile buried Ta Ta's face from view, he said, "There, that seems to be everything.

Politely, he steered her around the bed to the door, which he opened, and summoned Nana. To her, he said, "Did you find the shoes? No? I'm sure they'll turn up. Thank you, Nana. Good night."

As they left, Ta Ta thought to herself, a great king, Cha Cha. You will be a great king.

And as he watched them go, the Prince monotonously

repeated to himself, it doesn't matter. It doesn't matter. It doesn't matter.

***

Father ended the evening story telling at this point and put Tanya to bed. Later, when their parents were asleep, Charles went to his sister's room. That night he did not feed the thing in the closet. He talked to Tanya about her illness and about other things until she fell asleep. It was a difficult conversation. They both knew she was dying and there was so little to say that was not painful. He couldn't talk about school or about what to do when they, or rather he, grew up. Nor could he tell her what he had in mind, for he was sure she'd object. Even though he was doing if for her. He knew it could work if he did it right.

Strangely enough, the thing in the closet had made scarcely any noise that night—no scratching or growling, just a gentle, persistent knocking. Tanya had been too tired and worn down to notice, but Charles had. And he knew the thing knew he was coming. And it was waiting.

So, when he was sure Tanya was fully asleep, he crept off the foot of the bed and stealthily made his way to the closet door. The gentle knocking subsided, and he heard a pleasant buzzing on the other side. He tried to convince himself it sounded like a cat purring, but finally gave it up. It was a buzz.

Slowly, he opened the door and the buzz subsided to the threshold of his hearing. The orb hung there in front of him, motionless, the red at the center pulsating like a beating heart.

He stretched out his hands over the orb. The pulsating slowed down and became very, very slow. He let his hands descend slowly to the surface of the globe, almost but not quite, touching it. It emitted neither heat nor cold. This surprised Charles. He remembered how cold the doorknob had been the first time he opened the door. Also, he had expected the thing would be crackling with energy, or hot, or cold, or something. But it was nothing. Nothingness. That was the word. It was nothingness. How could that help his sister? He wanted to know. What was this thing? Why was it here? Why in his sister's closet? What connection did it have with her?

Slowly, cautiously, he let his fingertips drop to just above the orb. He remembered what had happened to the creatures he had dropped into it. But, he sensed that it would be different for him. Carefully, he let his fingertips touch what seemed to be the surface. It was a cloud, but it was perfectly round, and at a certain point he felt a slight tension, like the surface of water. He yanked his fingers back.

Interesting. Other than the slight tension he'd felt nothing. He looked at his fingertips carefully in the light given off by the orb. They seemed completely normal. Slowly, cautiously, he let his fingertips graze the surface once again. Nothing. Again he inspected his fingertips as well as he could in the dim light. Again they seemed normal. He took a deep breath. Okay, he thought, this time let's hold them in there.

He held his fingertips to the surface and kept them there. He heard his heart beating faster and he realized he was shivering. The globe began to buzz a little louder, but still, he felt nothing. Cautiously, he let his fingers sink lower into the globe of light. He sank his fingers into the first joint and he felt nothing. The excitement left him and he found himself becoming more detached and analytical about what he was doing. Coldness of mind was stealing into his awareness, and he discovered he rather liked it. Suddenly, he felt his fingers pushed out of the orb. It didn't bother him. The orb went dark, and the buzzing faded away. That was all for the night it seemed. He knew there would be more tomorrow night. He shut the closet door quietly, not noticing his sister's eyes staring at him from her bed. He went to the bedroom door. There was no point in staying in his sister's room. The thing wouldn't hurt her.

Not that it mattered.

From her bed, Tanya watched her brother leave.

Why, Charles, she thought. Why did you let it have you? Don't you see what it is? What terrible thing inside you brought it here? How long have you been seeking it? She was too tired to cry, too tired to protest.

But things were beginning to take shape in her mind. Things were beginning to occur to her. There was something, something very important, that she hadn't noticed. And she had to find out what it was. Quickly, before it was too late. Then, she fell asleep.

The next morning was cold. Charles bundled up when he awoke and took a walk out to the cave tree. Unexpectedly, it seemed to be dying. It did not upset him. It seemed fitting to him. Everything died. Sometimes sooner, like his sister, sometimes later, like this tree. It really made no difference. It was all hollow inside in the end. He felt a curious twinge of excitement rising up inside him. Things were opening up to him he hadn't ever imagined. No wonder God hadn't answered his prayers and healed his sister. Why should He? It really made no difference in the end, did it? Life and death were all the same.

Nothing.

It was exhilarating. A sense of power of knowledge was

growing in his stomach and spine. There were answers.

Yet, something soft and unappealing was tugging at him. A persistent warning was eating at him. Don't do this, it told him.

The two voices warred within him.

His heart beat faster and faster, and he did not notice the sky growing dark around him or the dropping temperature.

What was he to do? This feeling of power was something outside his experience. It felt wonderful. But the other voice said it was wrong.

Finally, he told himself, it's to help Tanya, and the matter was decided.

He felt empty inside. He felt that way the rest of the day until that evening when Father resumed the story.

Chapter 15

The Red Bishop Moves

Once back in Nana's room, Ta Ta related her brief conversation with her brother. The wizard stared grimly into the fire as she spoke. He sat on the stool, elbows on his knees, hands clasped together under his chin, his body hunched forward.

"As I expected," he said when she had finished. "It is the end game. But all we know is it involves the royal family and it's tomorrow night."

He ran his fingers through his hair in frustration.

"That's not enough!" he said. "We're playing a game and we only know where three of the pieces are. What else is on the board? Where are the other pieces?"

He slammed a fist on his knee.

"If there were only some way of getting the information."

"Begging your pardon, sire. There might be one way."

It was Emily, speaking nervously and timidly and looking, Ta Ta thought, very afraid.

The wizard looked up surprised and asked, "What way, Emily?"

Then, suddenly, he said, "No, Emily. Absolutely not. I won't hear of it."

"It's much too dangerous," protested Typhus.

"Please, sire, I don't mind. It has to be done," Emily pleaded.

"No," the wizard insisted. "Who knows how it will end up?"

"But," Emily countered, "it's much more dangerous not to know."

"What? What's too dangerous?" Ta Ta asked.

She saw her friends exchange secretive looks and Typhus said, "To leave this room, Princess."

"Exactly," said the wizard.

"But it must be done," said Emily, her eyes moist with passion.

Then Nana stood in front of Ta Ta with a tray of food, and the others drew apart and carried on their conversation in hushed whispers. Nana offered her a bowl of warm soup which she eagerly accepted. She suddenly realized how tired and hungry she was and how grateful to be in her father's castle once again. As to the others argument, she sensed it was not time for her to know their secret. She trusted them to tell her when they were ready. She felt sleepiness and fatigue overcoming her.

When she awoke the next morning all seemed normal. It was bright daylight. Typhus and Emily lay huddled in blankets on makeshift beds of straw. Nana was gone, obviously attending to her daily duties. Only the wizard was awake, slumped in a chair, his legs stretched out in front of him, his arms dangling, staring into the remains of the fire.

She had the impression he'd been sleeping in the chair and had only recently awoken. He heard her stirring and motioned for her to join him. She sat beside him in front of the fire, and as she warmed her hands, he spoke to her in a low voice.

"It's very much worse than I imagined. Typhus and Emily spent a very busy night. Griselle has spun her web everywhere, from the scullery to the highest reaches of the court. There is much talk of something happening tonight. Your brother was right on that point."

"But what?" asked Ta Ta.

"A general rebellion, but somehow a bloodless rebellion. There will be mostly a quiet takeover."

"How were they able to find all that out? They're strangers to the castle."

"They have their ways. Now, you must stay out of sight for the rest of the day. Attend to Emily. I'm afraid she's very ill. She's to have complete rest. I've prepared a special remedy for her. See to it that she takes it. Under no circumstances is she to have any other remedy. It's in that little pot by the fire. One teaspoon every two hours until it's all gone."

Ta Ta eagerly nodded her agreement, then asked, "Can we stop Griselle?"

The wizard stared into the fire again.

"It will be a narrow thing at best. Griselle holds the center of the board. Typhus and I will spend the day exploring. Perhaps, we can turn something up. Our only advantage is surprise which must be maintained at all costs. Do not answer the door. Speak to Emily only in whispers. When the fire goes out, leave it out. There must be nothing to arouse suspicion."

He turned his head to look at her, and a hint of excitement and hope appeared in his voice.

"I don't know what your brother is up to, but he appears to have remarkable presence of mind. Tonight we shall follow his hint, cut your hair and disguise you as him. I have absolutely no idea why, but perhaps, he does. Do you consent?"

"Of course. But why weren't these quarters watched if Griselle has so many spies? Why didn't they see us come in last night?"

"A hopeful oversight. I wonder if there isn't some power that blinds the wicked at crucial moments and leads to their downfall. It's quite arrogant of her. I suspect she mistakes Nana's simplicity and goodness for stupidity and doesn't bother to spy on her."

Typhus began to stir. He got up, covered Emily with his blanket, and joined them. Together, they ate a pot of stew which hung over the dying fire. He filled in the princess, naming the various spies in the palace and those who were loyal. Ta Ta was amazed at the ability of Typhus and Emily to gather so much information and was beginning to realize that wizardry was somehow involved. But, it was clear they didn't want to talk about it, almost as if they were somehow ashamed of their secret, so she made no attempt to penetrate the matter.

With breakfast done, the wizard hid his long red hair under a brown hat and cape. He covered his red robe with the cloak of a merchant and concealed most of his beard under the cloak. Typhus posed as his servant. They left, promising to be back after dark, but in time for the banquet.

Once out the door, the two began to wander about the huge castle. The wizard did his best to fight off a growing sense of despair. He had so far attempted to hide the depths of his misgivings from the others, though he was sure Typhus had no illusions about how vastly his master was overmatched by Griselle. Was this really to be his end? Had it all come down to this? What had he been thinking all these years? With brilliant clarity he now saw he'd only dabbled at wizardry. Basically, it had all been show. He had only skimmed the surface. What of his dream to discover the secrets of the universe? That had been lost to a desire for esteem, position and popularity--and he'd achieved none of these. And now, when he needed resources instead, he had none to draw upon.

A nagging part of his mind wanted to quit, to go back to the way things were. How was this his quarrel? It was unfair. As usual. He had been comfortable enough in the Fourth Kingdom. He could return and go back to the old routine. Make a go of it this time.

He shook off the notion. It appealed not a whit. Well, the old Rigirus was dead it seemed. Some sort of miracle had been wrought by the Princess in her own little way. And now, the new Rigirus was facing almost certain annihilation. And, almost certainly, for a lost cause. Strangely, it did not trouble him. For the first time in his life he felt inner peace. He had something he'd never had before; he had a noble purpose, something to strive for that was undeniably good and worthy. Something worthy of sacrifice, even the sacrifice of his own life. That noble purpose, he would not give up.

Moreover, he cared for what Typhus and Emily and Princess Ta Ta thought of him. He did not want to betray them. The idea of the hurt his betrayal would cause them was reason enough for him to stay.

His thoughts turned to Emily. So good, so simple, so brave. She was in great danger. There was something wrong with her formula. Her condition would not stabilize.

No matter how much he and Typhus jiggled the formula they could not get it to work as well as it had for Typhus. Typhus's reversions to his rat state were as predictable now as clock work. Better still, he could be maintained in a human state as long as necessary by added small dosages of the formula. And, he progressed steadily in his human state. He had developed a first rate intelligence, even, as the wizard had finally learned, making improvements in his formula on his own. He was phenomenally healthy and energetic. Emily was proving to be the opposite. Her reversions were still unpredictable, her intelligence only average and fundamentally simple and childlike. Perhaps worst of all, sometimes when she returned to a rat state, she kept her human size. If she reverted at the wrong time, in the wrong place, before humans, as she did in the camp that night, she would probably be instantly killed. Still, she was undeniably sweet and, while she seemed resigned to her eventual permanent return to ratdom, Typhus could not bear to lose her. And neither, the wizard had to admit, could he.

So, best to take stock of his arsenal and develop some semblance of a plan. First, what did he have? Prince Cha Cha had obviously managed to retain some sort of self control. The corollary was that Griselle had some means of controlling minds. Typhus and Emily had both reported that the conversations of the rebels had been singularly dull and unexcited. Actually uninterested, as if little was at stake. Therefore, if that control could be broken, perhaps, the back of the rebellion could be broken as well. Or, if Griselle were eliminated, so too, was the control. Therefore, the need to maintain control was her weak point. Also, they still had the element of surprise. He doubted if Griselle had more than an inkling of his existence. Certainly, his career had never come close to matching hers, so there was no reason for her to pay attention to it.

But, there was the rub. Her power was legendary among wizards and magicians. She had much more than the best fireworks which so bedazzled the populace. She was rumored to be a shape shifter with the ability to transform herself into an animal almost at will. Moreover, it was said she could change the weather, mix devastatingly effective love potions, make the barren fertile, increase or decrease crop yields, ensure wealth to merchants and power to princes and all in ways that made it clear it was her spells and potions, and not coincidence, that did the trick.

All of these, of course, were the standard truck of wizards, but no one had the reputation for results that the Wizard of Fandon did. As for himself, well, he'd tried, but his results had been mixed at best. Indeed, no one, least of all himself, was really sure it was his efforts that produced the results. Too much time usually elapsed before the event and sometimes even opposite effects seemed to be the result. Hence, payment was often slow in coming, if it came at all. Of gratitude, there was none.

So, why had Griselle left Fandon? Nasty rumors had circulated. Fandon had become a kingdom of strife, contention, rivalry and jealousy. The more successful the Wizard of Fandon was, the unhappier the kingdom seemed to become. It seemed the happiest kingdom of all was the Seventh Kingdom where there was no wizard at all. The notion made him uncomfortable, but then Typhus caught his attention with a gentle nudge.

"Please pay attention, sire. That fat fellow in the blue jerkin. Don't look."

"Oh, what? Yes, of course not. What about him?"

"He's one of the traitors."

The wizard made a pretext of studying the wares in the

market square. Unobtrusively, he observed the man. A stout, powerful man, he kept a stall in the market where he sold leather goods. He seemed uninterested in selling his goods. He went through the motions, but there was no keenness when approached by customers. There was no bustling, no eagerness to please. The wizard noted the eyes. Nana's phrase for the Prince had been apt. It was as though there were closed shutters over his eyes.

"Do you notice his eyes, Typhus?"

Typhus pretended to examine a piece of stained glass.

"Aye, sire. They're all like that."

They moved on, taking a slow stroll through the city. Once you knew the trick, it wasn't that difficult to spot them, the wizard noted with a sigh of relief. The numbers were disquieting, but if you kept careful tally, they were not overwhelming. Still, it must require considerable resources to keep them all under control. Perhaps, that was why Griselle was not waiting to acquire more rebels. Perhaps, she was at the limit of her powers. It was a ray of encouragement. They made a thorough sweep, from the shops, to the smithies, to the stables, to the open air market, to the ale houses and to the residential lanes. Her people, he observed, were not necessarily in key positions. But, of course, they would be if she took power. Still, she would need a few key players to pull off her power play. Would they be as easy to spot at court? The wizard hoped so.

Still, what could he do? Although he hadn't told the others, he'd given up all intention of going head to head with Griselle in a duel of wizardry. If he knew the secret of secrets, the unifying principle, perhaps, that would give him an edge.

But he didn't.

The outcome of a duel was certain destruction.

"Do you think she'll be all right, sire?"

The wizard looked at Typhus. He was studying some rings and bracelets with a worried look. He was asking about Emily, of course. No, the wizard didn't think she'd be all right, but he wasn't about to give up on her. He put a reassuring hand on Typhus's shoulder.

"If she can hold out until this unpleasantness is over, we can put all our attention on her. Then, perhaps, between the two of us, there's a chance."

He felt a twinge of guilt that he had not been more encouraging, but Typhus was nodding his head firmly, so it seemed to be helpful.

"Go ahead and buy her that bracelet," the wizard said. "It'll cheer her up and that's the sort of medicine she needs right now."

They were both so intent on the happiness of the purchase they failed to notice the dull, shuttered eyes of the woman who sold it to them.

They continued to wander the streets, and when they had surveyed as much as they could, with the fading daylight, they made their way for Nana's lodging. Each was tired and wrapped in his own reverie, Typhus thinking about Emily and the wizard about how to defeat Griselle. As they neared the quarter where Nana lived the wizard noted the sun was setting and the moon had appeared already. The streets themselves were in deep shadow. As they passed through the center of a small courtyard, a sudden gust of wind blew the wizard's hat off. Without thinking, he plunged off in pursuit, not noticing that Typhus, lost in his own thoughts, did not see or follow him. He reached down to pick it up when another gust sent it skittering out of his grasp. He ran after it again and another gust sent it into a dark alleyway. Without hesitating, he sprang after it and grabbed it. Satisfied, he put his hat on and adjusted it snugly. He turned to go, but an ox cart pulled up in front of the alley and blocked it. Suddenly, a dim light from behind him lit up the alley. He turned around and saw an open doorway, which was the source of the light, at the end of the alley. He stared, dumbfounded, sensing that he had fallen into a trap. A dark, regal, feminine silhouette stepped into the doorway. A soft, crooning voice drifted over to him.

"You know you have to face me sometime. Why not now?"

***

After his parents had gone to sleep, Charles stole down the hallway to his sister's room. She eyed him warily when he entered but said nothing. Charles realized he had nothing to say and only nodded at her, then curled up on the foot of the bed.

Tanya didn't know what to do. Part of her wanted to save Charles from what she suspected he was going to do. But that same part that loved him was also increasingly repelled by him. She wanted to kick him out of the room and keep him from the closet. But, she sensed the futility of it. This thing had to be dealt with. For some reason her brother had to confront it. Why it was in her closet and not his eluded her. One way or another he must face this. And there was another reason. She was simply too frightened when he was not there. She couldn't bear the thought of going back to being alone with it at night. Even if she was sure now it was not there for her, it scared her, and she was relieved to have her brother on the foot of the bed.

Slowly, her eyes shut and she faded into her dream.

She passed through the valley of fairy lights. She was no longer afraid of the dark window and let herself be drawn up to it without any resistance. She hung there in front of the window. There was no sense of being trapped now.

Cautiously, she let herself float into the center of the room. A feeling of complete peace came over her. The darkness comforted her. She rested within it and let it wash over her and soothe her. Her feeling of safety and comfort was complete. She lost all sense of time and had no idea how long she floated there.

Then, she felt something uneasy stir within her. This wasn't complete, something was missing. She looked about and saw something she hadn't seen before. A door.

Charles waited until he was sure his sister was asleep. He sensed she knew he was up to something, but it didn't matter. He was doing it for her so it was okay. When she was asleep he snuck back to his room and got a jar out from under his bed. He hurried back to his sister's room. After checking again to make sure she was still asleep, he went to the closet and slowly opened it. He took a little garden snake from a jar and held it over the gaseous orb. A snake's not really an animal he told himself. It's a reptile. Strangely, the snake did not seem frightened at all. He let it go and it fell straight into the circle all the way through and disappeared without any sign of a struggle and without being tossed up and down like the mouse and the spider. Charles felt unsettled but vindicated. Just like he thought. It wasn't an animal.

He stood in front of the orb and wondered what to do next. He thought about just sticking his fingers in again, but somehow it didn't seem like enough. So he began to speak to it in a whisper, being careful to keep his voice low enough that Tanya couldn't hear.

"Listen, thing, whoever, whatever you are."

The buzzing stopped completely and the slow pulsing of the red center slowed. As it slowed, Charles felt himself becoming heavy and lethargic.

"I don't know why you're here. But you're different. You're way different. So, I figure you must know how to help my sister."

The pulsing of the light and the buzzing stopped entirely. Charles became afraid the thing would go away and began to hurry his words.

"You've got to help her. I mean, nobody else will. So, go ahead. I mean, what do you want?"

There seemed to be nothing more to say. So, he put his hands over the cloud and let his fingers in.

Nothing.

He slowly put in his hands down to the wrists. He began to feel excited and realized he was sweating. The red center began to pulsate again. He pushed in his forearms, and a strange tingling warmth flooded up his arms to his shoulders. He put in his arms up to his elbows.

His fingers were now touching the pulsing, shining red center.

The tingling warmth flooded past his arms into his chest, stomach and head in waves that matched the pulsing of the red center. He felt almost unconscious, light and weightless as if he was falling and tumbling in space. Then, he panicked, pulled his arms out and shook his head to clear it.

He realized he was setting on the floor, legs outstretched, his arms supporting him from falling. Mentally numb and shaking, he got up, closed the closet door and curled up on his sister's bed and fell asleep.

He dreamed he was back in the field with the kites.

Tanya's kite hadn't drifted off. It was still there. The

tiniest white speck against the blue. As he stared at it, it seemed to become larger. He concentrated and he began to pull the kite back with his thoughts. It was becoming larger, coming closer and closer to them but Tanya was shouting at him, tugging at him, trying to stop him. Why? Couldn't she see what he was doing?

The next morning he woke up well before his alarm went off and went back to his room. He felt keenly alert. Everything seemed more intense, vivid, possessed of an energy. Even his hearing was more acute. Clearly, then, the creature was a good thing.

He remembered a slightly wilted flower in a vase in the hallway. He left his room, went softly to the flower, and touched it with his finger. He half expected, more than half actually, that the flower would blossom back to life.

It didn't.

But, it didn't wither completely away either, like he'd seen on a TV show when some vampire or something like that had touched a plant, like it should have if the creature were a bad thing.

Nevertheless, Charles was nonplused and a trifle disappointed. He felt that he had made some sort of deal with the creature. He had made it his friend and had let it do whatever it did when he touched it, and it should therefore help him cure his sister. But he didn't worry about it. He found he was ravenously hungry and made himself a huge breakfast.

Later, he went to his tree. Tanya didn't want to go which he put off to her illness. When he got there, he saw the tree was dying faster than he imagined possible. The wood was actually splitting. He looked inside the hole and saw the inside was crawling with insects. Termites he supposed, but he wasn't really sure.

He had a sudden urge to try his hand at healing again.

He put his hand on the tree. He held it there, closed his eyes and concentrated hard. The insects inside the tree began to buzz loudly. At last, he opened his eyes, stepped back and looked. The tree looked the same. He closed his eyes again, put his hand back on the tree and this time spoke as he held it there.

"Thing, whatever you are, where ever you're from, please heal this tree. Just like you're going to heal my sister. Please."

The buzzing became very loud. He stepped back from the tree. Still no change.

He went into a sudden fury and he kicked the tree several times and stomped off, heading back for the house. On the way he calmed down. Maybe it takes time, he thought. Maybe it takes days or even weeks.

Despite his newly regained appetite, Charles found dinner unsatisfactory that night. He couldn't put his finger on it, but everything tasted slightly off. The food looked somehow waxy and unreal. Strangely enough, his parents skin also seemed slightly waxy and unreal. It made him glad that his sister was eating her special meal in her room. If his parents looked that bad, he hated to think of how bad her illness would make her look to him.

Maybe that was why he was so surprised when he saw her at story time. For now, the pallor of her skin and her drawn face struck him as exceedingly beautiful.

Chapter 16

The Black Queen Moves

"He couldn't have just disappeared!" Ta Ta said.

She felt a panic rising within her. She hadn't realized how much she had come to depend on the wizard. Once again, she just wanted to go back to being a little girl.

"I don't know. He was there, then he was gone," Tyhpus said.

"Think! That's not possible."

Typhus was sitting on a stool, clutching his hair in his fingers, his face torn with remorse.

"I know. I know. It was just very windy all of a sudden."

"Wind? I heard no wind today."

They both had the same thought.

"Griselle!" Typhus said as he sprang up, his remorse now replaced by anger.

"But how?" Ta Ta asked.

"It doesn't matter, Princess. The important thing is, she knows something's up. Our surprise is gone."

"Will Rigirus talk?"

"Who knows if he has the power to resist, Princess. Maybe he can hold out until the banquet. That will have to do."

Princess Ta Ta sat down, trying hard not to, but beginning to lose her composure. She fought back a sob and said "What do we do now?"

Suddenly, she felt a gentle, reassuring grip on her shoulder.

"We do exactly as planned."

Ta Ta looked up in disbelief. It was Emily who spoke. All day she'd been sick in bed, cuddled up, kept warm by Ta Ta who piled blankets on her and spooned her medicine to her and held her hand. Now, she was up, face drawn and pale, but resolute.

"You shouldn't be up," Ta Ta protested.

"I have to be up."

"Should we go through with the plan?" Ta Ta asked. "What if Rigirus gives it away?"

Emily answered, her voice barely above a whisper, "What if he is counting on us to keep it?"

Ta Ta and Typhus fell silent.

"Your brother is counting on us to follow his hint," Emily continued. "We must trust Rigirus, and we must hope that he trusts us."

About this same time, Rigirus was seated comfortably in a soft, high backed chair in a large, underground room. Facing him, sat Griselle on a tall throne like chair which sat upon a raised platform. He had followed her out of the alley rather than try to escape. He had sensed resistance would be futile. Besides, if Griselle knew they were there, he reasoned it was better to confront her directly rather than run away. He must find out what she knew and keep her occupied and hope the others could muster the resources to do without him. It was a desperate gamble, but he knew there was no other way.

Since he'd been with her, Griselle had been eyeing him closely, playing cat and mouse, keeping up a crooning stream of inane chatter about how she planned to redo the castle once she took over. Apparently, she now felt she'd sufficiently studied her victim, for she leaned forward, smiled and spoke.

"So, tell me, Rigirus, how did you plan to stop me?"

Rigirus smiled back.

"You know my name."

She laughed what she apparently thought was a pleasant laugh.

"Of course. I know all about all the wizards of the Seven Higher Kingdoms. And the Lower and the Middle. Especially, such a great wizard as yourself."

The last statement was delivered perfectly. It was intended not as flattery but as insult. Odd, thought the wizard. Two weeks ago that remark would have crushed him, but now, it had absolutely no effect. But, keep her busy and play games if that was what she wanted.

"Griselle, you honor me. I had no idea you considered me a great wizard."

She laughed again, this time with no pretense at pleasantness.

"But, of course, I don't. You are the laughingstock of the entire Seven Kingdoms."

In spite of himself, he laughed.

"And the Lower and the Middle?" he asked.

Griselle bridled, and he cursed himself for his lack of

control. He should have pretended to be hurt. Conceal as much as possible.

"Your meager reputation does not reach that far," she said.

He managed to appear crestfallen. That seemed to mollify her a little.

"Perhaps, you lacked proper instruction. Who was your teacher, Rigirus?"

Rigirus shrugged his shoulders. Perhaps, an honest answer would be best here.

"I'm largely self taught."

Her mouth fell open in astonishment.

"Self taught!" she gasped. Then she laughed uproariously. It wasn't pleasant, but this time it was genuine.

"What did you do, Rigirus? Read books?" She was shaking her head in disbelief.

"It seemed the best way."

"Best way? Best way? It's no way at all. It's impossible to learn anything without a master to apprentice yourself to. No wonder you're so pathetic."

Easy, thought Rigirus. Let her enjoy herself.

"I thought the books were rather interesting."

"Interesting?" She slapped one hand loudly against the arm of her chair. She seemed horribly irritated. "Those were the most boring books in the world. It's all mumbo jumbo without someone to explain it to you."

Ah, thought Rigirus. A weakness. Difficult reading, yes. But boring mumbo jumbo? Most definitely, no.

She stood up, her voice threatening.

"Did you really think you could best me in a magic duel?"

Of course, that was by now the farthest thing from his mind, but he saw no point in letting her know that.

"The thought had crossed my mind."

She laughed again and sat back down.

"Crossed your mind? Tell me, did this ever cross your mind?"

She closed her eyes and wind began to blow, gently at first, then picking up intensity. Faster and faster it blew until he was forced back in his chair, and the chair itself began to slide across the room. Despite the fury of the wind, he forced himself to stay observant, and he noticed that the wind blew only on him and the chair—the rest of the room was completely still. It stopped when his chair came to a rest against the wall.

Griselle eyed him with contempt.

"You're too far away. Come back here," she said waving her hand in a summoning motion.

At high speed the chair sped back to its original spot and stopped so abruptly Rigirus was tossed to the floor. He got slowly to his knees, then his feet, all the time making a great show of dusting himself off in an attempt to hide his fear.

"Oh, are we dusty?" Griselle crooned. "Some water to wash you off then."

She snapped her fingers and, out of nowhere, water drenched down upon the wizard's head, leaving him soaked. Her laugh now became a cackle.

"Oh, you made a mess washing yourself, little Rigirus. Let Mama dry you off."

An intense, blazing heat surrounded him, a heat so intense he was sure he would suffocate or burst into flames. When it became so terrible he thought he would scream, it abruptly ended. Slowly, he came back to his senses and found he was completely dry.

He looked at Griselle's eyes. They were triumphant,

gloating, but—what else? Applause, he realized. She wants applause. Just like the rest of us. So, he shook his head side to side as if in grudging respect and began to clap his hands.

"Bravo! Bravo, Griselle. Marvelous. I've never seen anything so brilliant."

Griselle looked startled. It wasn't the reaction she'd expected, but she did seem pleased at the appreciation. She nodded her head at him. "It's only a small part of my repertoire."

"Oh, I believe you."

He ambled over to her dais and sat down on the edge with his back to her. He took his hat off and played with its brim as he spoke.

"Why, Griselle?"

"Why what?"

"Why do you destroy when you could create? You could do so much good."

"Oh, posh. You know the answer to that. We all become wizards for the same reason."

"And what is that reason?"

"Power. Pure and simple."

The wizard sighed. Yes, he'd been guilty of that. But there had been another reason.

"What about loneliness, Griselle?"

"Loneliness? You sound like old Sarnus."

"Who?" he asked, keeping his voice as flat as possible.

"You never heard of him, Rigirus? He was my master. Marvelous wizard and magician but too sentimental. Made him so easy to manipulate."

"But, you must be doing these things out of lack, out of need."

"Oh, you are weak! So was he. You do not understand

the desire to bend others to your will, to dominate, to subdue."

He half turned and looked up at her, searching her face for some clue to help him understand.

"There's no satisfaction in hurting others," he said.

"Oh, but there's tremendous satisfaction in it. However, you're missing the real point."

"Which is?"

"Which is, I choose to do it."

"But your wizardry brought you sufficient income, I'm sure."

"Income is not enough. Beyond a certain point, it's only a symbol. I want to dominate others. Just because I want to, Rigirus. I will not sacrifice that desire so I can feel warm and syrupy inside."

"And how much is enough, Griselle?"

"That's the great secret, Rigirus. There is no enough. For anybody. And aren't we all grateful for that?"

She shook her head and studied her fingernails.

"I don't know about you, Rigirus. Asking how much is enough, worrying about hurting others. That is weakness."

"No, Griselle, that is strength."

She shrieked in amusement.

"You sound just like Sarnus. You know what he thought? He thought my problem was that I was unloved. I bet you were thinking the same thing."

He nodded and said, "I confess, I was thinking along those lines."

"You know what I think?" Griselle said, leaning forward and poking him in the shoulder with her finger. "I think it was you and old Sarnus that were unloved. Love. That's your big answer to everything isn't it?"

He smiled regretfully and nodded again.

"Yes, I suppose so."

She returned to admiring her nails while she spoke.

"Me, I've had plenty of love. Doting pappa, tender mama, lot's of security. But, they couldn't buy everything for, or give everything to, their little Griselle that she wanted. Little Griselle didn't like that. So, when little Griselle became big Griselle, she set about rectifying the situation. How many men have thought they could save me by offering me love? Fools! Don't they know that every beautiful woman, and plenty of not so beautiful ones, gets all the offers of love she wants. Griselle's had plenty of love. Griselle likes power better."

The wizard expelled a weary breath and shook his head sadly.

"So, Griselle, there is to be no peace between us?"

"That, Rigirus, is up to you."

So at last, they had come to the real business. Easy, Rigirus, he told himself. Move your pieces carefully.

"What do you mean, Griselle?"

"What is the Queen's plan?"

He hid his jubilation. She didn't know about the Princess and thought the Queen had imported him. It stood to reason she would be more alert to that possibility. Best to answer with the truth.

"I cannot tell you that."

"Why not? She obviously brought you here to try your magic upon me. You should give her money back. That, would be a sign of your love."

"I'm afraid I can't do that."

"Ha! See, we're not so very different. Join forces with me, and I'll teach you some real wizardry. Not enough to topple me, of course. I'm not the fool Sarnus was. But enough wizardry to get you money and respect. Not to mention power. Come on, you know that's what you really want. Everybody does. Even that sanctimonious king and queen. Always prattling about the good of the people. Hypocrites. It's all for their own good if you ask me. At least, I'm honest."

"And what do I have to do?"

"Say you'll join forces and have a cup of wine with me. It's very simple really."

"You barely know me. How do you know I won't try to betray you?"

"Those who are honest about their need for power, know who to trust and who not to trust."

The change in her voice told him she was lying. He was sure the wine must be drugged and also had a strong intuition that it was the key to her control. And, for some reason, people had to consent to drink it. Otherwise, she could have called her henchmen, who were doubtlessly lurking well within earshot, and had them force it down his throat. And, if the Prince were still capable of resisting, then he must have given only partial consent. Did he dare to pretend to consent? Wasn't he being coerced? Wouldn't he be able to still maintain a partial control?

"Just a tiny, little sip, Rigirus. That's all, just one," she crooned.

Just one sip. Then this potion must be very, very powerful, he reasoned. Better not to give even partial consent. Better to risk all. He shook his head, stood up, dusted himself off with his hat and turned to face Griselle.

"It's a tempting offer. You must have some fantastic machines."

Griselle looked as if she'd been slapped in the face.

"Machines?"

"Yes, yes, wind machine, hidden tracks for the chair,

tiny trap door up there for the water, forced heat apparatus. I'd really like to see that one."

Griselle was on her feet.

"Machines? Cheap tricks? You think I use cheap tricks?"

"Cheap? Good heavens, no. They must have cost you a fortune. I doubt if you're still in any position to pay me as much as the Queen."

Griselle's face turned red, and she trembled with rage.

"I do not use cheap tricks! What about the wind that blew your hat off and led you to the alley?"

He chuckled.

"Coincidence, Griselle. Don't try that on me."

"Coincidence? How was I going to get you down here?"

"Obvious. You were going to present yourself in the doorway and entice me over."

"What!"

Griselle shrieked so loudly it hurt his ears, but he pressed on.

"Oh, yes, I daresay you were quite the looker in your day. And, in the shadows, I suppose you still entice your share. But," he looked her slowly up and down, ignoring her cold beauty, and said, "well, let's just say you're lucky the wind blew my hat over there."

Griselle was so enraged she forgot all about her magic and flew at him with her fingernails. Rigirus caught her forearms in his hands and laughed in her face. It was dangerous, but he wanted her too mad to think clearly. Indeed, she couldn't even speak but just emitted a series of shrill shrieks. He heard footsteps running up behind him and then found himself being pulled away. Too bad he hadn't had time to kill her, he thought. It would have solved everything neatly.

Her hands free, Griselle slapped him hard across the face. Then, she brought the same hand back across his face in a backhand slap and once again in a forehand slap. It hurt, but the wizard exulted inside. Good. She wasn't thinking straight, she was wasting valuable time, and she still had no idea of the existence of Ta Ta or Emily. There was still hope.

Griselle pulled away from him and sat down on the edge of her chair, her hair in disarray and a wild look on her face. Her eyes were unfocused, and her jaw hung open. Her jaw began to shake and, suddenly, she spoke.

"Take him away and kill him."

The guards began to hustle him off which was fine by him. He wasn't a great wizard, but he could handle these two dolts when he had them alone away from her.

"Wait!" she cried. She had stood up and was pounding a fist angrily against her thigh. A light seemed to have gone on in her eyes.

"Ooh, you think you're a clever one don't you? Well, Sarnus thought he was clever too. I fixed him and now I'll fix you."

She began to pace about her dais and kept pounding her fist against her thigh. Rigirus saw she was still distraught and trying to think. Suddenly, she grabbed a little box out of her sleeve and took a tiny white pill out and advanced on him.

"Hold him still," she commanded her lackeys.

She forced the pill into his mouth and held it shut until she was sure the pill had time to dissolve. Then she said, "Clever are you? Let's see how the Queen likes it when she sees me with you. And let's see how you like it when you and she die together. For treason."

***

That night, in Tanya's bedroom, Charles began to talk.

"What's it like being sick?"

"It's just there."

"I think I know what you mean," he said.

"About what?"

"About not minding dying."

Tanya shivered. She'd been wondering how to explain it to Charles. Now that he said he understood, it frightened her.

"What do you mean?" she asked.

"I mean maybe death is a beautiful thing, a good thing, like you said."

"I didn't say it was good. I said I didn't mind."

"If it's not good, how come you don't mind?"

"Because it just is. I didn't plan it. It's just happening, so I don't mind."

"It's not fair," he insisted.

"Just because it's happening to me instead of someone else doesn't make it unfair."

"I didn't say it would be fair if it was someone else."

"If it was someone else would you care?"

Charles shrugged. This was too complicated. He tried another tack.

"What if I died too?"

"Charles!"

His sister was staring at him in shock.

"Why not?" he asked. "Maybe it's beautiful."

Suddenly, Tanya was his big sister again and had him pinned to the bed, one hand around his throat, the other holding his head down by his hair.

"Listen you little twerp, you stop thinking like that right

now, or I'll beat your brains in."

"Why don't you mind," he gasped.

"Because it's just the way things are. I'm not making it happen."

"But you want it to happen."

"Do not!"

"Do too! You want out," he said and, tearing himself away from her, ran out of the room.

Tanya fell back on the bed exhausted and breathless. Inside she was sick. Was Charles right? Did she want to die? Did she just want to escape the effort of living? Was she really trying to evade something? That would be wrong. But she accepted dying. That was what was beautiful. Not really caring. She didn't want to go back to caring. The uncaring made it all bearable.

Chapter 17

Endgame

"Do you remember where we left off? Do you remember how Griselle had forced a pill into Rigirus's throat?"

Tanya and Charles both nodded. How could they forget?

"And do you remember how, before that Ta Ta and Typhus were ready to give up but didn't."

"It was Emily, Daddy."

"That's right. It was Emily. And do you know why?"

"Why, Dad?"

'That's what we're going to find out tonight. It was like this."

***

In the meantime, while Rigirus was confronting Griselle, Ta Ta, with the help of Emily and Nana, had cut her hair to match Cha Cha's and disguised herself as a serving page. Underneath the page's outfit she wore the blue doublet her brother had mentioned. Nana removed the white piping so it would be identical to the one her brother would wear. But, how to hide her face until the right moment? Nana procured a black wig to hide Ta Ta's blonde hair and with cotton placed under her lips to distort her mouth they hoped it was enough to disguise her face from the casual observer. The dinner and entertainment, also, should provide enough distraction to keep anyone from paying her much attention. Emily and Typhus were dressed as servants. They would all keep close to Nana who as governess to Cha Cha, while not part of the banquet, would be expected to be close by in the wings.

Before they left, Ta Ta made sure Emily took her remedy. Then she took the remainder from the pot and poured it into a small vial, sealed it and handed it to Emily.

"There's only one dose left. Make sure you take it."

"There's no worry, of that, Princess. It means ever so much to me."

Then they left and Nana let them through the scullery and kitchen and hence to the banquet room. Ta Ta and Typhus had wanted Emily to remain in bed, resting, but she had insisted, logically enough, that now that Rigirus was probably a captive of Griselle she felt safer with them. And moreover, she wanted so much to see a grand royal banquet while there was still time, and who knew but what she might be of some use.

The part about "while there was still time" disturbed Ta Ta, but a glance from Typhus warned her not to pursue the matter. Besides, with Rigirus gone, she found the presence of Emily comforting. So, they all made their way to the servers section of the royal banquet room, to the end of the royal dais upon which the royal family and favorites would eat.

The banquet room was filled with light, color and music. A large square of tables around the room seated the highest nobles. The interior of the square was filled with tables of lesser nobility. These tables within the square were placed in lines parallel to the dais. The ladies wore their finest silks and satins and the men their formal festive attire. Emily was quite taken with the scene and clutched Ta Ta's hand tightly, oohing and aahing with the arrival of every lady of the court, each of which seemed to be more gorgeously dressed than the last.

Ta Ta, of course, had seen all this before and was not so easily impressed. She was anxiously awaiting the arrival of the royal family. Would they recognize her and give her away? And what did her brother have in mind? "Be ready to do whatever needs doing." Did he have a plan? Had Rigirus compromised them? Their lives were in the balance. So she stayed as inconspicuous as possible, sandwiched between Typhus and Emily and trying to see out between them from the shadows. She wanted to see without being seen, fearful that her disguise was not good enough. Indeed, Nana stood away from her, worried that someone might make the connection if they stood together.

Then, at last, there was a blare of trumpets and the royal family was announced. In they came, in stately procession. Princess Ta Ta sank back into the shadows. As much as she longed to run and throw herself into her parents' arms she knew this was not the time. But, she did want to get her brother's attention and let him know she was there. He might be counting on it.

Other servers took the food and wine to the royal family and guests. Ta Ta and her companions merely served the servers. Typhus carved meat, Ta Ta poured wine from casks into flasks and Emily refilled plates of delicacies. Emily started to curtsey to the servers, as they were so splendidly dressed, but a quick word from Ta Ta and a stern look from Typhus stopped her. Besides controlling Emily's propensity to ooh and aah at all the beautiful costumes and curtsey at every opportunity, Ta Ta also kept a careful watch on the royal family. Her brother seemed indifferent, gazing into space as if nothing important was happening. But her father truly worried her. He seemed agitated, miserable, tense and uncertain, as if his mind held black, unpleasant thoughts.

Finally, her father's face brightened as he looked across the room. He smiled broadly, and as Ta Ta followed his gaze, she frowned. Advancing across the room was Griselle with an equally broad smile of her own. Then, Ta Ta, Typhus and Emily all gasped at once, for escorting Griselle, arm in arm, was Rigirus.

As they came into the hall, Rigirus was surprised that he could walk so well. Griselle had removed his hat and the disguise he had on over his red robe, but that didn't really affect the way he walked. He felt heavy and slow, and his vision was distorted, as if looking through the bottom of a glass. He tried to speak once or twice, but the effort was so great he gave up. Still, he walked well enough, with Griselle supporting him while pretending to be on his arm. His thinking was as heavy and slow as his attempts at speech. He kept swallowing and taking big gulps of air in an effort to clear his head which seemed to amuse her, for he could hear her chuckling to herself. It was peculiar that his hearing was so acute. Indeed, all the sounds were crystal clear and so loud that it was maddening. Desperately, he strove not to give way to the drug entirely but to retain some presence of mind. He did this by trying to deduce what drug he had been given. After running through a list of the different drugs he knew of, this occupied him all the way from where he had been drugged to the banquet room, he decided he knew of nothing that fit. It must be some sort of combination.

He was about to try deducing the combination when he noticed they had halted. He attempted to peer ahead. Dimly, he perceived blurs, with golden heads up above him. He heard every word clearly, however.

"My Queen, allow me to present my very special guest and dear friend, Rigirus, great wizard of the Fourth Higher Kingdom."

He heard the malice and triumph in Griselle's voice.

"Rigirus, the Seventh Higher Kingdom bids you welcome."

The Queen's voice was stiffly formal, full of distaste for any friend of Griselle, but if Griselle was hoping for shock or dismay, she was disappointed.

Rigirus remembered he was supposed to bow, and feeling no pain, he bowed very deeply, his forehead touching his knees. He wanted to say something grand and eloquent, but it seemed like too much trouble, so he just said "Likewise I'm sure," only, since his speech was slurred, it came out "Lahws a shus."

He said this while his forehead was still touching his knees and would have stayed there all night if Griselle hadn't pulled him up by the collar and led him away.

"She pretended not to recognize you," she hissed.

"Sh veah clv…clv…clva."

"She doesn't fool me at all."

"Y smah enbdy."

Back at the serving table Ta Ta and her companions watched Rigirus in horrified fascination. It was obvious to her, and she was sure it was obvious to the others, that he was drugged. What had he told Griselle in that condition? She gulped and shrank back a step when she felt a reassuring hand on her shoulder. She looked up and it was Emily. Back of Emily stood Typhus, with his hands on her shoulders. They were right, Ta Ta realized. We have to take our chances and see this thing through.

Prince Cha Cha meanwhile, had noticed his sister as soon as he had entered the room. When he was seated he noted with approval that she stayed in the shadows. Not that it mattered. And, something else that didn't matter caught his eye. Those two, standing next to her, were obviously friends of hers. Where did she get them? What were they competent for? Was the man a soldier? Was the woman a spy? And who on earth was this strange, bright red creature Griselle drug in? And why was she showing him off like some sort of trophy? He was missing something here, but what?

Moreover, did any of these people have a plan? He'd told his sister to be ready to do whatever needs doing, so she and her friends would probably be waiting for him to implement his plan. The problem was, he didn't have one. Not that it mattered, he insisted to himself, as he felt a spark of excitement within him threaten to burst into flame. It doesn't really matter, but Griselle seems to be fully occupied with the guest and something else. He couldn't feel the presence of the mind probes like he normally did. Doesn't matter, doesn't matter he repeated, but what if, he began to wonder.

From her position way down past the end of the table,

Ta Ta caught the change in her brother's demeanor. She was both encouraged and alarmed. Encouraged, because she was sure he'd spotted her and was beginning to implement his plan. Alarmed, because the change in his face was so obvious. Surely, Griselle would notice that. She looked for Griselle and saw her and Rigirus making their way down the long line of diners on the dais. It was a slow process because it was crowded, and Rigirus kept bumping into people and chairs. Then, he would insist on making a deep bow and a long, slurred apology. Sometimes he apologized to the people and sometimes to their chairs. Griselle prodded, pushed and pulled him along, but everyone knew she had brought him, since she'd made such a big show of introducing him to the Queen, and so he was a terrible reflection on her, and so everyone he bothered with one of his apologies, she had to apologize to for his clumsy apology and, although Ta Ta couldn't be sure, it seemed that Griselle was trying to pretend that inviting Rigirus wasn't really her idea but hadn't really worked out a good lie to explain him away. At any rate, by the time they got half way to their seats the entire banquet room was laughing at them, except for the Queen, who only smiled serenely at her plate. Griselle finally gave up trying to explain Rigirus and pushed, tugged and pulled for all she was worth the last third of the way. But Rigirus seemed insensible to her efforts and insisted on making all his apologies. In the meantime, Griselle's face became red and sweaty and tears made her makeup run. When they finally reached their seats, Griselle dropped into her chair beside Cha Cha and, with her elbows on the table, buried her face in her hands.

From her post at the serving station, Ta Ta thought she saw a smirk quickly appear and disappear on Rigirus's lips.

Well done, Rigirus, she thought.

Well done, whoever you are, thought Prince Cha Cha. And, not that it matters, he also thought, but now I have a plan.

Abruptly, Griselle's face came up out of her hands. Ta Ta gasped. She'd never seen Griselle unmasked before. Her face was red, her lips pulled back in a snarl, her eyes wolf-like. She was glaring at the Queen as if she were somehow to blame for her humiliation. Without warning, the face disappeared and the mask was on again. Slowly, the red left her face and she resumed the crooning voice. A quick look in her highly polished, silver goblet's mirror-like surface, a few quick, expert flicks of her fingers, and both makeup and hair were swiftly repaired.

Griselle began to daintily eat her food while indulging in inconsequential table talk with some of the other diners. Then she turned to the Queen and said, in a voice loud enough to be heard by everyone on the dais and in the front rows of the hall, "So my Queen isn't it a most magical evening? Almost enchanting wouldn't you say?"

The Queen's fork stopped in midair and a perplexed look came over her face, but she answered, "Yes, I suppose it is."

"As enchanted as you had hoped?" Griselle pursued in her sweetest croon.

The Queen looked even more perplexed. Then she smiled and gave a courteous, courtly answer, which meant nothing and was obviously intended to end this strange conversation.

"I'm sure it will be the most enchanted evening of all before it is over."

Ta Ta saw Griselle suddenly tense up and fall silent. She began picking at her food, and after a moment of looking down at her plate, her eyes began to furtively dart about the crowd. Ta Ta guessed the meaning. She thinks Rigirus was brought here by my mother. That explains the questions, and because of my mother's answer, she thinks there may be more wizards in the crowd.

This was good. It meant she didn't know about the rest of them and would be distracted looking for other wizards. The bad part was she might spot Ta Ta herself while she was looking about. She shrank deeper into the shadows and kept Emily and Typhus in front of her.

Rigirus, too, noticed the questions and the change in Griselle's demeanor. Drugged, his mind worked very slowly, but it did work. The problem was, he felt so tired. Not enough to fall asleep but too tired to resist, now that he was sitting down and not in movement. But he exerted his will power and forced his mind to focus, at least a little. Slowly, he was forcing his mind to work on the problem of what drug he'd been given when he had a sudden insight. She might be giving the King the same drug she had given him, albeit in much smaller doses. From what he had learned from Ta Ta and from the general reputation of the Seventh Kingdom, it was inconceivable that this King could have allowed Griselle to gain so much influence if his obviously powerful mind had been clear. But, after this moment of clarity, he became fatigued again and was forced to allow his mind to rest.

Prince Cha Cha noticed that Griselle's mind probes were entirely absent tonight. A little bit of excitement began to build, and he carefully shifted his attention to a coat of arms on the back wall. He was seated right next to Griselle. Not just yet. Still, one part of his brain noted that the man in the bright red robe was drugged, not drunk, but still subtly resisting Griselle's authority. He saw the lines of struggle etched in the man's face. He stole a glance at Griselle. He knew her very well by now. She was obviously struggling with a decision, weighing and calculating strengths and balances, deciding if it was safe to do something. And he knew what. And he knew it wasn't the time to interfere. Not yet. Not now.

Griselle, took a deep breath, sat up straight, beamed a treacherous, spidery smile and spoke.

"My King, my Lord, I propose a toast."

There were murmured hear hears from the audience. It was a little early to start the toasts, as most of the guests were still buried in the third course, but the mood was cheery.

Griselle stood, lifted her goblet and beamed at the King.

"To your Majesty's health and ease and to the undying loyalty of all his subjects."

Another round of hear hears and Griselle continued the toast.

"May the royal family live long and well and may they always be loyal to their King."

Prince Cha Cha tensed. This was it. Doesn't matter, doesn't matter he told himself.

A few in the audience looked puzzled at the reference to the royal family being loyal to the King. That seemed strange. Did they hear right? But their thoughts were drowned out by the loud cheers and clamor of Griselle's stooges.

"I myself swear undying loyalty to the King. Wheresoever you are, is all the charm of life. Indeed, I would rather forfeit life itself, than be disloyal to you."

Cha Cha noticed his father's lip was sweating.

Griselle lifted her goblet high and extended it in the direction of the King.

"My King, I pledge my undying loyalty to you though it should cost me my very life."

She took a small sip, then slid back her chair and made a formal curtsey and her flunkies in the crowd roared their approval and also stood and drank. Once they were up, of course, the rest of the crowd felt obligated to do the same, even the ones who found this toast rather strange. The royal family, following protocol, remained seated.

"Again, my King, my undying loyalty to the death."

Griselle took another sip and curtsied and her flunkies cheered.

"Oh, twice is not enough. One more time," she said as she half turned to the crowd. She swept the cup around to take them all in.

"All of us, do we not pledge our undying loyalty and our lives to our wonderful and wise King?" Then she took another sip and curtsied again.

Her followers hollered and stamped their feet and waved their cups and said things like "Our undying loyalty," and "Love and loyalty." Again the rest of the diners followed suit. Then Griselle sprang the trap.

Looking puzzled, she asked, "But, what is wrong my dear Queen? You have not joined us in pledging loyalty to the King."

You could have heard a pin drop. The crowd became tense. Everyone caught the import of the words and everyone saw the unfolding drama. How could this be? It all depended on the King.

The Queen, however, was taken completely by surprise. She seemed to be the only one in the room who didn't understand what was going on. She stammered her reply.

"But, but I'm the Queen."

It was so evident to the Queen that no oath was needed

from her that she could think of nothing else to say.

"Yes, my beloved Queen," Griselle crooned, "you are the example of the nation. You are not to be outdone. Show your loyalty to your King as we have done. Three times, curtsey before his Majesty and pledge your undying love and loyalty. Give us all an example to remember."

Slowly and uncertainly, the Queen came to her feet, her face red with consternation as she began to realize what was asked of her. She turned to her husband.

"This is outrageous. Who is she to make such demands?"

The King looked miserable and befuddled. His face was sweating profusely and he rubbed his eyes with both hands. He looked trapped. Finally, he waved a hand weakly about.

"It's just a small thing," he said.

"What!" the Queen said in shock.

"Surely, you can do as the rest of the people," he said in a soft weak voice.

"But, I am the Queen. My loyalty is beyond question."

"And so it should be," Griselle said as if imploring the Queen. "Put an end to all the rumors, all the accusations."

"What rumors?" the Queen said aghast. Her hand flew up over her heart and she began to wilt like a leaf before a fire.

From the back of the hall a few voices, male and female were heard.

"She is disloyal."

"May the King be preserved from her."

"A traitor Queen."

"Treason!"

And then, the Queen's defenders began to shout back and in a moment the hall was in an uproar, tables, benches and chairs were being overturned and weapons drawn.

Ta Ta looked on in horror. Her brother had said, "Be ready to do whatever needs doing." But when was he going to act? Surely, she must reveal herself now. It was worth the risk. She could explain everything despite Griselle's henchmen. She took a step forward, but suddenly, her way was blocked by a dagger. She looked around and saw Typhus and Emily were also guarded. Griselle's men had spotted them after all. The men made no effort to kill them or lead them away, no doubt, Ta Ta thought because they had no orders to that effect. Ta Ta watched the scene in the hall unfold.

"Silence!" roared the King.

The hall fell still and all eyes turned to the King and Queen.

"It is a small thing," he said, softly again, but this time with firmness and resolution.

The Queen's voice quavered as she spoke and tears began to form in her eyes. She bent to the King with both hands up in supplication.

"No, my Lord and King. Please, no."

"I command it."

The whole hall watched in horrified fascination. Everyone knew that the fate of the kingdom hung in the balance. Griselle kept silent.

Prince Cha Cha felt the gnawer in his mind searching frantically for just the right bone to bite into, and fought down the urge for action that was so essential a part of his makeup. Not just yet, not now he repeated to himself. Doesn't matter, doesn't matter.

"I said I command it!" the King roared. As he had never roared at their mother before, both Cha Cha and Ta Ta knew it was because he knew he was wrong, but didn't know how to turn the course of events.

"My Lord, my husband, my King, do not command me to this humiliation, I beg you. Surely, my love, my devotion, my loyalty are already known, already proven."

"I command."

"I am your Queen, your wife."

"Do you disobey my direct command? Then, in what else do you disobey me?"

"Nothing, my Lord. I swear it."

"Then swear your loyalty," the King said, rising from his chair.

Suddenly, the Queen's tears ceased. She took in a deep breath, stood tall and regal, her shoulders and back straight and spoke in a whisper heard by everyone in the hall.

"I cannot."

While his body was still sluggish, Rigirus's mind was returning as he listened to the conversation. No, you cannot, great Queen, he thought. You are true royalty. And though you haven't articulated it, you know that you cannot betray your lineage, your kingdom, your people or your husband and king by abjectly groveling before this ludicrous test. And, Griselle, how little you know the measure of your foe and the terrible strength that you mistake for weakness. The unifying principle, the secret of secrets, if only I had it, I would lay you low.

And Prince Cha Cha at last had the thing he wanted, the thing he had waited for, for so long. At last, the gnawing part of his mind found the right bone, bit deep into the marrow and pulled it out. Now! Now it was time. Now it mattered. He jumped up and shouted, "The duty of love and the love of duty."

Everyone turned to him in disbelief, especially Griselle.

"Father, have you forgotten? The duty of love and the

love of duty make a good king."

His father blinked at him as if being awoken from a deep sleep. Cha Cha felt a sudden rush of anger coming into his mind from outside. It was one of Griselle's mind probes, but this was the plan he had made, and in one motion he plunged his table knife at her. She fell back but he was able to run it through her hand pinning it to the table. She screamed and the mind probe vanished.

"Father, have you forgotten? Your first duty is to love your subjects and your Queen." His words came out in a torrent, long dammed up, waiting for the right opportunity, and also, because he wanted to get them all out before she launched another probe.

"Do you not love your Queen enough to trust her? Is that not your duty, to love and protect your kingdom, your subjects and your Queen? And do you not love that duty, that great and holy duty, which rests upon your head with the crown?"

"Don't listen to him!"

It was Griselle, screaming like a demon. She'd pulled the knife out of her hand and held it aloft as it dripped blood. She held up her wounded hand from which blood streamed down her wrist and into her sleeve.

"See what he did to your loyal subject, my beloved King," she screamed. "They're together against you."

But it was too late. The King was wide awake now and enraged at being played for a fool.

"Seize her!" he yelled and motioned for a couple of guards to grab her.

Griselle howled in rage. All her plans were blasted. But, she was not through. She'd anticipated even this eventuality.

"Now!" she shrieked. "Now, arise, my subjects. Fight

for your Queen!"

The hall exploded in chaos. Griselle swung the bloody knife down at Cha Cha, but he rolled away and the blade swished past his throat. He retreated before her, and she pursued, slashing repeatedly as he backed away.

Ta Ta looked at her guard. He was transfixed, inert and seemingly useless without some sort of order. She looked at Emily who nodded at her. Ta Ta grabbed a pitcher and smashed it against the guard's knife hand, knocking the knife away, then ran for the dais and her brother, ripping off her wig and server's costume as she went and spitting the cotton out of her mouth. She stole a quick look over her shoulder and saw Emily had her own guard down on the ground and was mercilessly beating him on the head with a silver plate. Typhus's guard lay sprawled motionless across the serving table while Typhus was landing a solid right on the jaw of Ta Ta's guard.

Ta Ta jumped up on the royal table on the dais. She saw an enraged Griselle pursuing her brother slashing at him over and over, narrowly missing him each time. Farther down the table she saw her father fighting off three attackers and protecting her mother. She looked back to her brother. Griselle had caught up with him. She held him by the arm with her knife raised high. Ta Ta ran full speed down the table and hurled herself headlong into Griselle's midsection with a flying leap that sent them both sprawling on the floor. Griselle sprang back up enraged, but her face turned pale when she saw two Prince Cha Cha's facing her. She raised her dagger but turned from one to the other in total confusion, unable to move.

"What sorcery is this?" she cried.

Cha Cha gave his sister a shove in one direction and took off in the other. Ta Ta understood and moved as fast as she could through the brawling crowd.

Cha Cha, when he had put some distance between himself and Griselle, leapt up on the table and looked across the hall. He saw his father coming over to protect him, his dagger drawn, but Griselle had fled from sight. Cha Cha glanced around the hall and saw the King's forces were in disarray. The traitors knew each other and who the loyalists were, but the King's forces had no idea who they were supposed to fight. So, they did not know who to defend against and who to attack and were being quickly overwhelmed by the well organized traitors.

"Father, follow me," the Prince shouted. "I know who the traitors are."

Cha Cha jumped off the table to the floor below, followed closely by his father who had no choice but to hope his son was right. The Prince picked up a dagger someone had dropped on the floor and hurled himself into melee after melee, each time picking the most important traitor and plunging the dagger into his side, his father following through after him. Instinctively, the loyalists began to coalesce around Cha Cha and his father. Any traitor who tried to blend in was quickly pointed out by Cha Cha and dealt with by the enraged loyalists. Hot tears streamed down the Prince's face, for he was still but a boy, and he saw many a formerly beloved figure that had been seduced by Griselle fall by his instruction.

Meanwhile, Typhus and Emily fought their way over to Rigirus and pulled him to a position of relative safety closer to the King's loyalists. While they were doing this, Ta Ta found that, while she didn't know the identities of the traitors, the loyalists on her side of the room would instinctively rally around her, taking her for the Prince, and the traitors would attack. Soon, two distinct battles raged in the room. One, surrounding the Prince and the King, the other Ta Ta and her protectors.

Slowly, the tide turned as Griselle's subjects were separated and identified. Once the loyalists were organized and knew their enemy they fought with the white hot fury of the betrayed. Inch by inch, they stabbed, thrust and slashed their way across the hall as the traitors fell beneath their dirks and daggers. At last, they had the surviving traitors pinned in a corner of the banquet room from which there was no exit. One last rush and victory would be theirs.

Then, they heard a sound which froze their blood. Faintly, at first, like rustling leaves, then louder and louder, the unmistakable sound of slithering. The sound of a horde of slither hither and thithers. They burst into the room, Griselle walking insolently at their head, her face an ugly, sneering gloat.

The king's men fought hard, but their dirks and knives were no match for these ferocious beasts who fell upon them tearing and slashing with their razor like teeth, their powerful jaws and knife like claws. With pikes, spears, broadswords and cross bows the King's forces could have made a fight, but as it was, they were doomed to a gruesome death. Ta Ta's band disintegrated under the pressure and a slither hither and thither captured her and carried her to Griselle who seized her by her hair. Quickly, the rest of the loyalists and the royal family were pushed back to the far wall. There they stood, the royal family protected within a large semicircle, cornered on one flank by the traitors and on the other flank and center by the slither hither and thithers.

In the middle of the Royalists stood Rigirus, Typhus and Emily. Rigirus was almost back to normal. Normal enough to eye Emily with concern.

"Quick, Emily take your remedy. You're starting to change back."

And sure enough, her nose was just slightly longer and her eyes slightly smaller.

"They've taken the Princess prisoner," she said, ignoring him.

"Please, love," Typhus begged. "It's now or never. Who knows what will happen?"

"Take it now, Emily," Rigirus implored. "It's the last we have. It looks dark, but we may still be able to get back to the fire and make you some more. But if you change back now you may be a rat forever."

"No, sire, I will not take it."

"Please, love. Quickly!"

Emily looked at Typhus and Rigirus with a strange smile and said, "I know the secret of secrets."

Without warning, before they could say another word, she whirled about and disappeared into the crowd, which closed around her. Typhus tried to follow her, but the crowd was too thick. Rigirus sadly took Typhus by the arm, and gently turned him to face the front.

The creatures had ceased their advance. Everyone knew it was the end. The royal family stepped to the front of their followers.

Griselle stood before them, holding Ta Ta by the hair, her voice dripping contempt.

"So, my King, you could have done as I wished and lived. Now, you shall die with your wife."

"An honor of which I am not worthy," the King said.

"And you, you insolent whelp," she pointed a bloody dagger at the Prince, "I could have made you a great King."

"Only my father could have made me a great King."

"And, Princess Ta Ta, a most clever disguise. It fooled me just long enough. It was you that brought Rigirus to the kingdom wasn't it? I had no idea you were so resourceful. But, not enough. You chose Rigirus? Really!"

"He's a better wizard than you," Ta Ta shouted. "He knows about the secret of secrets and you don't."

Griselle cackled loudly.

"You don't believe all that blather, do you, Rigirus? That will o' the wisp?"

"With all my heart" he replied stepping up beside the royal family.

"Then what is it?"

"If only I knew, Griselle, I could defeat a hundred of you."

She tossed her head back, cackled again, then said, "And what does that mean?"

"It means you will lose in the end," he said.

"In the end? Rigirus, I am so worried. But in the meantime, I have business to attend to."

Griselle held her dagger to Ta Ta's throat.

"Here's a little magic. All it takes is a little innocent blood."

The Queen screamed. Cha Cha, the King and his men hurled themselves forward, but the slither hither and thithers easily knocked them back.

Then, in the back of the room there was a horrible scream. A huge brown figure in women's clothing bounded across the room. It jumped across the slither hither and thithers and leaped at Griselle whose face contorted in terror. She let go of Ta Ta and threw her arm up to protect herself, and with her other arm, plunged her dagger into the bounding figure. The brown figure and Griselle rolled over and over on the floor. Suddenly,

Griselle's severed head rolled away across the floor. The figure rolled off Griselle. Everybody gasped in disbelief.

It was a gigantic rat dressed in women's clothing with a dagger stuck deep in its ribs.

Ta Ta suddenly knew the truth.

"Emily," she cried. She flung herself upon the creature and cradled it in her arms.

"Dear Emily. Please don't die. I love you, Emily."

The rat looked into her eyes. One paw reached for the brass bridle bit around Ta Ta's neck and clutched it. Then the rat pulled it to the button she wore around her neck and enclosed them both in her paw. The rat's face began to soften and change. Gradually, her form became human and lovely. More lovely than that of any woman in the court, more lovely even than Ta Ta. Her nose was no longer too pointed, but soft and round, nor her eyes slightly beady, but large and soft. She gazed up peacefully at Ta Ta, then closed her eyes and died.

A great shudder rolled through the hall and all the slither hither and thithers began to roll over, shudder three times and die. The traitors were dropping their weapons and shaking their heads as if waking from a sleep. Some, the ones that had willingly joined Griselle, were turning into slither hither and thithers and dying along with the others. But the traitors that had tried to resist Griselle fell to their knees and cried in relief at their release from thralldom.

"Rigirus," Ta Ta cried. "What's happening?"

"It seems that the slither hither and thithers were only kept alive by Griselle's malice and now that has been destroyed."

"But how?"

"Emily deduced the secret of secrets, the unifying principle."

"What was it?" she asked.

"The only thing it could possibly have been. Look."

He walked up to Ta Ta and Emily, bent over and opened up Emily's palm. Resting in her palm, instead of the button and the piece of brass, was a beautiful, white diamond, the loveliest anyone had ever seen.

"The rest of us were too sophisticated to see it," he said. "It took the simplest to see the obvious. It is love that takes the commonest things and turns them into the most enduring and beautiful. 'The duty of love and the love of duty.' They," he pointed at the dying creatures, "chose to live without love and its duty and became the most horrible of animals."

He turned to the King.

"Where did you learn that phrase, your Majesty?"

"Why, when I was a young lad, I became lost from a hunting party. I was lost two days and nights and down to my last food and water when I came across an old beggar who was dying. Naturally, I gave him my food and water and sat by him all night to keep him company while he died. But I fell asleep, and when I awoke the beggar was gone. There was fresh food and water where he'd been lying, and a parchment with that phrase, and only that phrase, written upon it."

"Was the beggar's name Sarnus?"

"Don't know. He didn't say and I didn't ask. Why? Is it important?"

Rigirus shook his head and said, "No, not really. I think I know the answer."

He turned his gaze to the beautiful, peaceful countenance of Emily.

"Emily instinctively lived by the secret of secrets, by love and duty, with all the sacrifice that they demand.

Thus, though born an animal, she became fully and beautifully human."

"And now she sleeps," said Typhus, his head bowed in sorrow.

Rigirus put a comforting arm around his shoulder.

"No, Typhus. Now, she awakens from this shimmering dream we call life. Even as we speak, she lives forever with the Prince of Love in the Abode of Love."

"Is there really such a place, Rigirus?" Ta Ta asked.

"Just as surely as there are right and wrong, just as surely as there are love and its duty, there is an Abode of Love. And if you, Princess Ta Ta, and you, Typhus, do as she did and love unto the end, just as surely, Emily and the Prince of Love will be there to greet you. And, so it is, for us all."

"And that, my children, is the entirely true story of Prince Cha Cha and Princess Ta Ta."

"Oh, Daddy, you made it up."

"Only a few details. The most important parts are true."

***

After Father carried Tanya to her room, Charles lay staring at the ceiling, building up his nerve for what he knew he was going to do. The idea had excited him earlier, but now he was flooded with second thoughts. But, he wanted to know, had to know what this thing was all about. Besides, it was to make his sister well, so it had to be okay. Charles waited until he was sure his sister was asleep, then stole into her room. He walked over to her bed and made sure she was sleeping by softly calling her name three times and getting no response.

Satisfied, he went to the closet and quietly opened the door. It hovered near the bottom. A glittering, incandescent cloud. Why had he found it so repulsive, so fearful at first?

Not that he now found it beautiful. It was something else. Alluring, compelling, hypnotic, exciting; like a bad friend at school who kept getting you into trouble, but was fun to hang around with. But, why was it in his sister's closet? That's what he didn't get. It should be in his closet. Everything would be so much simpler that way.

He took a deep breath, then plunged his hands and arms in all the way. He let his fingers enter in all the way to the dark red center. It began to pulse at the same rate as his heart. With each pulsation, waves of emotion coursed through him; waves of elation, warmth, relaxation, nausea and revulsion, in no particular order, that overwhelmed his entire body. He inhaled deeply of the odor of the cloud. It was as if he and the creature were changing places, as if there were some mutual transfusion of essences. He was almost there, almost at the core of the secret. He was sure he could cure his sister. Then a voice, not his own, seemed to be speaking to him from inside himself and told him what he must do.

Meanwhile, Tanya had progressed well into her dream, and she was not enjoying it.

Tanya was before the doorway. Cautiously, she floated towards it. Was it going to open? Now? Tonight?

A tremor of fear swept through her. What was on the other side? Did she really want to know? She tried to leave, but couldn't. Something attracted her, pulling her to the door. She waited, tense.

She smelled something strange. What was wrong? A rotting smell was filling the black room. A winding, curling, gray smoke was rising up from the floor. It made her heavy, and she could feel her fairy light dimming. She was slowly sinking. She looked down and saw the smoke that covered the floor waiting to engulf her. She saw a pair of red eyes in the smoke below her that stared hungrily at her. She was overcome by terror and opened her eyes.

She was staring into Charles's eyes. They were only an inch from hers. Then they receded as Charles straightened up. His eyes were vacant, and she realized he did not see that she was awake now. She made no sound but watched, her heart pounding, as Charles walked back to the closet. There, he stared at the cloud, then bent over and put his head into the gaseous orb. She could hear him take in a deep breath. She realized with a silent scream that the cloud was getting smaller. He turned and walked back to her, oblivious to the fact that her eyes were now wide open. He bent over her again and let his breath out in her face. He exuded a gray smoke out of his nostrils and mouth into hers. Horrified, Tanya covered her mouth and nose. The smoke seemed to come out of him in an unending stream, filtering through her fingers and burning and scratching at her mouth, nose, throat and lungs as it went. Wasn't it ever going to stop? How much did he inhale anyway? How much had she already inhaled? She wanted to scream, to fight back, but felt weak, drowsy. She was dreaming, she must be. Go back to sleep a voice told her. Whose voice? Not Charles's. Not hers.

She took her hand off her mouth and punched feebly at Charles's face.

It was enough.

He stopped, straightened up and turned for the closet.

She managed to find the strength to sit up and grab him by the arm. He stopped and turned to her.

"What are you doing?" she asked. "Are you crazy?"

"They're our friends. They want to make you well."

"They?"

"They're going to live inside us and drive out the sickness. They told me you feel better already."

Startled, Tanya realized that she did feel better. The tension in her lungs was gone and her throat felt warm and comfortable. Charles noticed her expression.

"See. You're going to be all right now. Just like they said."

"They. Who are they?"

"Inside the cloud. It isn't just one. There's hundreds of them. And they're going to live inside us."

Charles tore away from his sister and walked back to the closet. He put his face into the cloud and began to inhale deeply. Just a little more and he would understand. He would know. He could feel it filling his body and mind. His being. Warming, soothing.

Then, he was lying on the floor. What was he doing down here? Then, he saw his sister standing above him, tears in her eyes, holding his baseball bat.

"Why are you doing this, Charles?"

"I'm trying to save you. It's for you."

"It's using you. It isn't going to cure anybody."

Charles looked longingly at the now closed closet door.

"Just a little longer," he pleaded.

"Get out!" she whispered as loudly as she could through her tears, and waved the bat at him.

Charles was slowly coming to his senses. He realized his left shoulder hurt terribly. She must have hit him there.

"I had to hit you. You wouldn't answer me. Now, go!"

Charles got painfully to his feet, his head spinning, and staggered out of the room. Charles feelings hurt even more than his body. Why didn't this thing work? He had let it into him. And it would have cured his sister. He was sure of it. But his sister didn't want to be cured—had recoiled in horror and revulsion. He now had the feeling he'd made a horrible mistake but couldn't figure out why. After all, hadn't he done it for the right reason? Hadn't he been just like Prince Cha Cha in the story? Trying to save his sister? He'd done the right thing. He'd done it only, he insisted to himself, to help his sister. And, now, he felt drained, helpless. God hadn't done anything, so he had.

Once back in his room, he collapsed into his bed, and his head started spinning. He saw a kaleidoscope of figures in his mind. It seemed like they were all each other at the same time—him, his sister, Mom, Dad, the creature, other kids at school. It was as if they were all the same. He couldn't tell which or who they were or who he was, where they began and he left off. That, he was sure, was how the creature could cure his sister—go inside and become her and fix her from the inside out. But there were other figures too. Strange people, not people really, something else with strange voices he didn't recognize.

Suddenly, he didn't want to be here anymore. He wanted to be himself again. Normal. It was all so complicated. Why didn't Tanya mind?

Tanya lay in her bed, spent and breathless.

Why did you lie, Charles? To yourself? Why did you say you did it for me? It was just a big shiny toy to you. Something to play with. Something to set you above the others. It was power and things we're not supposed to know yet. It was a bad thing. You saw that at first. Then you looked too much and you got attracted.

She lay motionless trying to recover her strength. She thought about the story Father had told. She was glad she'd heard it. It was such a beautiful story. But, she didn't really believe there was anything after you died. No

Abode of Love. It was just nothing. And, she didn't mind. It would be good just to rest. To not cough away the nights and the days, to not see her mother cry or her father grow old or her brother corrupted. She looked at the little manger in the glass by the bed. She looked at the imitation snowflakes. It would have been nice to have seen one last snowfall. She reached her arm out to turn it over. But a burst of pain in her side, that was new to her, made her stop. It frightened her, and she knew that she was much, much sicker than anyone had guessed. Her breath wouldn't come, and as her eyes closed, she looked at the glass bubble and at the closet door where the creature lurked and wondered how she could have made such an obvious mistake.

She was moving down the dark valley again. But, this time she felt unbearably light, free, not even one of the fairies, freer than that—just a body of pure light.

She paused but briefly in the window, and then she entered the dark room, vibrating, floating. At last, the dark door in front of her began to open. It swung open and she saw another room, filled with a light which centered around a baby in a rough, wooden crib.

She floated over to the baby which looked up with gentle, intelligent eyes. She looked into the eyes and began to talk to the baby.

"I'm sorry I didn't want to believe. I'm sorry I was afraid to love. That day, when I was in that church and I saw your grown up body hanging there and bleeding, I was afraid of what you would ask me to do. It was stubborn of me, I know. Especially, after you let the creature come. I should have known what it was. I'm sorry I blamed the creature on Charles. It was really mine."

"I don't mind dying. I'm so very tired. So, I really have nothing to give you. No sacrifice to make. I hope you'll make Charles well. He really didn't understand."

The baby smiled and held up its tiny hand and pointed at her with his index finger. Tanya smiled back and stretched out her hand and touched her index finger to his. A flood of warmth ran up her finger through her hand and arm and flooded her whole body. Her chest felt warm and open.

She realized she was being healed. The healing, she sensed, would not be a quick or painless one. Now, she would have plenty of sacrifices of love to make. And the greatest sacrifice she would make was to not join the child just yet. And she knew there would be one more sacrifice—the gift of acceptance would soon be taken away. Soon the days would no longer be one special, golden, treasured gift at a time.

She heard crying and she opened her eyes. She saw the little manger under the glass. Up above, on the window pane she saw the large snowflakes of a very early snowfall sticking to the window. She heard her brother, coughing and vomiting and the sound of her parents running down the hallway to his room. He's trying to drive the cloud out of you, Charles, she thought. He'll heal you. If you want it. If you let him.

For herself, she thought, the days will no longer be precious gifts. They will be plans, schedules and parts of plans. They will be goals met and unmet. And no day will be judged on good given and good gratefully received, as a precious gift complete and entire of itself, but on how it fits into the plan. And her job, her last sacrifice of love, she knew, was to remember. Remember somehow, through the years, and then, when the time was right, tell the others. To explain what couldn't be explained.

She could hear her brother sobbing in Mother's arms.

Someday, maybe, just maybe, she would find a way.

THE END